Only One Knight

Knight in Damaged Armor Series Book 2

Kendy Ward

Printed in the United States of America

This book is dedicated to my family – Daddy, Mummy, Denise, Philip, Quincy, Shantae, Zylen, Zaire, Zeden, Zion and Zaq.

One

Priscilla gripped the steering wheel and pulled into the parking lot of Renaissance Lounge. She desperately needed to win. In dire need, all she could think about was the $5,000 grand prize. The stage of Nassau's newest hot sport for the thirty and older crowed was usually lit with some of the island's most talented musicians. But tonight, instead of the Bahamian bands Visage or Baha Men taking the stage, the country's most talented wordsmiths would get on the mic as the lounge hosted the Bahamas' ultimate spoken word show down. This was Priscilla's fourth appearance in the Bahamas National Spoken Word Competition, and she hoped it would be her first win.

She opened her door to a merciful island breeze carrying a faint salty fragrance of the ocean. Her skirt billowed in the night air. The restaurant, located in the Palmdale area of the island, was sufficiently inland and the ocean breeze was not that common. But tonight the wind gracefully ruffled the palm trees in front of the building. She inhaled the familiar scent that brought with it images of gently rolling waves, lapping against her bare feet as her toes sank into the white sand. She lived where people came to vacation, yet it had been eons since she'd been to the beach. *Maybe I'll have some time next weekend.*

She exhaled her thanks to God for getting there without incident. Her "lil bubbler" had not randomly shut off from any of the million things that was wrong with it. She needed a new vehicle, but a single sister with a mortgage and a mission to open a youth center couldn't afford a new car, especially when the import tax on cars was seventy-five percent. Chile. No, she was riding this car until the wheels literally fell off. Priscilla picked up her pace and hurried to the entrance.

Not for the first time she wondered why the owners chose a location away from downtown. Nassau had millions of tourists that visited the island, who for the most part spent their money downtown. Maybe they had considered that locals needed a place to unwind that was not targeted toward tourist, and money could be made from that market also.

The lounge was in the island's bustling business district. The folks that worked in the nearby banks, insurance companies and doctors' offices were enthused about a quality place to have lunch or hang out after work, making it an immediate success. Open a little over year, she had frequented Renaissance several times with her girlfriends. Although this visit would be much different from any of those times.

Inside, the restaurant décor transported you to a 1920's speakeasy. Decorated in black and white, the space had a huge stage with a band stand. The red curtain behind it set a striking contrast. Old-fashioned mics set in mic stands on the stage. Priscilla smiled as she imagined the likes of Duke Ellington and his orchestra commanding this room, causing feet to tap on the black and white checkered tiled floor.

Priscilla took a seat in one of the booths. The leather seats were black and so were the tables. She was surprised to see each table decorated with a bouquet of live red roses. She watched the band take the stage for sound check. It was an hour before the lounge opened for the evening. The restaurant closed at three o'clock after the lunch and opened again at seven for dinner. She looked around wondering who else would be getting on the mic tonight. She'd received instructions to be at the venue an hour early for sound check but didn't see any of the other poets or the event organizers, for that matter. That wasn't unusual. People and things in Nassau were never on time. They called it island time. She called it disrespect.

The band had been jamming for about twenty minutes when the event people started to trickle in. She recognized the tall dark-skinned brother with the afro as Will, one of the island's most popular poets. No, not one of... *the* most prolific and influential poet in the Caribbean. Her stomach took a dive. This guy had won the Commonwealth Poetry Prize (CPP) five years running. First place in the entire Commonwealth of Great Britain. There were sixteen countries in the British Commonwealth, and Will came first out of the thousands of poets from these sixteen nations. As the winner of the Bahamas National Poetry Competition, Will represented the Bahamas well at the CPP with his five consecutive wins, but she wanted to win. She wanted his spot. As they said on the island, she wanted it bad, bad.

She recognized a couple of other poets she had seen at some of the spoken word events she'd been to. *Lord, please help me. I want this and I know that I can do all things through You because You have empowered me.* Priscilla looked up from her quick prayer and Chris Dorsett, one of the producers of *Avery in the AM* radio show, waved at her. She wondered what he was doing there. The show was a morning show, and it wasn't morning. She wished Avery of *Avery in the AM* and one of her best friends, would have given her a heads up that Chris would be there; it was always awkward seeing him after rebuffing his advances.

She smiled and waved back. Chris was cool. He was a dope, down to earth guy, but she wasn't interested in him romantically. He was very... boring. Unfortunately, he had been trying to get with her since the first moment he met her seven years ago.

Priscilla noticed he was headed her way, and her eyes darted about looking for an escape route. Praise God he was intercepted by someone who looked like he'd just walked off of the pages of *GQ* magazine. He wore brown shoes that looked spit shined and a blue suit that had to be custom made. It fit the stranger as if it was made for him alone. The gentleman wore a yellow, blue and white plaid shirt paired boldly with a yellow paisley tie. A yellow pocket square folded with precision rested in his left breast pocket and a little yellow flower adorned his lapel. Priscilla spied cufflinks. *Men still wear cufflinks?*

Mr. GQ made Priscilla feel grossly underdressed in her t-shirt, maxi skirt and sandals. This brother looked like he ran stuff. Actually, he looked like he ran everything. Like he could run the country, if it was based on nice suits, cufflinks and commanding a room. He looked up from his conversation with Chris and their eyes locked; Priscilla felt as if all the air had been sucked out of her. The intense gaze of his piercing eyes took her breath away. Corny, yes, but it was true.

The man was handsome – tall, at least six feet three, fit in that go to the gym and workout kind of way, not in that acquired from manual labor kinda way (No, this dude didn't look like he was into any kind of manual anything.). His skin was the color of hot chocolate, her favorite thing to drink. He was fine, but it wasn't just beauty. Something else that she could not yet identify or name caused her heart to race a little faster when their eyes met. When someone tapped her on her shoulder, breaking her connection with the handsome, well dressed stranger, she felt relieved. The stage manager introduced herself and let Priscilla know that she'd be up for sound check in five minutes.

***

Priscilla felt the butterflies in her stomach take flight as she stood center stage. Her head bowed, legs slightly apart, fist raised. In the darkened room the stage lights behind Priscilla cast a shadow on the wall in front of her that made her afro appear as a halo, which seemed the perfect visual for the spoken word piece, *Ghetto Angel*, that she was about to share with the audience.

The low timbre of her voice captivated the listeners as she gave them an education on the current state of the Bahamian ghetto, a place of crime, carnage and hopelessness. She gave a charge to those who would hear the call to be a ghetto angel. Who was going to save the country from itself? Corrupt politicians could not be the answer. The answer had to be the people of the community. After throwing down the challenge Priscilla dropped the mic. The intensity of the silence in the lingering space afterwards caused her heart to pound loud in her chest. *Did they like it? Did they get it? Did they get it and not like it?* So many thoughts raced through her mind. Anxiety tried to creep in, but truth pushed it away. She'd spoken the truth with conviction, and if it convicted that's what it was supposed to do.

A burst of applause exploded throughout the crowded room as people stood to their feet. Priscilla bowed before standing at attention and raising her fist once more. She walked backstage and was greeted by the other contestants, who offered appreciative nods and some fist bumps, before being consumed in a group hug by Avery and Reign.

"Girl, you decimated the competition."

Reign's excitement was contagious, and Priscilla felt like maybe she had finally won. She glanced over at Will, the reigning spoken word champion, and wondered what he thought of her piece. He nodded his head, which she took as a sign of approval and respect. Her confidence soared.

"That Will sure is fine."

Priscilla rolled her eyes at Avery.

"I'm just saying the guy is fine. How come you never took him up on any of his numerous offers to dinner?"

"The first and only reason is that he doesn't know Jesus as his personal Lord and Savior."

"My goodness, he can get saved. Suppose Vince had said that about me when we first met?"

Priscilla didn't want to remind Avery that her husband had said that about her and wouldn't come anywhere near her. And although Priscilla would not bring that up, Reign had no qualms about reminding Avery of all the trouble she caused a man who was just trying to love God and do the right thing.

"Okay, Reign, that's true, but it turned out okay in the end. I'm saved. So, I'm just saying Will can get saved."

"You do you see him over there with all his groupies, right?" Priscilla nodded her head towards Will. "That is not my ministry nor my calling. When he's good and saved he can come holler at your girl, but until then I'm not interested. Actually, I'm not interested in any man who isn't interested in God."

"I hear you, Mother Theresa. I'm going to get back out there. The radio station is broadcasting live and I've been gone for a minute."

"I thought your show was *Avery in the AM*. How'd you manage to take over Andre's spot?"

"I asked nicely."

Priscilla believed Avery when she said that. She had a way of wrapping men around her little finger with ease that usually made Priscilla sick.

"Reign, are you coming?" Avery asked.

"Nah, I see someone I need to talk to for a minute."

Priscilla gave Reign a pointed look. An investigative journalist, Reign was well known for causing a ruckus on occasion as she chased down a story.

"I promise I am only going to talk to this cat. That's it. I don't even have my gun."

"Gun?" Panic filled Priscilla's voice. She stopped short of patting Reign down when she noticed Reign laughing. "That wasn't even a little funny. You two get out of here. I'll see you after they announce me as the winner."

"Where's your humility? You sure you saved?"

"Bye, Reign." Priscilla playfully shoved Reign toward the

exit before focusing her attention on the stage where Kendrick Thompson was doing his piece.

He was the second to the last contestant, and he was good. But she felt that she was better. She wasn't being conceited as Reign had alluded. She felt confident. She'd left it all on the stage and hopefully the judges recognized that.

"Excuse me."

The deep voice startled Priscilla. She turned, surprised to see the handsome guy in the nice suit from earlier standing behind her.

"Yes?" Under his intense gaze, Priscilla didn't recognize her own voice. It sounded like he had taken her breath away... again.

"I'm Randy Knight."

When he said his name, Priscilla recognized it immediately. Like most people on the island she knew of the Knight brothers. Jason was a professional model; Rome was a professional basketball player and Dave was the face of Renaissance Holdings. The twins, Randy and Storm, however, were the recluses of the family. You never read about them in the papers or saw them on the news. Everyone knew of them, but no one ever saw them. They didn't even attend the annual fundraiser Renaissance hosted to benefit the children's home. People from all over the country came to support the home, but not Randy Knight or his twin brother.

He extended his hand toward Priscilla, but she knew if their hands connected there would more than likely be some sort of sparks flying, and there could be no sparks flying between her and this self-made multi-millionaire, who also happened to be the MIA father of one of the students at the school where she was the guidance counselor. When she didn't accept the handshake he offered, he withdrew his hand and rubbed it along his pants leg.

"Ah...Well, I just wanted to compliment you on the amazing piece you did. My brothers and I used to be involved in our community. You reminded me that we need to get back to doing that. Thank you for sparking that within me tonight."

Why'd he have to say spark? There wasn't supposed to be any sparking. However, her poem was supposed spark something in people and that it sparked something in one of the wealthiest men on the island who had the resources to make a real impact in the community was almost as much of a reward as winning would be tonight ... almost.

"You're welcome." Priscilla smiled and he smiled back.

"It was a pleasure meeting you, Lyricist. Please let me know if there is any way that we can help your cause."

With that, Mr. Randy Knight turned on his heels and disappeared. She could not believe that was Randy Knight, CFO of Renaissance Holdings. The conglomerate owned nearly every business establishment downtown. On their small island, he was a celebrity. She rolled her eyes. He was just talking. He couldn't even find enough time in his busy schedule to attend a parent/teacher meeting. Priscilla forced her attention off of Randy Knight and back to the competition just as the contestants were being called on stage. She heard her name and followed briskly behind Will as they hurried to get in place.

Back on the stage, Priscilla had an opportunity to really look at the crowd. She saw her cousin, Pedro, being his usual loud self. He was with two of her other cousins, Tonya and Monique. The girls waved and Pedro threw up a peace sign. She shook her head. Of course, Reign and Avery had somehow found a way to be front and center. Reign's brother, Sky was sitting with Avery's husband, Vince. She even saw one of her co-workers from Bahamas Christian Academy. She was happy that her friends and family had come out to support her.

She zoomed in on the panel of judges. Timico Sawyer, known by most as Sawyer Boy, was a local celebrity comedian.

Then there was Tracey Ann Perpall, or TAP as she liked to be called, a blogger, vlogger and social media influencer. And to complete the trio of judges, Sasha Laurel, a foodie and host of the local food show, *Happy Foods 242* sat with the others. Priscilla almost laughed out loud when she saw Avery giving the judges an exaggerated wink. Each had been a guest on her morning show, and she looked to be pretending to call in favors.

Priscilla almost passed out when the MC called Randy Knight to help present the trophy to the winner. She tried to smile, but she was pretty sure it looked like a grimace. If... when she won, she was going to have to hug him. *Jesus, be a fence around me tonight!*

"Ladies and gentlemen, the winner of this year's Bahamas National Spoke Word Competition is Lyricist!"

The world moved in slow motion around Priscilla for about ten seconds and then it seemed like everything sped up as if someone pressed fast forward. The applause of the crowd faded into silence when Randy walked toward her with the trophy. The only sounds she could hear were her heart and his footsteps. She could see his mouth moving and kinda figured he was saying congratulations, but she couldn't hear him over her pounding heart. He leaned in and before she knew it she was trapped in his embrace. She was sure the world had completely stopped for all of five seconds or maybe it was just her breathing that had stopped. She felt safe, secure in his embrace for the whole five seconds it lasted.

Priscilla commanded herself to get out of the Randy Knight galaxy and back into the Milky Way so she could bask in her long-awaited victory. She had won the money! She now had enough for a down payment on the building she wanted for the youth center. Tears filled her eyes, and she gave God thanks. Then she started to do a little two-step. That was all the invitation her family and friends needed to get up on the stage to join in her victory dance.

"I'm coming with you to Toronto." Reign volunteered.

"Me too," Avery added.

"Wait. Who invited either one of you?"

Reign and Avery stared at Priscilla like she had spoken a language they did not know. Reign squinted at Priscilla, and Avery frowned.

"Joking," Priscilla laughed.

"We're going to Toronto." Priscilla, Avery and Reign shouted in unison as they jumped up and down.

Two

The words of the accountant faded as the image of the graph on screen in front of him was replaced with the face of the woman from last night's poetry competition. Instead of the CPA's monotony, he heard the warmth of her voice with a rhythm and cadence that made him want to dance to her beat. Like the music of the Pied Piper it called him away from reality. It invited him to fantasize about things he hadn't thought about since Kimberly left. Things like happily ever after, but he knew first hand that didn't exist. So, he pushed those thoughts aside and refocused on the presentation.

After the meeting Randy walked over to the boardroom's glass wall. His mind was still elsewhere. Renaissance Tower was the tallest building on the island, and he was on the top floor. He had a bird's eye view of the island. Although he'd stood in the exact spot many times before, today he saw more clearly. He saw beyond the colonial architecture of downtown Nassau, the modern structures of the newly built Baha Mar on Cable Beach and the affluence of the gated communities on the west side of the island. He saw the ghettos of Kemp Road, East Street and Bain Town with their desperate looking houses in which resided desperate people. He saw the young men who resorted to violence and drugs because when milk costs nine dollars a gallon, there was no other choice. She was right. Something had to be done.

He quickly texted his administrative assistant to have his brother's driver bring the car to the front. He turned and shook his head; his brother, Dave, sat hunched over his laptop with his face nearly touching the screen. He wondered when

Dave would admit that he needed glasses.

"Let's take a ride." Randy started to walk toward the door. He felt Dave look up. He knew he had a raised eyebrow because he had more "twinergy" with Dave than he did with his twin, Storm. "We won't be late for our meeting with the Minister of Tourism."

"Where are we going?"

"For a ride."

Randy stepped off the elevator and walked with purposeful strides across the marble floor. He kept his gaze on the door ahead of him to avoid making eye contact with anyone. They didn't have time to stop and chat as they usually did. Outside, Randy squinted against the rays of the sun. He slid on his Gucci sunglasses and approached the waiting car. Unlike Dave, his preference was to drive himself. He liked cars, which was evident in the eight that lined his driveway. He liked the way his hands felt on a steering wheel as he took control of the journey and the destination. Being alone in the quietness of his car allowed him to think, solve problems and get ideas. For this ride, though, he wanted to concentrate on what was around him instead of what was inside him. Being driven instead of driving would allow his focus to shift.

Mitchell held the door open. Randy paused before getting inside and gave him instructions on where he wanted to go.

"Are you going to tell me where we're going now?" There was a hint of impatience in Dave's voice. As the oldest of the five brothers, Dave was used to being in charge. Their relationship had taken on a different dynamic when they went into business together. Randy knew Dave trusted him implicitly. That's why he had followed him to the car without question, but Randy supposed the abruptness of his request was kind of on the impulsive side and Dave did not like to do things on impulse.

"Kemp Road and some other places."

Dave looked like he had tasted something sour.

"Why in the world are we going there?" Dave leaned forward in his seat.

"I want to see it with my own eyes." He turned to look out the window and away from Dave's gaze.

"You could look at photos or a video. Wasn't there a video circulating the other day on WhatsApp?"

"I'm not on WhatsApp."

"Not the point. The point is you...we don't need to go there to see it."

"I want see it in person. Feel it. Smell it."

Randy knew he didn't sound like himself so he didn't dare say his last thought, which was connect with it. He didn't rely on his senses and emotions. He relied on facts and figures. Emotions lied to you, but facts always spoke the truth.

Dave exhaled and shrugged his shoulders. He sat back and let his head fall against the leather seat. Randy watched his brother close his eyes before muttering, "Whatever."

They drove down Bay Street, the main thoroughfare of downtown Nassau. The bumper to bumper traffic on the narrow streets was not something Randy would ever get used to. Normally he would be gritting his teeth in frustration, but today their slow-moving pace gave him a chance to take in what he saw.

Randy forced himself not to focus on the jewelry stores, clothing stores and perfume stores filling up Bay Street that carried his name. He focused instead on the driver of the late model Mitsubishi Lancer in front of them who was honking incessantly at the Western Transportation bus beside it. The bus driver stopped abruptly when he noticed the Lancer, and then the Lancer stopped abruptly. A woman in a gray blazer slowly got out of the car and into the bus. Randy smiled, knowing the driver of the car was probably relieved that he didn't have to make the drive out west in this traffic. It would take forever.

Getting to work early and leaving late helped him avoid the grueling traffic from his house out west into town. However, this school year he decided that instead of the car service, he would take his daughter to school himself. It was only day three of the school year, but after an hour and ten minutes of sitting in morning traffic he was fighting hard not to change his mind about taking her to school. You could drive around the whole island in less than an hour; he didn't understand why it took him that long to get to her school or anywhere for that matter. She would be seventeen soon and he was strongly considering getting her a car so she could drive herself. The only thing was, he wasn't sure if Eden was responsible for getting herself to school that she would go. She'd been exceptionally good during the summer, though. Maybe she had changed.

A teenage girl in a deep yellow uniform skirt with a matching cross tie caught Randy's attention. She was running with the speed of a track star, trying to catch a jitney. Randy's eyes bulged when she caught up to it and jumped into the moving vehicle. *Wow.* He was certain that she was indeed an athlete. She was lanky, like Eden, but there was power in her strides. Eden's idea of exercise was sitting courtside at a South Florida Suns game to watch her uncle Rome play basketball.

The driver turned onto Village Road and then onto Shirley Street to get to Kemp Road. Randy noticed the old arena where boxing matches took place was abandoned. Graffiti marred the building that was once a place of prominence on the island. As they continued the drive down Kemp Road, the landscape was a drastic contrast from Bay Street and Shirley Street where tourists frequented. There was a reason tourists were warned not to stray too far from the "tourist" areas.

Randy's eyes rested on a group of young men standing on a corner. Two were leaning against an old, gutted out car. The taller of the two took a long drag on the blunt he held between his index finger and thumb as he looked at the charcoal Rolls Royce Ghost. Despite the car's dark tint Randy felt their eyes connect. Not able to withstand the intensity of the resentment he saw, Randy looked away to get Dave's attention. He was surprised to see that Dave was not asleep. He seemed transfixed on something outside the window on his side.

"What are you looking at?" Dave's large frame was blocking the window and Randy couldn't see. Dave sat back. A little girl at a water pump on the side of the street was filling a gallon water jug. Beside her was a shopping cart with several empty gallon water jugs. Randy felt his heart constrict as memories flooded his mind, and he was sure Dave was having the same flashbacks. They knew this meant that wherever this girl lived there was no running water because whoever she lived with couldn't afford to pay the water bill.

"I see why you wanted to take this ride." Dave almost whispered. "We came up, and even though we promised that we wouldn't, we forgot."

Randy nodded in agreement before giving Mitchell instructions to take them directly to their meeting with the Minister of Tourism. He and Dave had an idea that would be a tourist magnet for both domestic and international travelers, but they needed the Bahamian government to free up some Crown land they had their eyes on.

Crown land was land in the Commonwealth of Great Britain that belonged to the British Crown. This land could be leased or sold by the British Crown to the Bahamian Government; in turn the government could lease or sell to whomever they liked. Randy and Dave had influence, but unfortunately, their influence did not reach as far as the British Crown. For that reason, they had to influence where their influence reached.

After their meeting Mitchell took them back to the office, and Randy headed over to the Renaissance Resort job site. This was by far the largest undertaking Renaissance Holdings had engaged. He didn't know how they dared to dream that they could build a Bahamian owned resort to rival Atlantis Resort and Baha Mar. This project, if it did not succeed, would bankrupt them. It made him nervous, but he knew he had to take a risk to make a gain. This, however, was a ginormous risk. This was the keep you up at night type of risk and it had done exactly that.

Randy was satisfied with the progress of the project, and it seemed like they would be opening on time. Opening weekend at the resort was already booked, and at seventy-five percent capacity, that was better than their projections. He was excited about succeeding. Randy knew Dave was excited about making money; that was the way Dave measured success. For him, success didn't necessarily equal dollar signs.

Randy was headed to a meeting with the tenants at Renaissance Mall Nassau, and then he had to stop by their three Renaissance Cinema locations. When his phone rang en route to the tenant meeting, Randy swore before answering the phone.

"Randy Knight." He barked. How in the world could Eden get into trouble on the third day of school?

"Mr. Knight. This is Ms. Deveaux from Bahamas Christian Academy. I'm calling about Eden. We need you to come down to the school."

"What has she done now?"

"I would prefer to discuss it with you when you get here."

"Look I'm headed to a meeting. Does this have to be right now? Can I come after school?"

"I need you... The school needs you to come now. If not, we're going to have to call the police."

Blood rushed to Randy's ears. *Police? What did Eden do?* He felt himself morphing into his father. His dad never hesitated on a butt whooping, and Randy was about to show up on that school campus with his belt swinging. Maybe that was why

Eden was the way she was; he did hesitate in giving her a good old-fashioned butt whooping.

"I'm on my way."

It took Randy less than ten minutes to get over to the school from Renaissance Mall on Robinson Road. He haphazardly parked the Mercedes Maybach and jumped out of the car. As he walked the outdoor campus, he felt the urge to remove his jacket, but couldn't figure out if it was because of the temperature or his anger. He was the calm, cool and collected brother. There was not much that ruffled his feathers, but he was at his wit's end with Eden.

Prior to enrolling her in Bahamas Christian Academy she had been in boarding school. That is until she was expelled for stealing. Stealing? What in the world did she have to steal for? It had to be the thrill. He gave her everything. He had only sent her to the boarding school because before that she had been kicked out of four schools in two years for anything from fighting to purposely flunking her classes. She'd been a model teenager over the summer. He thought she was done with the getting in trouble phase. She'd promised that she had changed. If she got kicked out of this school, he didn't know what to do. Randy walked in the school's office acting like his father.

"Where is she?" He felt like he was seconds away from pulling off his belt.

"Mr. Knight, I presume?" The older lady looked up from behind the partition with a smirk.

Along with Eden's behavior, the slow and unbothered way the woman said Randy's name annoyed him. He looked down at the receptionist. "Someone else's child acting up in this school today?" Randy's uncharacteristic sarcasm caused the receptionist to look at him like she wanted to take off her belt for him. "Yes, I'm Mr. Knight." He softened his tone and tried to smile a little.

"Please follow me." The lady opened a door that led further into the office and motioned for him to follow. They passed several offices before coming to one marked "Principal." In all his years in school Randy had never been to the principal's office, but with this child he felt like she was there more than in class. Randy walked in the room. Not bothering to look at the other occupants in the room, he focused on Eden.

"Come here." She didn't move. Randy started to walk toward her, but someone walked in front of him. He looked down into the face of... Lyricist. He felt like he was in the opening scene of *Black Panther* when T'Challa saw Nakia for the first time. He froze. *What is she doing here?* Randy tried to rack his brain for the connection. He wished he'd been able to make any one of the umpteenth meetings that had been called because of all the havoc Eden caused the previous school year. Unfortunately, he had always been busy with work. His mother or Dave's wife, Victoria, usually sat in for him.

The calm he saw in her compassionate brown eyes, along with the surprise of seeing her there, de-escalated him. Staring into her eyes, he felt peace envelop him. She rested a hand on his arm and his anger subsided. His blood pressure went down. In her presence, instead of the heat he'd felt earlier, he felt a breeze.

"Mr. Knight, welcome. Please have a seat." She gestured toward the seat next to Eden. Her words caused him to come out of the semi-trance he was in. He took the seat she offered and watched her take her seat. They were seated on either side of Eden.

"Good Afternoon, Mr. Knight." Principal Kilpatrick greeted, taking Randy's focus off of Lyricist. "Have you met Ms. Deveaux before?" he asked.

Randy took the hand she extended and received her firm handshake. She was the one that had called him. He couldn't remember who she'd said she was. Kilpatrick's administrative assistant maybe. She didn't look like an admin person, though.

Her 'fro was gone. Now she wore faux locs. They framed her heart shaped face perfectly. An admin person was usually the suit type and she was anything but that.

"I have not. My pleasure."

"Likewise," she smiled.

"Ms. Deveaux is our school counselor and also deals with all disciplinary matters."

Randy gave Eden a look, and she shrank in her seat. Lyricist-Ms. Deveaux reached over and squeezed Eden's hand.

"Would someone fill me in on why we're here?" Randy didn't want the formalities or the small talk. He wanted to know what Eden had done.

"She stole all the lab animals." The principal answered.

"What?" Randy thought he had misheard.

"I didn't steal them. I freed them."

"Freed them? So, you're PETA now?" Randy sucked his teeth.

"Daddy, I had a moral obligation to free them. We were going to dissect the frogs, and I wasn't sure what we were going to do to Polly."

"Polly?"

"The pigeon we kidnapped. Then there were the mice and the rabbit. I couldn't do it. We shouldn't do it."

Randy had never heard Eden speak about morality or speak with such conviction. Last school year she'd been suspended five times. Three times for fighting, one time for hustling some kids playing cards, and the last time was for calling the math teacher stupid because the lady made a mistake on an equation.

"Did you sell the animals?"

"No! I placed them back in their natural habitat. Except

the rabbit. I took him home."

Randy had wondered why Eden kept making frequent trips to the backyard. He wanted to laugh. This girl was a trip. This was something the old Eden would have done. The Eden who hadn't been abandoned by her mom. She'd always loved animals. Although technically she did steal school property, he couldn't help feel like he had his little girl back.

"Mr. Kilpatrick, I'm sorry we won't be able to do our classwork when the time comes later this term, but I'm not sorry for freeing the animals. I will donate $1,000 of my own money to the school's lab." Eden glanced at Randy for permission. He nodded his head. She'd made a lot of money from her hustling. "But you can't use it to buy more animals. Maybe there's some educational videos that we can watch. I don't know. And I'll take whatever punishment you give me."

The principal seemed speechless and so was Randy. On one hand he felt proud of Eden for standing up for what she felt was wrong, but on the other hand she was going to more than likely get suspended again.

"You will have a three day in school suspension." Ms. Deveaux said.

Randy wondered if he asked her out would she say yes. It was something he should absolutely not be thinking about while he was sitting in the principal's office with his child. He should be thinking about what he was going to say to Eden when they got home. Lyricist-Ms. Deveaux hadn't given him any indication that she was interested, but there was a vibe between them. He felt it even now. It was this vibration of connectivity between them that he wanted to explore, and when he wanted something, he got it.

Eden nodded her head and frowned. It was apparent she wasn't happy about the suspension.

"When does it start? I have two teachers who've already

said we'll have a quiz next week. I don't want to miss them."

Randy's neck swiveled towards Eden so fast he felt like he got whiplash. Last school year Eden's grades were so terrible she was on academic probation and almost repeated eleventh grade. What had gotten into her?

I've gotten into her.

Randy knew no one in the room had spoken, but he had clearly heard a voice. He dismissed it, chalking it up to his lack of sleep the last couple of weeks.

"Your suspension will start tomorrow. We'll work on your teachers letting you make up the quizzes."

Randy noticed that Ms. Deveaux was still holding Eden's hand. She gave it another squeeze and Eden nodded before sighing.

"Well, that's it then. Thank you, Mr. Knight, for coming. Hopefully, we won't be seeing you like this again this school year." Mr. Kilpatrick said.

"You won't," Eden said quickly. "My goal is not to do anything else that my father wouldn't like. You know how He says that in Him we are new people. The old me has passed away."

Both Mr. Kilpatrick and Randy looked taken aback. Randy thought she was talking about him, but she was talking about God and the Bible. *When did this happen? She must've been talking to Dave or Storm or Jason. No, it was Rome. She's closest to him.*

Never mind which of his brothers was responsible for Eden's transformation. Right now, he needed to wrap up this conversation with Kilpatrick so he could talk to Ms. Deveaux before she left, but this man was not getting the hint. Finally, Randy just excused himself from the conversation when Mr. Kilpatrick was mid-sentence. He approached Eden and Ms. Deveaux. He smiled at her choice of outfit. She was wearing a black and white striped maxi skirt and a black blazer, which seemed too conservative for her. He imagined that she liked bright, bold colors. Her simple black t-shirt was her statement. It was read Queen (noun) and for the definition it said, "Me."

"Nice shirt, I agree." Randy smiled appreciatively. Priscilla lowered her eyes and a tiny blush crept into her cheeks. She swiped her faux locs away from her face. "Thank you, Mr. Knight. You have an exceptional daughter."

No one – no teacher, no principal, no counselor had ever said that to him about Eden in recent years. "I would have to agree with that also."

"Daddy, stop it." It was Eden's turn to blush, and she was a lot fairer in complexion than Ms. Deveaux. When she blushed, her whole face straight up to her ears turned red.

"I'm glad you were able to come today, Mr. Knight. I need to schedule a meeting with you to discuss how we're going to help Eden stay out of trouble this school year."

Eden rolled her eyes. "Ms. Deveaux, I told you that I don't have any intentions of getting in trouble this year."

"And that was before this little episode of Free Polly."

Randy liked her humor. "We definitely should meet. Lunch or dinner?"

Both Ms. Deveaux and Eden gave him a quizzical look.

"I mean. You can call my assistant. She will be able to tell you better than I can when I'm free." Randy handed her his business card.

"Ok, I'll do that." When she took the card, her hand grazed his and her eyes widened. He knew she had felt the same jolt as he. Their eyes met and held.

"Ah, are you guys ok?" Eden's look said that she thought they were two weirdos.

Randy cleared his throat.

"Yeah. Why?"

"Because you're just standing there staring at each other."

"I look forward to our meeting, Ms. Deveaux."

She looked like she was going to say something but simply nodded her head instead. Randy smiled.

Three

Priscilla tried to push down her irritation, but she was at school at six o'clock on a Friday. She had a right to be irritated. Did he not know that Friday was the last day of the work week, precursor to the weekend? Why had she agreed to meet Randy Knight at five thirty on a Friday evening anyway? *Because you really want to see him again.* She ignored the thought. That was not the reason. He couldn't seem to find any other time in his schedule for his only child, that was the reason.

When his assistant told her that he didn't have any openings on calendar for the next six weeks that's when she asked to speak to him. Instead of being called his assistant the woman should have been called his gatekeeper because she was not letting Priscilla through to him. She acted like he was the Prime Minister of the Bahamas. She'd been put on hold many times when she refused to take an appointment date in November. It was the beginning of September. No. She did not want to speak to his secretary, his administrative assistant, his personal assistant or his scheduler. The man had so many layers of staff she was surprised they hadn't offered up his barber and the cook.

She needed to speak to him concerning his daughter. She didn't care what he was doing. He could be in a meeting with the Pope. He needed to take her call. Finally, after twenty minutes of being transferred from person to person, Randy came on the line, and despite the hint of annoyance in his tone his voice sounded like late night calls and pillow talk. Everything that she had been delivered from by the grace of God. His voice was so distracting she forgot why she had called, which only further annoyed him, but his impatient words on the other end of the phone brought her back to reality. She didn't know if she was more disappointed in the fact that Randy Knight was the uninvolved, unresponsive father in question or the fact that he didn't seem to remember her, especially since she'd been daydreaming about that five second hug ever since the poetry competition. And didn't he tell her after their meeting with Mr. Kilpatrick that he was looking forward to meeting with her? Priscilla shook her head.

He couldn't meet in the morning. He couldn't meet during the day. He couldn't meet on Tuesday, Wednesday or Thursday. He could only meet on Friday at 5:30. Obviously, he didn't know that school got out at 3:30. But she needed to talk with him in person with Eden. So, she said fine. Now it was Friday at 6:08 and the man was a no show.

"Ms. Deveaux, I think we're going to have to reschedule this appointment. He probably got caught up at work."

Priscilla heard the disappointment in the sixteen-year-old's voice. This was Priscilla's second year at Bahamas Christian Academy as the school's counselor. After ten years in the public-school system, she noted there wasn't much of a difference with the private school kids when it came to acting out and getting in trouble. Even with it being a Christian school in the first two weeks of school she'd already addressed drinking on campus and a half a dozen fights. These kids kept her on her knees.

Eden had been Bahamas Christian Academy's live-in terrorist from the moment she stepped foot on campus as an eleventh grader, but over the summer it seemed like someone had a come to Jesus with her, and the girl came back to school almost like a new person. Priscilla wanted to ensure it stayed that way. That's why she wanted to meet with Eden and her dad to talk about how they could make sure that happened.

"I understand that your dad is busy."

"That's an understatement. He's a workaholic. Last week he went out of town on Tuesday. Got back late Saturday night. He's been driving me to school. His idea, but when I got up that morning he wasn't there. He texted me that he had to go the States right quick. Who does that? Who decides they have to go to another country 'right quick'? How do you actually go to another country right quick? He got back from his 'quick' trip on Saturday. That's Tuesday, Wednesday, Thursday, Friday and Saturday; I'm just seeing him. And he's supposed to be the parent? When does he have time to parent me? Let me go to live with my Grammy. He doesn't want me here. So why am I here?" Eden angrily wiped away her tears.

Priscilla was momentarily speechless. She really wanted to like Randy Knight, but he seemed like a real butthole. She understood busy. She understood drive. She understood that what he had accomplished came from hard work and sacrifice, but it seemed like the thing he was sacrificing was time with his daughter.

"Your dad is the only one who can answer that. That's why we all need to meet. Hopefully the three of us will be able to get together soon."

"I wouldn't hold my breath if I were you."

"I'm sure we'll—"

"Whatever. I don't want to waste any more of your time. I'm going to go."

Before Priscilla could respond, Eden stood and walked out of her office. Shocked by the girl's abrupt departure, Priscilla was staring at the door when it flung open startling her.

"How am I supposed to get home? My driver got off early because I was supposed to ride home with him today."

"You have a driver?"

"Yeah, how else am I supposed to get around? My dad is

way too busy to drive me everywhere."

"You have a driver, dred." Priscilla mumbled but her comment did not escape Eden.

"Did you just say dred?"

Eden frowned. Priscilla guessed the students thought that the teachers and faculty went around all day using the Queen's English and never used local vernacular like "dred," which was the same as saying "man."

"I'll catch the bus."

"Child, you have a driver. You don't know anything about catching the bus. If you did, you would know that the buses stop running right around this time."

"They stop running?"

"Are you sure you're from here?"

Priscilla tried not to laugh, but this kid had no clue. She had a driver. Priscilla used to have to walk home from school because her mom didn't have money to give her to catch the bus. She'd gotten a scholarship to St. Andrew's School, which was definitely God looking out for her when she didn't even know anything about Him, but the school was on the opposite end of the island from where she lived. It was a very long walk.

"Try   calling   him again."

Priscilla watched Eden call her father for the fourth time, and for the fourth time he did not answer her call. What kind of father didn't take his kid's calls?

"He can't wait until I turn seventeen so I can get my license, then I can drive myself wherever I need to go. He promised to get me a BMW X5."

Priscilla listened to Eden ramble and was mad that Randy Knight was a moron, a fine moron, but still a moron. Who tells their kid they can't wait for them to be able to drive themselves around because they're too busy creating a business monopoly on the island to be a parent? And he was purchasing her a car that cost almost as much as Priscilla's yearly salary. *Rich people.*

"I'll take you home. Unfortunately, I do not drive a BMW. I hope you don't mind being seen in a Toyota Prius."

"A what? Is that like the Japanese version of the Corolla?"

"First of all, don't be dissing my car. Secondly, a Toyota Corolla is Japanese. Lastly, you must feel like exercising."

"Exercising?"

"Yeah, keep talking 'bout my car and you will be walking."

"I'm not talking about your car, Ms. Deveaux. I just don't know what a Toyota Prius is."

"Mm hm. Get your stuff. Let's go."

~~~~~

"Oh, so this is a Prius." Eden said once she buckled in. "And a right-hand drive one at that. It's very quaint."

"Can a car really be described as quaint?"

"Of course. Especially one that looks like it's from before I was born."

"You must really want to walk."

"I'm joking."

"And for your information a right-hand drive car is safer to drive when you're driving on the left side of the road. You can see better. Those left-hand drive cars are made for American streets where they drive on the wrong side of the road. Make sure your dad gets you a right-hand drive BMW."

"Nobody else drives a right-hand drive car. You're the only person I know with one."

"Okay be unsafe out there in these streets. You know Bahamians don't know how to drive. Where am I going?" Priscilla pulled out the school's parking lot and onto Soldier Road.

"Lyford Cay."

"What? I should've asked you where you lived before I offered to take you home. That'll take us over an hour."

Lyford Cay was once a cay off the main island of New Providence where Nassau is, but developers filled in the water way between the cay and the island, connecting it to New Providence. Priscilla called the area the community of the rich and famous. Not only did local celebrities and politicians live behind the gates that hid multimillion-dollar homes, it was also the home of international movie stars, singers and business tycoons. Behind those gates Bacardi, Campbell and Heinz were last names, not just words you saw on labels.

"So, you understand the struggle I go through every day to get to school. I have to get up really early. Earlier than anybody else in my class. It's a sacrifice. I shouldn't have gotten kicked out of Lyford Cay School. I could sleep until eight o'clock and still be at school by eight thirty."

Priscilla shot Eden a look of disapproval. "You shouldn't joke about getting kicked out of anywhere."

"You're right. I'm sorry. I am trying to do better. I'm trying to exercise the fruit of the Spirit."

"Really? What part of the fruit is calling people names?" The day before Eden had gotten into a small altercation with one of the "popular" girls. Priscilla knew most of the girls in the high school felt somewhat threatened by Eden's looks, even though it seemed like Eden never even thought about her looks. Priscilla noticed the girl didn't seem conceited at all. It was everyone else that was tripping over it, especially the boys. She got a lot of attention from the boys, which was why the girls didn't like her.

Being dark skinned, Priscilla got teased a lot in school because dark skin wasn't considered beautiful. Back then she wished that she was lighter skin and had tried every skin bleaching product she could find. None of them worked. With Eden, it was the exact opposite. Her peers marked her light skin, light eyes and light hair as beautiful. The girl was nearly six feet tall and walked the hallways like it was her runway. Priscilla thought she looked like the girl from the Disney Channel that was in that movie with Wolverine, Zanisha... Zaria... Zendaya. Eden effortlessly and almost carelessly sported all the expensive brands that these kids only saw on music videos. Even though BCA was a private school, unlike Eden, most of the kids came from middle class families. This is why the other girls hated on her; they thought Eden thought she was too good for them.

Eden hung her head. "Yeah, that was not self-control for sure. I felt badly about it afterwards. I was really disappointed in myself for not listening to what God was telling me in my heart."

"Which was?"

"Forgive. I just kept hearing it over and over again, but I was like nah. Then the words were out of my mouth."

"I pray you learned your lesson."

"Definitely. My temper is to be controlled. It should not control me."

Priscilla smiled and glanced over at Eden. The girl had quoted something Priscilla had told her. "I'm glad you're listening."

"You look like you know where you're going." Eden commented as they got onto the East West Highway and then exited onto Independence Drive.

"I do. My mum has worked for many years as a housekeeper for different families in your community."

"I betcha she had more time to spend with you when you were growing up than my dad spends with me."

"No, not really. Most times she lived with the family that she worked for."

"Whoa. That had to suck big time."

"It did."

Just then Priscilla pulled up to the security gate. Eden leaned over her to flash a smile at the young security guard.

"Hi, Eden. Ah... How... how... how are you?" He stuttered as beads of sweat broke out on his forehead.

"I'm good, Joe. How are you?

The young man appeared temporarily stunned by Eden's question and couldn't speak to answer it. Priscilla thought she would explode from the laughter she was suppressing. This young man was obviously smitten by Eden.

"Okay," Eden said when Joe didn't answer. "Would you let us in please?"

"Sorry. Go ahead."

His squeaky response was about three octaves louder than it should have been, causing Priscilla to jump. The massive gates swung open, and Eden waved at Joe as Priscilla pulled off. Eden gave her directions until they pulled into a circular drive-way with a lighted fountain in the middle. The enormous two-story pale yellow house was surrounded by palm trees. Priscilla had admired this house often when taking her mom to work or picking her up. She always wondered who lived there and what it looked like on the inside, which is something that she did with the Lyford Cay homes she admired. She'd daydream about what it would be like to host a bomb Christmas party at one of these cribs.

Priscilla put down her window so she could inhale the scent of the salt in the air. She heard the faint sound of the waves teasing the seashore. She loved the quiet stillness of the neighborhood. There weren't any cars or buses driving by. No one walking in the streets. No stray dogs knocking down trash cans. Everything was perfect, like it was staged. But she knew that sometimes on the inside of these houses life was not as perfect as the outside. In some of them lived lonely little girls whose fathers ignored them.

"Thanks, Ms. Deveaux. I'll see you on Monday." Eden got out of the car.

"Is your dad home?" Priscilla got out of the car also.

"I don't think he's home yet. It's only seven thirty. That would be a pretty early night for him."

Priscilla recalled the night she first met Randy Knight at the poetry competition. It was during the week, a school night, and the event didn't end until after midnight. A car turning into the driveway captured their attention.

"That's Daddy now. This has to be some kind of record for him. He's never home this early. You must have been praying on the way over here."

Priscilla watched Randy get out of the car. He looked worn out, like he'd had a long month instead of a long day. Despite the wrinkle in his forehead there were no wrinkles in his clothes. The white and light blue striped shirt, matching blue trousers and brown shoes were immaculate. As he walked towards them, Priscilla wanted to curse her heart for beating faster. He was as fine as he was two weeks ago when she'd first met him.

Frowning, he crossed his arms over his chest. "What are you doing here? How'd you know where I live?"

What does he think I'm here for? Priscilla wanted to cut her eyes at him, but she was determined to remain professional. Of course, Eden was the only plausible reason, but he was glaring at her like he thought she was stalking him.

"Go inside." He said to Eden.

"Good evening to you too, Daddy."

"Eden."

"A'ight. Chill. I'm going. Good luck with him." Eden rolled her eyes before turning to go inside.

"I've had women do some crazy stuff to get my attention, but this is a first. Showing up at my house."

Priscilla silently counted to ten to keep herself from going off on him. Yeah, he was definitely a moron if he thought she was stalking him. She exhaled and forced a smile on her face.

"Let's start with proper greeting like Eden suggested. Good evening, Mr. Knight." When he just glared and didn't respond, Priscilla continued. "You obviously forgot that we had appointment today at 5:30. Since you didn't show up, I brought your daughter home. You're welcome." Priscilla watched Randy's expression change from anger to embarrassment. He closed his eyes and covered his face with his hands.

"That was today?"

"Yup."

"I'm sorry I missed our appointment. I got caught up at work on a project offsite. I left my cell phone at home. I called Eden from someone else's phone, but she has a habit of not answering numbers she doesn't recognize. I'm rambling. I apologize – and repeating myself."

If Priscilla wasn't so annoyed and disappointed with him, she would have found his chagrin cute. She wouldn't have guessed that he would be quick to apologize. She figured men of his success were too prideful to do so.

"I accept your apology, but I don't need an explanation."

"Thank you. I promise I am going to do better with being present for Eden. If you have time, we can meet now."

"No."

"No?" His furrowed brows and his puzzled expression made Priscilla think he wasn't used to people telling him no.

"It wouldn't be professional for me to meet with a student's parent after eight o'clock at night at their home. However, we can reschedule your appointment for a time that is convenient for me."

"Of course. I'll have my PA call you first thing in the morning."

"No."

"No?"

"We're going to do this now. I'm sure you know how to schedule your own appointments."

"Ah – I haven't had to for a long time, but I think I can manage." Randy took out his cell phone to have a look at his calendar.

"Next week. Early next week." Priscilla added.

"Next week is busy."

Randy's words caused Priscilla to frown and put her hands on her hips.

He bit his lip. "Ok, next week it is. What time Monday is convenient for you?"

"I'll see you on Monday at eight a.m., Mr. Knight. Have a good weekend."

"I'll see you then, Ms. Deveaux. Are you sure you don't want to come in for dinner? I brought take out from Renaissance Lounge."

"I'm positive."

"I'm not use to people telling me no, but I am used to a challenge, Ms. Deveaux. Drive safely and have a good night." He started to walk toward her, and Priscilla held her breath until she realized he was opening her car door.

"Thank you." She got in the car and quickly pulled off, wondering what he meant by he was used to a challenge.

Four

"E, turn down that music." Randy tugged on his seatbelt to make sure it was secure. The way Eden had taken the curve had him rethinking getting her a car for her birthday. "And please follow the speed limit."

"Daddy, I'm only going thirty miles per hour."

"The speed limit is twenty-five miles per hour, please slow down. Have you read that handbook from Road Traffic?"

"Handbook?"

"You sure you want your license?"

"Chill, Dad. I've read it."

"Then you know that you're speeding."

"I'd hardly call it speeding. I just want us to be on time for our appointment with Ms. Deveaux."

Randy pointed at the clock on the dashboard. It was ten minutes after seven. They had more than sufficient time to get to Bahamas Christian Academy for their eight o'clock appointment.

"Oh, I thought it was later than that."

"Sure, you did." Randy shook his head.

"I'm happy you didn't cancel again. Ms. Deveaux was starting to think that I'm not a priority for you."

"Of course, you're a priority..." The side eye Eden gave him made him swallow the words that were about to leave his mouth. If he had ever given Jaqueline Knight a look like that, she would have slapped it straight off his face, but instead of him chastising Eden he felt chastised as the words of Ephesians 6:4 came to his mind. *Fathers do not provoke your children to anger by the way you treat them.* He knew that one verse and text because he always wanted to throw it at his father when he was growing up. He and Eden were silent the rest of the ride.

Randy looked around as they made their way to Ms. Deveaux's office. He remembered hating having to change classes on rainy or cold days (and by cold he meant anything below seventy degrees). His brothers, Storm and Jason, would often skip classes on those days. Being the nerd, he never skipped class. He was like the US Postal Service; whether rain, hail, sleet or snow, he was there.

Eden knocked on the closed door at exactly eight o'clock. Whether by coincidence or by Eden's design, he was glad they weren't late. He didn't want Ms. Deveaux checking any more x's beside his name, and he was certain that he already had a few x's. Expecting to hear her hypnotic voice instruct them to come in, he was surprised when Ms. Deveaux opened the door.

"Good Morning, Eden. Good Morning, Mr. Knight."

She gave Eden a tight squeeze and him a firm handshake before ushering them into the office. Today she wore a pair of black wide leg pants and a black t-shirt with Team Jesus in white lettering. To keep himself from staring at her he looked around the room. The space wasn't big. He couldn't call it an office. It was more like a cubicle with a door. Her desk faced the door, if you could call it a desk. Two black filing drawers on either end created a base supporting a glass top. The wall behind the desk was filled with various framed quotes and Bible verses. For a second his eyes grew big when he noticed Ephesians 6:4 in one of the frames. It was the very scripture that had come to his mind on the ride to school.

"Is everything alright, Mr. Knight?"

"Ah, yes. Just admiring your wall."

"Thank you. Just a few of my favorites that I use to inspire students and parents."

Randy smiled and took a seat in one of the wicker chairs that faced the desk. He noted the chair cushions were pink and the plush carpet beneath his feet was gray. The office had character, like its owner.

"I'm glad you were finally able to make it, Mr. Knight."

Ms. Deveaux's smile made him feel a bit warm. He resisted

the urge to loosen his tie. Her hair was covered in a colorful and elaborate headwrap. Elaborate to him because he couldn't imagine how it was done. He'd never really paid attention to women in headwraps before. He thought it was kind of extra, but he liked hers.

"I'm glad to finally be able to make it, and I want to apologize to you and to Eden for not making this meeting a priority."

"I'm sure you know the adage actions speak louder than words."

Randy hadn't expected her response. She was more direct with him than most people. The only people who weren't afraid to pull any punches with him were his family. Everyone else was too afraid. He was tough to work with, but it wasn't like he went around biting people's heads off every day.

"Duly noted."

She cleared her throat. "I want to start by saying Eden has shown tremendous improvement since last school year. She is excelling academically. She joined the debate team and the peer tutoring program. She started a Bible study during her study hall, and she was a model student until last week.

"As you know the administration was extremely gracious last year and did not expel Eden after multiple disciplinary infractions. But there was a stipulation to their decision and that was that Eden behave herself this year. The administration has decided that if Eden gets into another mishap, she will be expelled."

Randy sighed. He expected as much. If Eden got expelled from BCA, it would be the sixth school she would have been kicked out of and that included boarding school in England. He didn't think another school on the island would accept her. What was the alternative? Send her to her mother? That thought made Randy determined an expulsion would not happen. Randy was about to respond, but Ms. Deveaux held up a silencing hand. His eyes widened. Nobody did that to him either.

"I said that because I had to. None us in this room want Eden to be expelled from BCA. For that to happen I think we all need to be honest with each other."

After their meeting with Ms. Deveaux, Randy did something he had not done since he and Dave started Renaissance. He took the rest of the day off and went home. He kicked off his shoes in the foyer. Then made his way to the kitchen and took a Kalik out of the stainless-steel refrigerator. As he chugged the beer, his frustration and anger with himself mounted. The can crumpled under the weight of his grip. He hurled it across the room, releasing the emotions he had bottled up for a long time. Screaming at the top of his lungs until he was spent, he dropped onto the floor in exhaustion.

He had failed his baby girl miserably. He had figured out how to run a multimillion-dollar company and amass wealth, but couldn't figure out how to be the parent she needed him to be. The truth was he had never tried. Instead of dealing with the heartbreak his ex-wife, Kim, caused, he threw himself completely into Renaissance. During his marriage his work took up seventy-five percent of his time. After the divorce, it took up 150% of his time, leaving the nanny to take care of a two-year old Eden. When she got older, his parents cared for her and when she started acting out it was boarding school.

Even though his relationship with his dad was nonexistent at the time, when his mom suggested Eden come and stay with them while he got himself together emotionally and mentally, he took her offer. An arrangement that was supposed to be a couple of months turned into a couple of years. When twelve year old Eden came back to live with him, she was as angry with him as he was with his dad.

The last four years had been tumultuous. He knew she was crying out for his attention, but he didn't know how to give it to her and he was too afraid to try. Two people he had loved without measure had hurled that love back in his face. He was afraid his daughter would wind up doing the same. Today's conversation with Ms. Deveaux confronted his shortcomings and put his failure on blast. It made him resolve to be the father Eden needed him to be. He had to fix their relationship. And although he didn't know how, he did know it was possible. He knew he could do it. Picking himself up off the floor, he headed upstairs to bed.

When he woke, it felt like it should be the next day but his phone indicated that it was still Monday, and according to his notifications, he had twelve missed calls, half of which were from Dave. The other half of the missed calls were from his twin brother, who was certain to show up to his house shortly in full tactical gear. He quickly texted his brother, Dave to let him know he was okay and he wished he hadn't told Storm that he hadn't showed up for work. Then he texted Storm, although he doubted it would detour his twin from coming over.

He ignored the dozens of text messages and email notifications on his phone and logged onto Facebook. He didn't remember setting up an account. It was probably something Eden or Dave or Melanie, his assistant, did. Whoever did it, right now he was glad they had. He typed Priscilla Deveaux in the search bar. The first person in the search results was her. He clicked on her profile.

She was thirty-five and her birthday was June 24th, two days after his. She went to high school at St. Andrew's School in Nassau and graduated from Clark Atlanta University. He didn't know why he was Facebook stalking her. He did know why. He wanted to know more about her and was almost certain she wouldn't provide him the information. At least not right now. He started browsing through her pictures, which were mostly of kids. He supposed they were her students. Some of them wore the Bahamas Christian Academy uniform and some didn't. There were also a lot of pictures of her with two women. He knew Avery Grant and the other woman from the poetry competition. No pictures with anybody he could readily label as family. *No boyfriend.* She didn't have a relationship status.

He went through her posts. The last post was from that

morning. It was a picture with Psalm 100:1. She captioned it "the passcode to His presence is your thanks." The one from the day before was another Bible verse with a word of encouragement. He went back three months, and the majority of her posts were a scripture with positive words. He was impressed. Weeks, even months, after the words had been posted he found comfort and encouragement in them. He sent her a friend request. *What did I do that for?* He quickly put his phone down to stop from canceling the request and found himself hoping that she would accept. He got out of bed when he heard someone in the hallway. With it being the middle of the day and Eden at school, a typical reaction would be alarm, but his "twinergy" was on high alert. So, he wasn't surprised when Storm walked into the bedroom.

"Bey, what you doing in bed?"

He rolled his eyes. He'd gotten out of bed just so his brother couldn't ask him that, but apparently being in the bedroom was the same as being in bed.

"You don't knock, aye?"

"What I have to knock for when I have a key? Are you sick?"

"What are you doing?" Randy squatted Storm's hand away from him.

"I'm checking to see if you have a fever. Mummy said I should give you some cerasee."

Storm referred to the bitter herb that grew wild all over the island. The leaves were boiled and given as a tea for medicinal purposes. Most Bahamians swore it cured just about anything.

"You called Mum?

"I didn't call her. I happened to be on the phone with her when Dave called. I conferenced her in. I didn't know he was going to say that for the first time in your life you didn't show up to work. For real though, what's up?"

"I'll tell you while we have lunch."

"Ok. Great. I'll have a crack conch."

"You're putting in an order? What do I look like, a restaurant?"

"Of course you're not a restaurant, but you do have some conch thawing out in your sink."

"How long have you been here?"

"Long enough to peep that conch and throw out the rest of your beer."

"You didn't have to do that. I don't have a problem with alcohol."

"I know, but you could develop one. It's just better not to touch the stuff."

Randy frowned at Storm. His self-righteousness got on his nerves. If there was such a thing as being too saved, Storm would win the prize. He shouldn't want this, but he wished Storm would get knocked off his high horse. Get a little dirty like the rest of the human race.

"Whatever."

They went downstairs to the kitchen. Randy looked at the conch and wished it wasn't his cook's day off. She came three times a week and cooked enough for the days when she wasn't there. He didn't want to eat the steamed fish she had prepared. Instead, he wanted conch. He started preparing the Bahamian delicacy while telling Storm about his meeting with Ms. Deveaux.

"I know that was rough for you to hear, but I think you needed to hear it. I'm glad Eden was able to get that out and say that she feels like you don't want her. Imagine carrying that around. We know how she feels is not the truth. Those are lies from the devil. Now you have to combat those lies with the truth backed by your actions."

"I know. I know. And I probably knew all along that she felt this way. It's just been so hard for me to connect emotionally after Kim left. It's not an excuse. It's just the truth. Kim's leaving totally ruptured my heart."

"You don't want to hear this, but you have to give that to God. Real talk, only He can heal your heart. You did therapy, but you're still broken. You went on that weird spiritual, finding your inner peace by walking on hot rocks retreat to Calcutta."

"Bali..."

"Wherever. my point is that it didn't work. You came back with burnt feet, angrier than when you left."

Randy frowned as he dipped the conch in the batter he'd made before putting it in a pot of hot oil. He had forgotten about the Bali thing. He had been searching anywhere and everywhere for something that would make the ache in his heart go away. And although the ache had substantially diminished, it was still there. The questions were still there. Why wasn't he good enough? Why had she left?

"Just come to church—"

"Storm, I'm not going to church; no one's laying hands on me or any of that mumbo jumbo."

"Ok." Storm backed off. "But I'll keep praying for God to heal your heart. He is the only One who is able to do that."

Five

Priscilla was pleased with how her meeting with Randy and Eden Knight went on Monday. She was certain real progress had been made. She hoped Eden's dad took her advice about attending family therapy. She didn't pry by asking about Eden's mom (even though she desperately wanted to know), but she suspected the woman's absence had a lot to do with the dysfunction of the dad and daughter's relationship. And although the meeting was a highlight in Priscilla's week, the week went downhill from there. She was relieved it was the weekend.

She loved her job and could not imagine doing anything else, but students tried you. They tried you just to see how far you would let them go. They knew she did not tolerate any foolishness, yet they still pushed the envelope. On Tuesday, one of the boys mouthed off at her. She quickly wrote him a detention slip. She could deal with fighting, but she could not deal with slick comments from students.

It must have been a full moon or something in the water the kids were drinking because they were awful that week. Someone put sugar in Mrs. Thompson's gas tank. The culprit was still at large. The fire alarm was pulled twice. An eighth grader jumped out of a window on the second floor and broke just about every bone in his body. At first, Priscilla thought the jump was a suicide attempt, but later learned it was the result of bullying. The poor boy was being chased by seniors, and jumping was his attempt at escape. The icing on the cake was walking in on two students dang near having sex in her study hall classroom. She wasn't naïve. She knew, Christian school or not, these kids were having sex. However, she didn't think she would walk in on them having sex.

A millisecond away from laying hands on them and cussing them out, she knew she would lose her job. She was so disgusted by the whole thing she had study hall outside. She read that little girl and had zero sympathy for her when she started crying. The boy was so nonchalant and unapologetic she wanted to tear his butt up. The typical popular jock featured in every teen flick, she could tell he was running some kind of game with the girls. The whole week had been too much. Her nerves were done, and it was only the first term. What would the rest of the year be like? *Jesus, please help me and help these children. This is why I need to get my center opened.*

She was happy to be home, happy for the mental break. At least that was the plan, but she could not stop thinking about the Facebook friend request from Randy Knight. Priscilla stretched in the bed and sighed. He needed to be working on his relationship with his daughter. That's what his focus needed to be on, not on liking almost all of her posts.

Before meeting Eden, she didn't have an opinion of the Knight family. After meeting her, she labeled, the whole family a bunch of entitled, rich people who probably thought more of themselves than they should. Eden was out of control. Her dad was missing in action. Her aunt Victoria looked like she thought she was on one of those housewives reality shows. Eden's grandmother was the only one who seemed normal. Judgmental? Absolutely. However, after the encounters she had with Randy, she wasn't so sure about her assessment.

She sensed that underneath his armor was a man with a gentle spirit. Something she didn't think was synonymous with being a business tycoon, but that night at the restaurant she watched him speak to everyone from the busboys to the waiter to the managers. He was attentive, even exchanging hugs with some. She'd caught a brief part of a conversation he had with one of the busboys when they walked by. He'd encouraged the young man to go back to school and get his diploma. In those few unguarded moments, she glimpsed his heart. Her pastor always said true character is what you do in your unguarded moments. If what she saw was who he was, she wondered why he was the way he was with his daughter.

She picked up her phone to accept his friend request, but before she could the doorbell rang. Priscilla looked at the time. It was nine in the morning. Who would be at her door this early on a Saturday? Priscilla assumed it was probably a Jehovah's Witness and decided to ignore it, but the ringing persisted. She got up and went to the door; through the peephole she saw Reign standing on her porch. She opened the door.

"What took you so long? You cannot still be in bed."

Reign didn't wait for an invitation as she passed Priscilla and headed straight to the kitchen. She pulled a box of cereal from the pantry, and then moved to the cupboard where she knew Priscilla kept the bowls.

"I guess you forgot that we're supposed to go with Avery to help her pick stuff for her baby registry. The shower is in a month. Invitations need to go out. She needs to get this done ASAP."

"I'm sorry. I did forget. I told you this week was super crazy. I was looking forward to chilling today."

Reign frowned at Priscilla, and then at the carton of soy milk she grabbed from the refrigerator. "You don't have any whole milk?"

"I tired telling you that I'm lactose intolerant."

"I thought that was Avery."

"You know what, give me back my soy milk." Priscilla snatched the soy milk out of Reign's hands.

"I'll watch TV while you get dressed." Reign relieved Priscilla of the soy milk and poured some in her cereal.

An hour later she and Reign were at Avery's house on Cable Beach. Avery's husband, Vince opened the door.

"Ladies, come on in. Avery is still upstairs. She's having a meltdown because she's pregnant and thinks her regular jeans should fit. Maybe you two can convince her to get some maternity clothes. See y'all later." He said before leaving.

Priscilla and Reign found Avery in her super-sized walk in closet in tears just as Vince had said.

"Ah, what's going on in here?" Priscilla asked slowly. The closet's floor was littered with dozens of outfits that Avery had probably tried to get in.

"I'm fat." Avery wailed. Priscilla stifled a laugh and Reign rolled her eyes.

"Sweetie, you're not fat. You're pregnant." Priscilla put an arm around Avery and rubbed her shoulder.

"I told your prima-donna butt to buy some maternity clothes." Reign was unsympathetic.

"They're not cute." Avery continued to cry.

"There are a lot of cute maternity clothes." Priscilla said.

"Just put this on." Reign handed Avery a simple black, maxi dress. Avery sniffled, took the dress from Reign and headed to the bathroom.

"This lying Christian told me that she had showered already." Reign said to Priscilla.

"I said that I was getting in the shower." Avery yelled.

Thirty minutes later the trio were finally on their way with Reign fussing the whole way about having to wait on Avery. Priscilla was thankful Avery knew exactly what she wanted so they only spent an hour in Kelly's Home Center. She was expecting Avery to take no less than three hours.

After leaving Kelly's, the ladies decided to grab something to eat. The hairs on the back of Priscilla's neck stood up when Avery suggested Renaissance Café. She knew it would be highly unlikely that the owner and CFO of the conglomerate that the café was a part of would be at the restaurant in the middle of the day on a Saturday. There was no way he would be there. As much as she wished for him to not be there to avoid another encounter with a man she had no business being attracted to, she also wished that he would be there. She made a counter-suggestion, but Avery got her with "the baby wants Renaissance's ribs." Of course, what the baby wanted the baby got.

"Thank you, Jesus, for allowing me to get here safely." Priscilla unbuckled her seatbelt and exited Reign's Jeep Wrangler.

"Yes, praise Him. I thought my water might have broken. She hit every one of the nine million potholes in these Nassau streets."

Reign folded her arms. "My driving is not that bad."

Priscilla and Avery exchanged glances before bursting into uncontrollable laughter; Reign pursed her lips and waited for their amusement to subside.

"Reign, need I remind you that you couldn't even pass your driver's test?" Priscilla wiped tears from her eyes. "You tried to buy your license." Priscilla and Avery's laugher erupted again.

"Priscilla, stop. My bladder cannot take all this laughing." Avery tried to give a serious look, but failed. Reign huffed and started walking toward the restaurant.

"Come on. Don't be mad. It was funny. We were fool enough to go with you to buy a driver's license like we didn't remember that your brother is a cop." Priscilla shook her head. "Avery was gonna drive off and leave you when your brother pulled up and got out of his police car, but I wouldn't let her. He grabbed you like you were a for real criminal. I almost passed out when he arrested you."

The three of them were laughing as they approached the hostess. She informed them there was a ten-minute wait. The restaurant was casual dining with a TGI Friday's type vibe, and it was usually packed especially on the weekends. Thankfully, they'd missed the lunch rush. With them chatting nonstop, ten minutes felt like ten seconds.

"You did what?" Priscilla slid in the booth next to Reign. She wondered if her friend possibly had a screw loose.

"I had to." Reign shrugged, picking up one of the menus the hostess had put on the table.

"You had to break into the man's office? Reign, what if you had been caught?" Priscilla wanted to mush Reign in the head. She shouldn't have been surprised, though. Her name should have been Reckless instead of Reign.

"Can I tell the rest of my story?"

"No, it's giving me indigestion." Avery rubbed her stomach.

"The baby is giving you indigestion, not my story."

Avery relented. "Fine, go ahead. I kinda want to know if you got the info you wanted."

"Please. You know your girl did, but that's not the best part of the story. The best part is when the fire alarm went off."

"Yeah, stop. I can't with you today." Avery held up her hand as if that alone would stop Reign from continuing. Thankfully, their server showed up, putting a pause on the conversation.

Priscilla ordered a cracked conch dinner, which she had been wanting all week. Island comfort food. She was salivating over the thought of her meal when she saw him walk in. Water sputtered out of her mouth and onto the table as she started to choke from the sip she'd just taken.

"Are you okay?" Avery handed her some napkins.

"Yeah, I'm fine. Reign, you can stop patting my back now. It was water not a piece of steak."

"Yes, he is that fine. If I was drinking water when he walked in, I probably would have choked too."

Priscilla felt heat rising to her face. How could she be mad that Reign said what she had thought many times? Randy Knight was fine.

"Hey, Randy." Avery called, beckoning him to the table. Priscilla tried to recall if Avery had any affiliation with Randy. Then she remembered Avery's brother lived a couple of houses down from Randy. After dropping Eden off the night Randy didn't show up for their meeting, Ahmed had honked at her as they drove by each other on her way out of the exclusive sub-division. Priscilla felt her face getting hotter with each step he took towards them. Then he was at their table, smiling down at them.

"Good afternoon, ladies."

The sound of his voice was like fire on Priscilla's skin. She felt beads of sweat form on her forehead. This brought a whole new meaning to saying that a guy was hot.

Avery smiled. "It's been a minute since I've seen you. I don't get to my brother's neck of the woods too often. How you been?"

"Can't complain. You?"

"Same here."

Reign cleared her throat, obviously wanting an introduction. Priscilla wanted to pinch her.

"How rude of me. Let me introduce you to my girls. This

is Reign Bryant, and this is Priscilla Deveaux."

"Ms. Deveaux and I are acquainted." Randy extended his hand to her. "It's good to see you again."

Priscilla reluctantly took his extended hand, remembering the jolt of electricity that shot through her body the last time they connected. He held her hand and gave it a little squeeze before releasing it. In addition to the sweat, Priscilla felt her cheeks getting hot, thankful for perhaps the first time that her complexion was darker.

"Likewise," she managed to say. She hoped her smile masked how shell shocked she felt. She didn't understand why she was acting like one of her students when they had a crush on one of the boys in their class. *Get it together, girl. Stop acting like you don't know how to act.*

Giving his attention to Reign, he bowed slightly and extended his hand to her. "Pleasure to meet you, Ms. Bryant."

"Of course, it is. Sorry. I meant to say same here, Mr. Knight. Where Avery is trying to be polite by not asking you to be on her show because this is not the time or the place, I have no such qualms. I personally believe when opportunity presents itself you should seize it, and I would like to interview you for *242 Magazine*."

"Oh, you're THAT Reign Bryant. I knew the name sounded familiar. I subscribe to your magazine. Let me tell you that article you did on human trafficking when you interviewed the director of *Cargo* was beautiful. It gave humanity to nameless, faceless victims. I have to salute you on that, but everyone knows that I don't do interviews."

"Not even for Ms. Deveaux's best friend." Reign draped an arm around Priscilla's shoulder and pulled her closer to her.

"Let me go, Reign." Priscilla shrugged Reign's arm off of her.

"Sorry about that." Reign moved over from Priscilla. "A wise person once said to me if you don't tell your story someone else will tell it for you and it might not be the story you want people to know. You have to be narrator of your story and I know that you have an amazing story. Think about it? Can I have your card at least?"

"Sure." Randy chuckled and handed her one of his business cards. "You're pretty convincing. I think everyone already knows my story, though."

"No, we don't. Not your story. We've heard the Renaissance story. We've heard your brother, Dave's story, but what's the Randy Knight story? What motivates you? What inspires you? What message do YOU have for up and coming young Bahamian entrepreneurs?"

"Dang, Reign, you're working this pretty hard." Avery interrupted. "I'm sure this is not what Randy is here for.

"I just believe in seizing the moment." Reign gave Avery a fake smile that said butt out. Priscilla wished both of them would shut up so Randy could be on his merry way.

"Let's talk. Give my assistant a call to set something up."

"Let's see how long that takes." The words were out of Priscilla's mouth before she could censor them. It was a mumble, but he heard her.

"Do you ladies mind if I speak to Ms. Deveaux in private for a moment?"

Avery and Reign exchanged puzzled looks, but they both nodded. Priscilla was stunned they had agreed so easily. He didn't even ask her if he could speak to her in private. Cute guy and they lose all sense of loyalty.

"Ms. Deveaux?" He extended his hand again. This time to help her out of the booth. After they'd walked a few paces away from the table he asked if she mind if they spoke in the manager's office. She did mind; she didn't want to be anywhere with him by herself. It was too physically taxing. She was already sweating like she had worked out. However, she felt like she owed him an apology for her comment and wanted to say that away from Reign's bionic ears that were now solely focused on them.

"That's fine."

Once inside the small office he offered her a seat. She shook her head. "I'll stand."

Randy shrugged and leaned against the edge of the manager's desk. "I want to apologize again. I was a jerk for blowing off your calls, taking so long to schedule an appointment and then missing it. I don't want you to think that's who I am. I may not be present all the time, but I am not a deadbeat dad. I hope our appointment the other day showed you that I care about my daughter."

"I know you care about your daughter. I should be the one apologizing for my comment. It was unnecessary."

"I'll accept your apology if you accept mine."

"I already accepted your apology."

"Great, then I accept yours. I'm glad we cleared the air since we're going to be working together to keep Eden in BCA until she graduates."

"I don't think that'll be hard. She wants to be there. She's really turned her life around since accepting Jesus into her life." Priscilla observed that he seemed surprised by what she had said.

"She didn't tell me about that. I speculated that one of my brothers probably got to her."

"Ask her about it. You know Jesus is the only one who could cause such a huge turn around in her."

"What Eden said in our meeting was a wake-up call for me. I had no idea she felt that way. I have work to do. We're going to see the family therapist you suggested, and we're going to have individual sessions as well. Thank you for being persistent with me."

The sincerity in his eyes gave Priscilla butterflies in her stomach. She commanded herself to remain professional and to not melt. "That's my job, and Eden is a really good kid."

"It's still special and it means a lot to me." Randy looked down at her and brushed his thumb over her cheek.

Priscilla felt like she should have squatted his hand away. Instead, she found her eyes drifting shut and a giddy smile tugging at the corner of her mouth. Despite her best efforts, she melted.

"I want to take you out to dinner to show you my appreciation."

His words brought Priscilla out of her fantasy and back to reality. There was no way she could go on a date with him. He was the parent of one of her students. There was nothing in the school's code of conduct that prohibited her from dating him. It was a rule she'd given herself. If it didn't work, it would be too awkward for all parties involved.

"I don't date my student's dad."

"Good rule to have and a good rule to break." Randy winked.

***

Back at the table with Avery and Reign, they bombarded Priscilla with questions.

"So, the poetry competition is not the only way you know Randy Knight." Avery surmised.

"Spill it," Reign demanded.

"His daughter goes to BCA."

"That's it?" Reign seemed disappointed.

"Yeah, that's it. His daughter is one of my students."

Avery gave Priscilla the side eye. "Priscilla, stop fronting. I saw the way that man looked at you."

"Nah, you need to check you contact prescription. He is strictly about his daughter." Priscilla repented of the lie, but she didn't want Avery and Reign getting any ideas about her and Randy Knight. They would be relentless in trying to hook them up if they thought there was something there.

"OK. What about the way you were looking at him? I saw you blushing."

"I don't blush, Avery." Priscilla folded her arms over her chest.

"There is absolutely nothing wrong with you being into this guy. Sometimes I feel like you think it's a sin to look at a man." Avery threw her hands up. "God forbid he show interest and ask you out, that's like committing fornication."

"Stop exaggerating. You know that's not what I think."

Reign rolled her eyes. "No, it's just how you act.

"A'ight, Lala. Keep it to yourself, but Reign and I are going to get to the bottom of those looks."

"For the record," Reign added. "I didn't notice any looks; I was too busy looking at the fineness that is Randy Knight, but if that's you I'll stop looking."

"There's nothing there." Priscilla repented again. *God, please forgive me another bold face lie, but You know I can't go there.*

Six

The smell of freshly baked Johnny Cake hit Randy's nostrils as soon as he walked into the house. He licked his lips and patted his stomach at the thought of eating the cake-like bread. He followed the scent to the kitchen where Ms. Gloria was preparing food for him and Eden for the next couple of days.

"Hey, Randy." She wiped her hands on her apron before walking over to him to give him a hug.

"How you doing, Ms. Gloria?" Randy took a seat on a stool at the island in the middle of the kitchen.

"Well, you know Charlene's boy still in the hospital. He gone and get mixed up with one of them gangs."

Ms. Gloria returned to chopping onions, and Randy noticed the extra vigor in her chopping as she talked about her grandson. He was afraid Ms. Gloria might hurt herself.

"He was raised better than that," *Chop. Chop, Chop.* "I know 'cause I helped raise him."

"I remember when he was in elementary school. He kind of reminded me of myself when I was that age."

"You mean nerdy." Ms. Gloria chuckled.

"I meant studious. What happened?"

Ms. Gloria was their neighbor for many years when Randy's family lived in Freeport. When she lost her job as a cook at one of the hotels, she moved to Nassau to live with her daughter, Charlene. His ex-wife would not lift a finger to clean, but he never expected her to since they had a cleaning service. And while she might not have been able to wash, iron or clean, Kim liked to throw down in the kitchen, so they never hired a cook.

After the divorce he threw himself into work and didn't have time to eat breakfast, lunch or dinner, let alone cook, so he hired Ms. Gloria.

"It's that neighborhood. I'm telling you it is like a war zone. I'm praying we can get up out of there soon, but Charlene doesn't want to move. Say it's our neighborhood, and we shouldn't let the thugs run us out." Ms. Gloria sucked her teeth.

"Things will get better."

Would they? Randy felt a tug at his heart. This was exactly what Priscilla-Ms. Deveaux's *Ghetto Angel* was about, saving their neighborhoods from crime. Why hadn't he taken Ms. Gloria's grandson under his wing? Why hadn't he become his mentor? Randy knew where he was from, and knew what he was up against. This conversation was another reminder that just because the crime and poverty didn't reach him personally didn't mean that he shouldn't be doing something about it. He did tell Ms. Deveaux he would be willing to help. He wasn't about just talking about a problem without being a part of the solution. He needed to be a part of the solution. He would reach out to her to see what her agenda was.

During his shower Randy recalled when he and his brothers used to come to Nassau with their father for revivals at their parent church. They would canvas the streets of Bain Town, Englerston and the Grove. He remembered knocking on doors of houses that looked like shacks – three to four rooms in the whole "house" with ten plus people living in them. Looking into the eyes of men and seeing emptiness, it seemed like they had no souls to save.

Randy recalled going to a house where two men were playing dominos. They weren't interested in hearing about Jesus, but they told them they could talk to the old lady inside. While Randy, Storm and their dad were inside they heard a commotion. Dashing outside, he saw one of the men they were talking to not five minutes before laying on the ground with a knife in his neck.

His dad and Storm immediately went into rescue mode, but he was frozen by shock. What would make one human do something like that to another human over a five-dollar bet? How did you reach someone who would do something like that? It seemed hopeless to him, but they continued to preach the good news. Randy scoffed. Lots of words and no action. It was time for some action. He quickly dressed and headed downstairs to the dining room where he found Eden already seated at the table.

"Daddy, I'm so proud of you. Three days in a row you made it home for dinner. That is definitely a record for you."

"It was a part of our deal. I'd spend more time at home. You'd spend more time staying out of trouble." Randy kissed the top of Eden's hair then tugged on one of her golden spirals.

"Dad! Come on. You know I don't like people touching my hair."

Randy looked at the mass of honey blonde curls that fell just past Eden's shoulders. He didn't understand why she made such a fuss about her hair. It looked like a get up and go kind of do and not one that required a lot styling. He'd never understand women and their hair. He caught himself wondering if Ms. Deveaux was as fussy about her hair and quickly returned his attention to Eden.

"I'm sorry. I forgot." Randy took his seat.

"I'm sure you didn't. How was your day?"

"Busy as usual. Nothing interesting. What about yours?"

"I'm glad you asked, but I am super hungry. Before I tell you about my day let's bless the food. Do you want to pray?

Taking Eden's hand in his, Randy shook his head. "You go ahead."

"Father, thank you for this food that I surely know Ms.

Gloria put her foot in. Bless this food that will bless my belly. Thank you for my dad and for strengthening our relationship. In Jesus' name. Amen."

"Amen." Randy gave Eden's hand a squeeze before releasing it.

"Amen." Ms. Gloria chimed in. "Just wanted to let you know that I'm leaving now."

"I thought you were going to join us for dinner." Randy pointed at the third place setting on the table.

"Oh no. That was just in case either one of you had company."

"Company?" Both Randy and Eden questioned.

"Yes, that's when you invite guests over to visit, and they have dinner with you. I can't remember the last time you had anyone over here for anything."

"I'm not the entertainer of the family. That's Dave's area. When I want to have company, I go over to his house. There's always a bunch of people at his house for dinner."

"You're right about that." Eden added. "On Sunday after church Uncle Dave invited ten families over for dinner. I was like Uncle Dave you are doing the most. There better be enough food for all of us."

"Eden, your mouth is too fast. Let that man do something good for those folks. Not everyone can afford to have a good Sunday dinner. Anyway, let me go. I'm going to stop and see my sister before I go home. I'm so grateful for that car you got me, Randy. I'm able to get around and see my family now." Ms. Gloria shook her head. "Depending on Charlene for a ride was not working. She's always busy. I'll see you all in a couple of days."

"Ok. Take care, Ms. Gloria." Randy stood and gave the older woman a tight hug. "Everything will work out with your grandson."

Eden stood, too and gave Ms. Gloria a hug. "I'll be praying for him."

"Thank you, Eden. I appreciate that. See y'all."

"What was it about your day that you were so anxious to tell me about?" Randy asked once they had retaken their seats.

"We're studying ecology in biology class this term, and Mrs. Lowe has arranged a field trip for us to go to BREEF, Bahamas Reef Environment Educational Foundation, to study ocean ecology. Well, just the ecology of the coral reefs."

"Shallow water snorkeling?" Randy took a sip of water. The stewed fish was little spicier than he could handle.

"Yes! I can't wait."

Eden loved anything to do with the water. She loved all water sports, especially jet skiing and was a certified scuba diver. That's what happened when you had an uncle who loved anything that could go over 100 miles per hour. Her uncle Rome had gotten her into jet skiing and parasailing. Her uncle Storm was Bahamian special ops, a highly specialized trained officer in the Royal Bahamas Police Force and could hold his breath underwater for almost three minutes. He'd taught Eden how to dive. Randy didn't like either of his brothers very much for getting his daughter involved in these very strange hobbies.

"You're excited to go snorkeling? You've dived to see the Andros Barrier Reef."

"I have, but I haven't done it with Da... my friends. Maybe after this I can convince hi... them to learn to scuba dive."

Eden's slip of the tongue was not lost on Randy. Who was this him whose name began with the letters d and a? Of course, Eden was at the age to be interested in boys, but he remembered what it was like to be a boy that age. He didn't trust D A with his daughter.

"I see. What's his name?"

"I'm not ready to share that information with you. You're going to tell Uncle Storm and have him arrested or something."

"Oh, I hadn't thought of that, but that's a really good idea."

"We've lost focus. Let's focus on the field trip. One of the chaperone's dropped out at the last minute. We need to have at least five. I told Ms. Lowe that you would be more than willing to accompany us. If you check your voicemail, you probably have a message from her."

"When's the field trip?"

"Wednesday."

"Day after tomorrow?"

"Yeah."

"I don't know, E. That's right in the middle of the week. My Wednesdays are usually jammed." Randy pulled out his phone to look at his calendar. He had a slew of meetings on Wednesday morning and a pow wow with his research and development team in the afternoon. He looked up to tell Eden that he couldn't do it. Her head was bowed.

"What are you doing?"

"Praying."

"Right in the middle of our conversation?"

"Ok, I'm begging. I'm groveling. Please, please, pretty please, Daddy."

Randy looked at his calendar again, which was synced with Dave's calendar. Dave was scheduled to be in those meetings as well. Both of them didn't have to be there, and he could reschedule the R&D meeting.

"Okay." Randy was stunned when Eden jumped up from her seat and started doing the Running Man. He couldn't do anything but laugh at Eden's antics.

"Thanks." She hugged him before sitting down.

***

Wednesday came so quickly Randy felt like somehow, he must have skipped Tuesday. There was usually some sort of debate with Eden when it came to getting her up and out of the house; however, this particular morning she was standing in Randy's bedroom at seven a.m. Randy looked up from his perch on his bed. Surrounded by his laptop, notes from his meeting with investors and breakfast, he had already put in what others might consider a half a day's work.

"We're leaving in ten minutes." Eden turned on her heels and left the room.

Randy roared with laughter. His mother had used a similar line on him when he was growing up and apparently on Eden too. She would say, "I'm leaving this house in ten minutes, and you better be in that car with clean draws on when I'm ready to leave." He would scramble out of bed and to the bathroom. There were many times he would race outside to the car and she would be gone.

"How many times have she left you?" Randy yelled so Eden could hear him as he got out of the bed.

"Plenty times."

Randy shook his head. His mom was something else. She did not play with them, and she did not play with the grandkids either. If they dared to get flippant with her, she would quickly remind them that "me and you ain' no company." She would tell them that she was their mother and not one of their lil raggedy friends. "Talk to your friends like that, but not to me."

Thankfully, he had the keys to the car and not Eden. So, when he got downstairs thirty minutes later, she was still there. The ride to the school was smooth. It was too early, and Nassau traffic hadn't reared its ugly head just yet. He let Eden drive again and this time he didn't have to hold on for dear life. She was getting better.

Eden pulled the car into the visitors parking lot. She wanted to back into the parking spot. It was scary. She almost hit the car next to her twice.

"Next time just drive in. Please."

"I have to practice. Practice makes perfect."

"Perfect practice makes perfect, and you'll be practicing with cones."

On the way to Mrs. Lowe's classroom, Eden was stopped by at least a dozen people. Randy felt like he was back in high school walking around with Jason. All of his brothers were cool and popular in high school, but Jason was the coolest and most popular. He hated going anywhere with him. If their mom sent them on a twenty-minute errand to the grocery store, it would take at least an hour with Jason. Randy would stand in the background fuming, thinking about how his time could be better spent.

The five-minute walk to the classroom took ten minutes with Eden. Randy was trying to figure out if any of the boys Eden had chatted with was "DA". She didn't give the "I like you" vibe to any of them, and he was very relieved because none of them seemed good enough for his daughter. He didn't know one thing about any of them, but that didn't matter.

A number of years had passed since Randy had been in a classroom. There were about thirty kids gathered around the high tables and stools in the science lab. Nostalgia provoked a smile as Randy noticed a couple of bulletin boards in the classroom. He remembered his eighth-grade history teacher had a bulletin board where he posted grades from test and quizzes in numerical order. He stayed at the top of that list, which made him feel proud, but at the same time he felt bad for the kids at the bottom of the list because they were often teased.

Randy was greeted by a petite elderly woman. She had

long dreadlocks that were almost completely white. If not for the texture of her hair, he probably would've thought that she was white. White Bahamians were not uncommon; however, Conchy Joes tended to stick together. As his grandmother used to say, "they don't mix." Apparently, there was some mixing in Mrs. Lowe's family.

"Good Morning, you must be Eden's dad."

Randy took Mrs. Lowe's extended hand. Her commanding voice seemed a contrast to her small size. Kids probably thought they could run over her and then her voice would stop them in their tracks.

"I am. It's good to meet you, Mrs. Lowe. I'm looking forward to today's activity."

"Awesome. I am too. Eden has really stepped up academically so far this year. She's a smart girl, but we always knew that." Mrs. Lowe pulled Eden, who towered over her by almost a foot, close giving her a side hug.

"I'll give you that hundred later." Eden's exaggerated whisper caused the adults to laugh.

"We're going to pray. Then I'll brief everyone on today's field trip before we head to the bus. We're just waiting on... Oh, there is our last chaperone now."

Randy turned to see Ms. Deveaux walking into the classroom. Randy had been hoping to run into her and had already planned to take a trip to her office if he didn't run into her. But her actually being on the trip was more than he could even imagine. She smiled and gave him a nod. He did the same. Before he could say anything to Ms. Deveaux, Mrs. Lowe asked him to pray.

"Ah... Umm... How about if we ask Ms. Deveaux to pray?"

"Sure." Ms. Deveaux shrugged before taking his hand in hers, signaling everyone to join hands.

"Heavenly Father, this morning we enter Your gates with

thanksgiving in our hearts and we enter Your courts with praise. We thank You and bless Your name because You are good and merciful always. We ask that Your perfect will be done in our lives today. We thank You for Your provision. For blessing us to be able to make this trip today. We seek Your forgiveness and release unforgiveness. Protect us and keep us safe. It is all for Your kingdom. We love you, Abba. In Jesus' name, amen."

Randy slowly opened his eyes and reluctantly let go of Ms. Deveaux's hand. She probably thought he was weird for that, but it was just that he had felt something he hadn't felt in a long time. It was genuine. Authentic. Pure. It wasn't loud. It wasn't showy. It wasn't huffing and puffing, just real and simple. In those few short moments when she was praying and he was listening he was forced to shut off all the hundreds of thoughts that were constantly running through his mind. Interested in hearing what she had to say, he had silenced his inner voice and concentrated on her voice. That singular focus brought stillness. In that moment of stillness, he felt peace, and that's what he had not felt in a long time.

Seven

Making their way from the classroom to the school bus, Priscilla walked alongside Mrs. Lowe. She had no clue what the biology teacher was talking about. Her mind was stalled on the fact that Eden's father was a chaperone. She remembered Mrs. Lowe mentioning one of the parents had cancelled last minute. She also recalled her being excited that another parent had agreed to take the vacant chaperone spot. Priscilla wished she had known who the replacement chaperone was. Then she wouldn't have been surprised to see Randy Knight standing in the classroom, or surprised when she felt excited about spending the day with him, although it was not really spending the day with him.

On the short walk to the bus her imagination had already conjured up five scenarios of how the day with Mr. Knight would go, and only one of those scenarios was positive. Worst case scenario, he would ignore her all day. She didn't really think he would, but what if he did? She'd also envisioned her doing something utterly embarrassing in front of him like falling. Just yesterday she had accidently closed the car door on her skirt. When she'd tried to briskly walk away from the car she got snatched back so fast she lost her balance and fell. She thanked God no one was around to witness that embarrassment. Suppose she had a repeat of something like that. And, of course, there was the scenario that Ms. Pyke, Alaina's single, pretty mom, would capture his attention.

Why should I even care if he is interested in Ms. Pyke? The question forced her to admit that she not only thought Randy Knight was attractive, she was attracted to him. Even though

Eden was one of her students, and she had a strict self-imposed rule that fraternizing with a parent was off limits, she would find it hard to turn him down if he shot his shot for real for real.

Her musings caused her to be the last one on the bus. Priscilla almost laughed out loud when she saw the only available seat was next to Mr. Knight. This could be God or it could not be God. She would only know for certain when she got to know him... if she got to know him. He smiled and stood, asking if she wanted to sit by the window or the aisle. She liked the window. Once she was seated, he took his seat. After Mrs. Lowe made some announcements and went over conduct rules for the day, he looked down at her.

"You know I'd already decided that I would pay you a visit today since I would be at the school, but as it turns out you are on this field trip sitting beside me."

"What were you going to visit me for?"

"Just to say hi and let you know how it's been going with me and E." Randy smiled and Priscilla nodded her head as if to convey that his response was an acceptable reason to drop by and see her without an appointment.

"How is it going? I know on the school front Eden has been keeping out of trouble."

"I've been spending less time at work, believe it or not. My brother, Dave, has this rule to not work after five o'clock that I've adopted."

"I need to do that too. I end up staying after school for games and helping out various committees. All kinds of extra stuff that people assume I have time for because I'm single, which obviously means that I have no life." Priscilla wanted to snatch the words back as soon as they left her mouth. Why did she tell this man she was single? She wondered if it came across as a flirting. *Nah... but what if it did?* She groaned inwardly.

He chuckled.

"Thank you for that bit of information." He winked. "My twin brother says the same thing. The church calls him all the time to do stuff and mostly last minute. They assume because he doesn't have a family that he is always available."

"I get it from all angles – work, church, my family. My family is the worst, though. Mama needs to go to her doctor's appointment. Call Lala. Someone's kids need babysitting. Call Lala. Someone's drunk at the club and can't drive themselves home. Call Lala."

"Lala?"

"My family's nickname for me. When my younger cousin, Troy was a toddler, he could only say the last syllable of my name – la. So, he called me La. Somehow the other La got added."

"I think it suits you. I like nicknames. I can't imagine calling toddler me Randolph. Seems too serious for a kid."

"You probably were a serious baby. Your mummy probably dressed you in little toddler business suits with glasses. I imagine you walked around with a pen and notepad."

Randy shrugged. "According to my mother I did scribble in a notepad that I carried around with me like it was a toy."

"The original Boss Baby." Priscilla quipped, and they laughed much louder than they should have. Mrs. Lowe gave them a disapproving look, which was followed by a look of curiosity from Eden.

"You're going to get us in trouble, Mr. Knight."

"No one should ever get in trouble for laughing, especially since I don't do it enough. And please, call me Randy."

"I can't do that," Priscilla shook her head, "not in front of the students."

"What about when we're not in front of the students?" Mr. Knight wiggled his eyebrows in mock suggestion.

Priscilla laughed loudly again. The gesture reminded her of an old man trying to holler at young chicks with some old whack line from back in his day. Mrs. Lowe gave them another stare of reprimand.

"Seeing that I have no intentions of being around you when it has nothing to do with school related stuff, I'll agree to call you Randy when we're not in front of the students."

"Oh, it's like that, ay? That's kinda cold, dred. You have no intentions. Ok. Can I call you Lala?"

"Absolutely not!"

"La?"

"No."

"Priscilla?"

"I guess. Same rule applies. Only when students are not around."

"What about if you come to my house for dinner and my daughter is there?"

"What? Why would I be coming to your house for dinner? Boy, bye." Priscilla motioned for him to get up. They had arrived at Cabbage Beach on Paradise Island, and everyone else had left the bus already.

On the beach, the team from the Bahamas Reef Environment Education Foundation were waiting to take the students shallow water snorkeling to observe coral reefs. As the BREEF volunteers gave out snorkel gear to the students, Priscilla stole a few glances at the camouflage swim trunks with an army green v-neck t-shirt Randy was wearing. *Lord, please don't let this man take off his shirt. Please, Jesus. I'm trying to be saved in my thoughts.* She had on a one piece as did all the girls. It was the school's rule. Over it she wore a floral wrapped skirt with a white tee that said WARRIOR QUEEN.

Once snorkel gear was handed out, BREEF had the students sit in a large circle in the sand near the shore and went through their safety rules before doing a presentation on the types of coral and fish they would see while snorkeling. They gave the kids a fun activity to try to identify at least five of the wildlife they mentioned while snorkeling.

It was ninety degrees, with a steady breeze that made the heat seem less hellish, the perfect beach day. Near the shore the blue waters were so clear it was transparent and seemed to sparkle when the sunlight hit it. Priscilla stood in awe of God's perfection; no man could ever duplicate the shade of turquoise. Further out, the water darkened into sapphire. Priscilla was mesmerized by the different shades of blue. She would never get used to how beautiful the water was.

"It's beautiful isn't it?" Randy walked up next to her.

"God is amazing. Imagine He spoke this into existence." Entranced, Priscilla continued to stare at the water. "This beautiful, complex ocean was spoken into existence. He said let there be and there was this."

"So, are you going to get in?" Randy handed Priscilla a pair of flippers, a mask and a snorkel.

"I'll admit that I'm a little nervous. I'm not the best swimmer, but the water is calm and shallow enough for me."

"Eden is like a fish. A real-life little mermaid. She gets that from my family. We love the ocean. Before we started hustling to make that paper, my brothers and I spent every bit of daylight on the beach every day during the summer. We dived, speared and trapped for lobsters. We went crabbing. My brothers would beg the jet ski operators on the beach to let us get a free ride when things were slow. Sometimes they would. We loved anything in the water. Matter of fact, Storm is a certified deep-sea diver. He is serious with his. He can dive hundreds of feet. I'm not that crazy."

"That is crazy. I'm just trying to snorkel in water I can

stand in." Priscilla laughed as she put on her flippers and secured her mask. Randy did the same.

They headed into the water with their group. Following the leaders from BREEF the students had no hesitation in getting under the water. It took Priscilla a minute, but she joined them. Randy and Eden were long gone by the time she immersed herself in the water. She stayed as close to the shore as possible. Then she saw Randy swimming towards her. Yes, even under the water she recognized him immediately. He took her hand, leading her deeper into the water. It was actually not that deep. Priscilla knew she could probably stand it, but she still felt anxious about going deeper.

With Randy's firm grip on her hand, she relaxed. Calm replaced fear, and she curiously looked around at the coral. She saw puffer fish, trumpet fish, flounder, and a lobster. She had no desire to encounter jellyfish or stingray, but knew those were on the top of the students' list. There were plenty of starfish, and she saw a real-life seahorse. She almost screamed her excitement when she saw that, but screaming wasn't possible underwater. Eden swam by taking pictures of Priscilla and Randy with her phone that she had protected in a water proof case. Randy was right. The girl moved as easily as a mermaid underwater. She signaled that she was going deeper and was off.

When they got out of the water almost an hour later, Priscilla was surprised to see a catered lunch waiting for them. A buffet table had been set up along with tables and chairs, and servers in Renaissance Café uniforms stood ready to serve the kids. Mrs. Lowe didn't have to tell the students twice. They raced towards the food once she was done saying the blessing.

"Mr. Knight, you really didn't have to do this. Thank you so much." Mrs. Lowe said.

"It's my pleasure. Think nothing of it."

All the chaperones sat at the same table. Priscilla sat between Mrs. Lowe and Mr. Johnson, the P.E. instructor. Randy sat opposite Mrs. Lowe, and Ms. Pyke sat between him and Mrs. Michaels, another parent. Priscilla had chosen not to sit next to Mr. Knight because she didn't want it to seem like they were spending the day together. She had already received curious glances from both Mrs. Lowe and Eden. Well, Eden's look was a big grin and a thumbs up when her dad wasn't looking. She shouldn't have felt any type of way when Ms. Pyke started flirting with him. Priscilla had to admit that on his part he was keeping it super professional with her. Ms. Pyke had shot her shot and he had blocked it. Priscilla found herself wanting to cheer.

On the bus ride back to school they kept the seating arrangements they had on the way over. Priscilla yawned about fifty eleven times. Randy joked and told her to stop; yawns were contagious. Before she knew it, she was knocked out and using Randy's shoulder as a pillow. It was the best thirty-minute nap ever, but it also meant they didn't chat as much as they had that morning.

They arrived back to campus right before dismissal, and Mrs. Lowe instructed the students to go to their homerooms. She thanked the parents again for chaperoning and also the teachers. Priscilla was tired; since school was almost over, she decided to call it a day and started to head for her car.

"Ms. Deveaux."

Priscilla turned at the sound of her name. She had contemplated whether or not she should say goodbye to Randy but decided against it because he was talking to Ms. Pyke and Mrs. Michaels. She didn't think it would've been a good look if she'd interrupted them to be like, "Bye, Mr. Knight" all sing-song like a fifteen-year-old who had a crush on one of her male teachers.

"I'll walk with you to your office." Randy said when he caught up to her.

"I'm headed to my car."

"I'll walk you to your car." He said, and she nodded.

"So, you were going to leave without saying bye?"

"You were talking." She shrugged, and it was his turn to nod.

"Were you actually trying to win that prize for spotting the fish on the list they gave at the beginning?"

"I wasn't trying to win." Priscilla started walking again, and Randy fell in step beside her. "I was just... You're right. I was trying to win that Starbucks gift card. These chirren don't need caffeine as badly as I do."

"They don't need a lot of stuff they're into. Who was that kid Eden was talking to at lunch? He didn't need to be sitting as close to Eden as he was."

Priscilla rolled her eyes. Eden was showing Dakari the pictures she had taken underwater. They were looking at her phone, not snuggling up.

"Dakari is one of our best students. He has a 4.0 GPA. He's a track and field prodigy. He more than likely will be representing the Bahamas at the next Olympics. He's a youth leader at his church. Without a doubt he will be a world changer. You have nothing to worry about. Not saying there's anything between them, but if there is, he would treat her right." Priscilla rattled off the boy's bio to which Randy snorted.

"He's a teenage boy. Teenage boys are only interested in one thing."

"He's a teenage boy who is on fire for Jesus."

Randy looked like he was going to say something but changed his mind. Priscilla didn't press him. They were at her car, and although the company was good, she was exhausted.

"Thank you for literally holding my hand through snorkeling. I ended up relaxing enough to really enjoy the experience." Priscilla found herself giving Randy a hug. *What am I doing? What am I doing? What am I doing in the school's parking lot!*

It was obvious she caught him off guard because he didn't immediately hug her back, but when he did Priscilla felt like she was in a place she never wanted to leave. His arms gave her a security she had not felt before. Living with a mom as flighty as hers, she never felt secure. Nothing was stable. When Randy returned her hug, she found herself thinking this is what it feels like to feel safe, secure and protected.

"You're welcome." Randy placed a gentle, lingering kiss on her forehead. Priscilla's eyes fluttered close, and she felt herself getting lost once again in his orbit.

"Dad, are you ready?"

Priscilla's eyes flew open. She thought she heard Randy curse under his breath before turning to address Eden.

"Yeah, I'm coming."

***

On Saturday Priscilla lounged on her sofa with a bowl of Honey Bunches of Oats. She put her feet up on the coffee table and leaned her head back. With her eyes closed she imagined being on the beach again like Wednesday except without the students. She could feel the gentle sway of the waves around her when she was in the water and could still smell the salt in the air. The combination was like a lullaby and she drifted.

Her eyes popped open and she sprang upright. What was his voice doing in her daydream! Listening to him was like hearing the *Miseducation of Lauryn Hill* for the very first time. She understood and connected with every lyric, every rhythm, every beat and wanted to play the album over and over again to savor it. That's what her conversations on Wednesday with Randy were like. They'd talked about poetry, music, business, finances, the community and of course, Eden. He quoted Hughes, Brooks, Angelou and Pintard. They even had a round of "Do you remember this song?"

She had a great time with Randolph Alexander Knight (she'd even learned his full name) and was looking forward to seeing him again. Priscilla groaned. *I'm looking forward to seeing him again? We weren't on a date. This is what happens when you're deprived of male companionship. Any lil attention and you think you're on a date. You thinking about making that man your man.*

Not to mention, she let him kiss her at her place of employment! It was on the forehead, but still inappropriate. She hoped none of the students or staff had seen them. She wanted to see where this attraction could lead, but this was not a good look for her. Snatched up in the school parking lot with her student's handsome, rich daddy. Looking like a gold digging predator. *Acting just like my mama.* Priscilla sucked her teeth. Yeah, she needed to shut this down.

Eight

Randy glanced at the time on his computer. It was 9:25. He was surprised Priscilla was calling him so late, especially since she had been ghosting him. He was also surprised to be in bed this early. After dinner he and Eden had watched a few episodes of the DC comic, *Arrow* on Netflix, and then called it a night. He set his laptop on his nightstand and picked up his cell phone.

"How may I help you, Lala? I didn't think I'd hear from you. You've been ignoring my texts."

"I'm with Eden." Her voice was serious and professional.

"Eden is in her room." At least she had been an hour ago when he'd stuck his head in to say goodnight. Randy threw his head back on his pillow. He thought they were done with these shenanigans.

"We were at Atlantis..."

"What?"

"It's a story I'll let her tell. I came to get her and my car broke down on the bridge."

"Ok. I'm on my way."

Randy disconnected the call before Priscilla could respond. He felt tension gather at the base of his neck. Maybe he should have taken his parents up on their offer to have Eden come live with them again. His decision to decline their offer was seventy percent determination to fix his relationship with his daughter and thirty percent not wanting to have anything to do with his father. But he was strongly reconsidering his decision.

On a small island the drive from his house to Atlantis Resort on Paradise Island was long enough for Randy's mind to fill with thousands of scenarios about Eden. Not to mention his thoughts about why she had called Priscilla instead of calling him.

For the first time in a long time Randy felt the urge to pray. Like he told Dave, he loved God and he believed God loved him. However, he was not convinced God was that concerned about his life. Did a God who created the whole, entire universe really care about whether he read his Bible or went to church regularly or listened to his prayers? Randy didn't think so; so many of his prayers went unanswered. Like his prayer that his wife would come back or that he would wake up from the nightmare with his dad.

Since Priscilla said they were coming from Atlantis that meant Randy had to drive across the new Paradise Island Bridge and then come back across on the old bridge. You took one to get on the island and the other to get back. He was thankful Priscilla had been able to pull her older model Prius on the side and wasn't blocking any traffic. After having lived in the UK and visiting the US, he knew for sure that Nassauvians didn't know how to drive. Traffic signs and traffic lights meant nothing and distressed vehicles received no courtesy.

Eden jumped out of Priscilla's car and ran toward him. It reminded him of when she was a little girl and he came home. She would run up to him and throw herself into his arms. Just then she jumped into his arms.

"Daddy, I'm so glad I got them out of there." Eden sobbed, and for a brief moment Randy just held Eden, wishing it could be like this more often.

"What are you talking about?"

"Kaley and Alex."

Randy looked over his daughter's head and saw Eden's two

friends standing with Priscilla. Even while listening to Eden he could not help but notice Priscilla. Two weeks had passed since he last saw her, and she looked better than he remembered. Tonight, she was wearing a pair of fitted black jeans with a black T-shirt that read "My Superpower is to Empower" in white lettering and army boots. She wore a printed head wrap and large hoop earrings.

"Slow down, E, and start over."

"Kaley and Alex..." Eden paused like she suddenly remembered something. She turned and beckoned for her friends to come over. Kaley, Alex and Priscilla walked over to where Randy and Eden were standing.

"Good evening, Mr. Knight."

"Ms. Deveaux." He wanted to say Lala just to get on her nerves, but she didn't look like she was in the mood for jokes. He looked at Eden's friends, remembering them as the girls who giggled every time he spoke, which annoyed him.

"Hi, girls." Sure enough they giggled. Eden rolled her eyes at Kaley and Alex.

"Like I was saying, I knew Kaley and Alex were going to Bing's party tonight."

"Bing?" Randy interrupted; he couldn't believe someone would actually name their child Bing.

"Teddy Bingham. Basketball star. He's a big deal, Daddy. Google him. After school I was in the library and I overheard a couple of the basketball guys talking. I was ignoring them at first because you know how guys are when they talk.

"They were talking about who they were going to get with, who they had already gotten with and what not. So then one of them said something about drugs. That's when I started paying attention. They'd planned to put drugs in girls' drinks so they could sleep with them. I started hitting up these two but couldn't get them. I went home, but I just could not let it go. I knew I had to do something, so I called Uncle Storm. But he wasn't answering his phone. Then I called Dakari and asked him if I could ride with him to the party because I knew he was going."

"The boy from the field trip?" Randy queried. Priscilla pursed her lips when he did. He shrugged his shoulders. He knew that boy wasn't any good.

"Daddy, he is not a major part of the story. Please, no more interruptions. We got to the party, and I started looking for these two. Thankfully they didn't have anything to drink, but we did see some of the track team guys with some girls who looked kind of out of it. I called the police. Yup, I sure did. Shut that party down. Anyway, somehow Dakari got taken in for questioning with the other guys, and that left us without a ride. That's when I called Ms. Deveaux. She'd told me that if I was ever in a tight situation to call her, and I couldn't call you because I snuck out."

Randy closed his eyes and pinched the bridge of his nose. He started to count backwards from 100. This new Eden wasn't stealing cars, burning stuff down or fighting. Her shenanigans were now for nobler causes, yet they still caused his blood pressure to rise. He chose not to address anything she had said and instead addressed Priscilla's car problem.

"I'll call a wrecker."

"I already called my cousin. He's sending someone to get it." She put on her super professional voice again.

Just then the wrecker pulled up to tow her car. In no time the guy had connected the car to the truck. After Priscilla gave him directions to her cousin's house, Randy gave him a tip.

"He's at work," Priscilla said as they walked to Randy's car. The girls had already gotten in the back seat of Randy's Maserati Quattroporte. Randy gave Priscilla a puzzled look.

"My cousin is at work. That's why he couldn't come and

get us. You were the next logical choice."

"You don't have to explain why you called me to come and get my child." He opened the car door for her.

Eden and her friends were talking a mile a minute on the drive to Kaley's house. He and Priscilla were not talking at all. She was sitting straight up in her seat looking out of the passenger window. He supposed that was her don't engage me in conversation position. He knew she didn't want to get involved with one of her student's parents, but how could she ignore that there was something beautifully potent between them? Yeah, he was attracted to her, but that wasn't only it. He liked her. He could be real with her. She didn't have expectations of him like everyone else did, and he could be himself with her.

He ran his index finger over the back of her hand just to be mischievous and because he really wanted to touch her. Her head spun around so fast he was sure she had gotten whiplash. She shot him a look that said, "If you touch me again, I'm a punch you."

"Stop it," she gritted out.

"I figured that would get your attention. I don't like being ignored, Ms. Deveaux."

"Oh well."

"Oh well? Come on, Lala —" The look she shot him cut his words short. "Ms. Deveaux, we have a connection. Don't ignore that."

"I have to." The look on Priscilla's face was a sad one. Randy wondered what it meant, but he didn't have time to ask. They pulled up to Kaley's house where Alex's mom was also waiting for her. They all got out of the car.

"Girl, it ga be me and you when we get home. You told me you were over here studying." "Mummy..." Alex hung her head.

"You better not say one more word. I don't work two jobs to pay your school fees so you can run around the island acting fast. Get in the car." Alex's mom then turned away from her daughter who was hurrying toward their car and toward the rest of them. "Ms. Deveaux, thank you for calling and for going to get the girls."

"It was no problem at all, Ms. Saunders. She really is a good kid. She just demonstrated poor judgment tonight."

"Yeah, don't be too hard on her." Kaley's dad advised. "I'm sure she's learned her lesson."

"I know she has. She won't be doing anything like this again. Good night, y'all. Thanks again, Ms. Deveaux." She nodded at Randy and Eden as she made her way to her car.

"Young lady, you can go in the house." Kaley's mom's voice was stern, but Randy pegged her as the strict parent although the girl's dad looked like he did not play.

"Mr. Knight, thank you for bringing Kaley home." Haley's dad extended his hand to Randy.

"You don't have to thank me for that." Randy accepted his handshake.

"Thanks all the same. Hopefully, we'll see you at church soon. The praise team really needs you." He smiled.

Randy squinted at the man, and the proverbial light bulb went off in his head.

"Kwame!"

"Hold on. You didn't know that it was me when we met last year at your house for Eden's sleepover?"

"No! I kept thinking you looked familiar, but I couldn't figure out why."

"I figured you didn't want to be bothered. You know how people get rich and switch."

"You know I'm not like that, Kwam. When did you move to Nassau?"

"As soon as your dad opened the church here. God sent me here to be a support to the ministry. Truthfully, I didn't want to. I felt hurt and betrayed like we all did. It was a lesson in forgiveness that I needed to learn."

The conversation made Randy uneasy. He wasn't going back to church, but he didn't want to flat out tell Kwame that.

"Well, it's good seeing you," Randy shifted his eyes from Kwame. "I'm going to get going."

Kwame nodded as he spoke. "Yeah, man, good seeing you. We'll play catch up another time."

Randy, Priscilla and Eden returned to the car, and Priscilla gave Randy directions to her house.

Priscilla looked over at Randy. "You sing?"

"Oh, you wanna talk now?"

"Curiosity is bugging the hell out of me." Priscilla quoted an old 90s song.
Randy smiled. "Jodeci, "Come and Talk to Me.""

"Mr. Rolle said the praise team could use you."

"I used to lead the worship team at my dad's church in Freeport."

Randy's revelation caused Priscilla's mouth to drop open.

"It's not that unbelievable."

"Yeah, it is. I saw you on the cover of *Island Vibe*. That dude doesn't look like he sings in anybody's choir."

"Girl, that thing is almost as old as Eden. How'd you find that?"

"I googled you." Priscilla admitted sheepishly.

"Stalker," Randy teased.

"You can't talk. You're a FB stalker. You went on there and liked all my posts."

Randy laughed. "That was kinda stalker-ish. So, you liked the cover?" Randy winked at her and flexed his biceps. The truth was he didn't feel comfortable doing that shoot at all, especially when they asked him to go shirtless for the cover. But he'd wanted to challenge himself beyond his comfort zone.

"I didn't mean it like that." Priscilla frowned.

"Yeah, you did." He flexed again.

"Stop doing that!"

"Doing what?"

"Nothing." Priscilla cut her eye at him. "I guess you like to workout too."

"Like? I don't know if I like it. It's just something that is a part of maintaining a healthy lifestyle. I'm definitely not like my brothers. They're all workout fanatics because of their jobs. Rome is a professional athlete; Jason models and Storm is whatever he is. He tells us he's a cop." Randy glanced in the rearview mirror. Eden had on her headphones and was looking at something on her phone.

"E." She didn't answer. "E." He said louder, but she still didn't answer.

"Look, what's the deal for real? I'm feeling you, shorty." He looked over at her. Priscilla groaned at Randy's lingo from back in the day.

"I'm feeling you too," she admitted softly. "But it can't happen."

"I can transfer E to another school."

"Randy!"

"Just kidding. No, actually I'm not. I'm saying whatever

the roadblocks are, let's move them."

"It's not just that."

"What else is there?" Randy looked over at her again, searching her eyes. There was that sadness again. This time it was mixed with fear.

"Randy, we live in two different worlds."

"I am from the same place you're from. I didn't always have money." This was a first. His money and status were usually things women liked, but of course, not Priscilla. She was different.

"You need to be with someone who lives in that lifestyles of the rich and famous world. I don't and I have no desire to." She turned away from him. He reached for her hand again, but she quickly moved it out of his reach.

Relenting for now, he sighed, "Ok." He was by no means going to give up. It was not in his nature to give up when he wanted something, and he wanted to get to know her. He wanted to explore the possibility of them and not find himself years later wondering what if.

He felt the tension leave Priscilla's body as she relaxed against the seat. She let her head fall back against the headrest. He guessed she felt like his response was him backing down. It wasn't though. It was him accepting that it was going to be a challenge to convince her to give him a chance.

Shortly after, they pulled up to Priscilla's house in a quiet neighborhood off Prince Charles Drive near where RND Cinemas, Randy and Dave's first business venture, used to be. They both looked back at Eden. She was still engrossed in whatever she was looking at on her phone. Randy reached back and tapped Eden on the leg. She removed her headphones.

"Yeah?"

"I'm going to walk Ms. Deveaux to her door."

"And leave me in the car alone?" Eden looked out the window inspecting her surroundings.

"You wanna come with us?" Randy asked, knowing good and well she didn't.

Eden's grin resembled the Cheshire Cat from *Alice in Wonderland*. "Nah, you two kids go on."

"Thanks," Randy said sarcastically.

"Good night, Eden. I'll see you tomorrow."

"See you tomorrow," Eden sang still smiling.

"Thank you for being there for Eden," Randy said once they were at the door.

"Of course, she's one of my favorites. Well, good night, Mr. Knight." Priscilla turned away from Randy to open her front door. Randy placed a gentle hand on her shoulder and turned her back to face him. She looked down, refusing to give him eye contact.

He lifted her chin, forcing her to look into his eyes. He knew he probably shouldn't, but he wanted to... needed to. A debate waged between his mind and his heart. His heart easily won. When his lips met hers, he felt alive in a way he had not felt in ages. Priscilla wrapped her arms around him as he deepened the kiss. When he ended the kiss, Randy took a step back from her. Emotions he hadn't felt since his ex-wife surged to the forefront, leaving him at a loss for words. So, he simply said good night with an emphasized "Ms. Deveaux." He felt her eyes on him as he walked back to his car. The reason he had kissed her was to make the point that what was between them was definitely not professional. He wasn't sure if she got the point or not, but he had discovered this woman could easily take his heart if she wanted to.

Nine

Priscilla was bummed that she was without a car and stuck in the house for the weekend. Reign was chasing a story and wasn't available to play the role of chauffeur. Avery was on imposed bedrest by her husband, and her cousin, Pedro was working. Priscilla plopped down on the couch. She had a laundry list of things to do.

She desperately needed to go grocery shopping. Her refrigerator looked like the only things she ate were baking soda and ice. She'd been buying take out every day or ordering lunch from the Gourmet Lunchbox delivery service. Doing that every day for the last two weeks was beginning to take a toll on her wallet. She also needed to do some last-minute running around for Avery's baby shower. Then there was a spoken word event that she wanted to go to tonight.

It would help her prepare for the Commonwealth Spoken Word Competition. Her stomach did a little dip as it always did when she thought of that competition. She had a lot riding on it. The money would help her be able to purchase the building she wanted for her youth center. *Lord, this is what you want me to do. Please help me with this.* She tried not to be anxious since God said she should be anxious for nothing, but... Priscilla stopped the negative thought before it could even properly formulate. Thinking of Second Corinthians 10:5, she took captive her thoughts.

Priscilla picked up the remote and clicked on the TV. TLC was having a *Four Weddings* marathon. She loved the show. Well, she liked all wedding shows, but TLC's *Four Weddings* was her favorite. She'd already watched every episode, but she could watch them over and over again. She just loved weddings, and with a family as big as hers she was always going to someone's wedding. In fact, her cousin, Stacey was getting married on her birthday in June. Stacey's wedding would be her ninth time as a bridesmaid. Obviously, she didn't believe in that twice a bridesmaid never a bride superstition.

As she watched the show, she tried not to think about Randy, but that was like telling herself not to breathe. Shutting him down had to be the right thing, but that kiss. She shouldn't have let him go there. A relationship between them wasn't possible. She could hear people whispering if they got together. What's he doing with her? He could do better than that. As the most eligible bachelor on the island, Bahamians expected him to be with a celebrity or a real live princess, someone on his level. They would ruthlessly drag her, and she wasn't into all that. Give her a regular brother. She'd be cool with that. Just when she was getting into the show, a text notification popped up on her phone. Randy.

Good morning. Since your car is out of commission is there anywhere you need to go?

God is this you? She had a lot to do, but did she need Randy helping her? She started to reply no but ended up typing the exact opposite.

GM... Actually, I was just thinking about the laundry list of stuff I need to do today.

Why did I type that?

I'll be there in thirty minutes. No strings attached. Just being nice.

The only thing Priscilla could think to respond was: **Thank you.** He replied with: ☺.

When the doorbell rang thirty minutes later, Priscilla sprang from her seat and practically ran to the door. She kept telling herself this was an answer to her dilemma. She managed to remember to look through the peephole first to make sure it was Randy and not her neighbor's daughter trying to sell her cookies again. She'd already bought five boxes. Seeing that it was indeed Randy, she opened the door.

"Good Morning."

Priscilla found it hard to think of what her response to his good morning should be. There was no way he should be standing at her front door in his white polo shirt and coral shorts complete with white Chuck Taylors. With aviator sunglasses to finish off the ensemble, he looked like he was about to walk down a catwalk. She checked him out, noticing that his shorts stopped right at his knees. *Hmm, nice legs.*

He looked sleek and polished like a clothing advertisement in a magazine. On the other hand, she was anything but sleek or polished. Reign had dubbed her fashion style as Bahamian Boho. She was wearing a pair of bell bottom pants she had made with some yellow and white floral print Bahamian Androsia fabric that she had bought on sale at Quality Fabrics and a t-shirt. She loved graphic t-shirts. It was kind of her signature thing that she always wore when she did spoken word. The t-shirt she had on was a basic white tee with the words "Got Jesus?" written in black. She also sported a pair of white Chuck Taylors. Instead of sunglasses, she had opted for a large straw hat and finished the look with a straw tote.

"I brought you breakfast." Randy continued after she didn't respond to his good morning. He held up a to go bag from Renaissance Café.

"Good Morning." She finally said as she stepped aside to let him in. "I'm so hungry, but all I have in the fridge is baking soda and ice cubes." She led him to her kitchen nook.

"Baking soda and ice. That's terrible. I guess grocery store is on your list of places to go today."

"It is." She smiled shyly. Priscilla wanted to roll her eyes at herself. There wasn't a shy bone in her body. *Girl, get yourself together. He's just a man. A fine man, but just a man.*

"Renaissance Café is actually my favorite Saturday morning breakfast spot. I would go there every Saturday if I could afford it."

"What do you mean?" Randy took containers out the bags.

"Those prices are steep."

"I got sheep tongue, pigs' feet and chicken souse because I didn't know which you preferred." Randy said instead of commenting on what she'd said.

"Oh, my goodness!" Priscilla refrained from dancing. "Sheep tongue is my favorite."

"Good to know."

Priscilla took a seat and Randy took the seat opposite her.

"You're not going to eat?"

"I had breakfast with Dave. It's our Saturday morning thing. Doing something away from the office. Not talking shop, just hanging out as brothers. I'm probably going to have some of this Johnny Cake, though." He took the foil wrapped sweet bread out of the bag, and Priscilla snatched it from him.

"You brought Johnny Cake too? I'm not sharing this."

"Really?"

"Really."

"I thought so." Randy took another foil wrapped Johnny Cake from the bag, which made Priscilla laugh. "I don't like sharing my Johnny Cake either. You really think the prices at Renaissance Café are too expensive?"

"When Renaissance first opened sheep tongue souse was twelve dollars. I know that was almost fifteen years ago, and I get inflation and all that. But y'all sell this for twenty dollars now plus VAT. Same size. I know sheep tongue didn't go up in price that much over the years. You're not even importing the meat. You have your own farms that produce most of the stuff you use at your restaurants."

"How do you know that?"

It wasn't public knowledge that Randy and Dave had bought an island where they farmed chicken, cows, sheep and other livestock along with growing all of the herbs, spices and vegetables they used at their restaurants. The investment they made in not only buying a whole entire island but also the technology needed to grow foods that didn't grow well in the lime rock soil of the Bahamas paid off in the long run. They avoided the heavy import taxes, and it also gave people work.

"Reign's been wanting to interview you and your brother for the longest so she's done her homework. That's how she was able to get your article in the current issue of her magazine. She'd practically already written it before your interview."

"She did a good job on that article. Maybe too good of a job. The attention has been a little bit too much for me."

"You know you like the spotlight."

"I don't. That's Rome and Jason's thing. Me, Dave and Storm like our anonymity."

"Yeah, people pegged you as the reclusive brother for years."

"I like that better than being called the most eligible bachelor on the island. Back to what you were saying though. I give each restaurant manager the freedom to set the menu, do the costing and set the prices. Honestly, once the restaurant is turning a profit I don't really interfere with the operations, but I'll look into it. We want to attract tourists because they're on vacation, and basically they'll pay whatever, but we also want locals to have some place they can go have breakfast on a Saturday morning. And we want it to be affordable."

"It's not affordable." Priscilla said after taking the last

bite of her Johnny Cake.

"Dang, girl, did you chew?"

"Very funny. The food was that good."

"Where do you need to go today?"

"Grocery shopping is number one on my list. I need to get some stuff for a friend's baby shower, and I have a spoken word event tonight. Car problems definitely were not on my schedule."

"Sounds like a full day. Let's go."

Priscilla was surprised to see that Randy was not driving the Maserati. She slid into the white leather passenger seat of a navy-blue Range Rover. The SUV was on her vision board. It was her dream car. She wanted to ask if she could drive but was content to be a passenger.

"I guess it would make sense to get the shower stuff before grocery shopping." Priscilla said, and Randy gave an exaggerated groan.

"You offered."

"That was before I knew shopping for baby clothes was involved." He joked.

"I'm not shopping for baby clothes. We're going to the party store for decorations."

"I guess I can deal with that. I may even be helpful. I have one request, though."

Priscilla gave Randy a skeptical look. "What is it?"

"You cannot be in there all day. I know how women go when it comes to shopping."

"Boy, please. You look like the shopaholic here." Priscilla gave Randy a once over.

"I don't have to shop. I own multiple clothing stores. I just get one of everything in inventory."

"I thought I saw this outfit on a mannequin at Coach and Carriage."

Randy laughed causing Priscilla to laugh too. She tried not to get too comfortable. It was hard though. Randy was easy to be around. She scolded herself for agreeing to let him take her around. She was having way too much fun and liking him more and more by the second.

After spending the morning shopping Priscilla was hungry. Randy suggested they stop at one of their upscale restaurants on Paradise Island. As they drove over the Paradise Island bridge Randy joked about the last time they were on the bridge when Priscilla's car broke down. She laughed in the right place but wasn't really listening to him. Looking out the window at the sail boats, speed boats and jet skis dotting the pristine blue waters, she wondered if she was under dressed. The Palace was one of those restaurants where women wore pearls and red bottoms, where Nassau's elite dined. She looked down at her clothes and squirmed uncomfortably.

Reign had featured the star-studded event for the Bahamian movie, *Cargo* in her magazine. Everyone was dressed for the red carpet celebration of the movie's premier at the American Black Film Festival, and Priscilla had never seen so many diamonds, rubies and pearls. It was like something straight out of Hollywood. She knew it was a special event, but on a regular day those were the type of people who dined at the Palace. Not her.

She wasn't there yet and already she was feeling out of place. Like Cinderella at the ball without her fairy godmothers' assistance. She wanted to tell Randy turn around, but knew she would have to explain why. She didn't want to say out loud the inadequacy she was feeling, and soon she was startled out of her thoughts when the valet pulled on the door of the SUV.

Randy had walked around to her side and was extending his hand to help her out of the car as the valet held the door.

She hesitated before taking his hand. She could pretend like she was sick. She didn't feel well. She felt a sheen of sweat on her forehead and had an uneasy feeling in her stomach. Her grandmother had worked as a maid in one of the hotels for forty years. Her grandfather was a cook. Her mother followed in her grandmother's footsteps, working as a maid for several families over the years. There were some families who were good to her, but for the most part they treated her like she didn't exist. Her aunts, uncles and most of her cousins worked at the hotels. Pedro had landed a job at the Royal Bank of Canada right after high school. They were the only two cousins who didn't work at any of the hotels.

She didn't think she was better than her cousins, as they often accused her. She was proud of them for not turning to the streets and deciding to make good lives for themselves. She knew how hard it was to resist the streets. Her unease came from not feeling like she belonged. Her family didn't belong at a restaurant like this one. They were always taught not to mix.

"Don't mix up yourself with them rich people. They like use people. Take what they want and then throw you away like trash when they done. Look what happened to your ma."

Priscilla's grandmother's words caused her to stumble as they approached the two gigantic golden lions that flanked the entrance. Randy's steady arm balanced her.

"Are you okay?" He asked. She nodded, but she was not okay.

Her feet sank into plush red carpet as they approached the double doors that were opened for them by two doormen dressed in tuxedos. The wait area was more like what she imagined a foyer at Buckingham Palace to be. The ceiling was high, and there were gold and white marble floors with a gold desk where a woman who looked like a beauty queen stood. Her eyes lit up when she saw Randy.

"Good day, Mr. Knight. Good day, Ms. Deveaux."

How does she know my name?

"Good day, Monica."

"We have the Throne Room prepared for you, sir. Please follow me."

Monica glided from behind the desk to lead them to the dining room. Priscilla nearly gawked at her dress. The black fitted sheath was something Priscila would wear on a very special occasion, not in the middle of the day on the weekend. As they walked through the restaurant, Priscilla was in awe of the off-white walls that were trimmed with gold and decorated with huge paintings that looked like Christopher Columbus might have brought them on his maiden voyage from Spain to the "new world." Crystal and gold chandeliers hung from the ceilings and the rooms had wall to wall red carpet.

The Palace really did look like Buckingham Palace on the inside. Priscilla's grandmother was a royal family enthusiast, so she knew more than she cared to know about the royals and everything royal. Her unease went up another degree. She tried to tell herself that she belonged in a place like this, but her mind wasn't receiving the message.

"We designed it to replicate some of the features of the ballroom at Buckingham Palace." Randy seemingly read her thoughts.

"It's beautiful." Priscilla took the seat Randy had pulled out for her.

"Bryce, your server, will be right with you," Monica said after Randy had taken his seat.

"This dining room is designed to look like the throne room." He remarked.

Priscilla looked around the room. It was extravagant, and this was just a small-scale replica. "So, you've been to the palace?"

"I have. Being a nerd pays off. I attended Cambridge on scholarship and lived in London for a year after I graduated. I loved living in England." He smiled.

Priscilla smiled also. She now had an explanation for his unique accent. It was a mixture of Bahamian and British.

Randy continued, "I think it's a must do trip, especially since so much of our history as a country is tied to Great Britain."

Priscilla tried another internal pep talk. She was there because she belonged there. This was an experience to be enjoyed and she was going to enjoy it. She laughed, "The Commonwealth Spoken Word Competition was in England last year. I wanted to win, if only for that all-expense paid trip there."

"Where is it this year?"

"Toronto," Priscilla said dryly.

"What do you have against Toronto?"

She shrugged. "No palaces."

"It's a great city too. I've visited a few times."

"I'll let you know my opinion on it when I get back."

"Have you travelled much?"

Before Priscilla could answer the server showed up. He bowed slightly before removing their napkins from the table and draping them over their laps. He then poured them each a glass of water."

"Thank you, Bryce. How's everything going?"

The young man looked to be no older than eighteen and seemed nervous. He was sweating and there was a slight tremor in his voice as he spoke.

"Good, sir."

"Relax. You're doing a great job." Randy smiled at him.

Relaxing slightly, the server returned Randy's smile before he took their drink order.

After the server left, Randy continued. "You didn't get to answer my question. Have you travelled much?"

"I went to school in Atlanta and I've been to a couple of US cities: New York, Dallas, New Orleans, Charlotte and Los Angeles. I want to see more of the world, though. After I graduated and started working, I thought I'd have the money to knock some places off my list, but I decided it was more important to save my money."

"What are you saving for?"

"First, I was saving to buy a house. Once I got that out the way, I started saving for the youth center I want to open."

"May I ask what kind of youth center?"

Priscilla explained to Randy how she almost got caught in that wanna be thug life and how Ms. Bethel's youth center saved her. She'd always wanted to pay it forward by having a place where young people could come to learn life skills and see that there are opportunities for them to have a better life.

"That's definitely needed. I'd invest in that. Have you thought about investors? Or a grant? The government might have a grant for something like that."

"I'll have to research that. I hadn't thought of a grant, but you're right. The Ministry of Youth, Sports and Culture would be probably be willing to offer some sort of assistance or have a partnership."

"Let me make a few phone calls and see what I can find out."

"You'd do that?"

"Why wouldn't I?"

"Thank you." Priscilla said when she didn't have an answer to his question.

"By the way, your poem really inspired me. The next day I took a drive through Kemp Road, Bain Town, and the Grove. Then I visited Pinewood, Elizabeth Estates and Nassau Village. I really feel like if we give people a better alternative, they will take it. I'm working on a proposal to the Ministry of Education to provide training for students in the hospitality industry starting in primary school and continuing in secondary school. Then I'm working on an idea for a post-secondary hospitality school. It will be totally free. I know there's the Bahamas Hotel Training College, but it has tuition that some can't afford."

"I was just going to mention BHTC. Why not partner with them?" she asked.

Randy pursed his lips; he appeared to be weighing his thoughts. "I was trying to find a way to say this without sounding like a rich, arrogant, know it all, but I can't. I can do it better. The Renaissance brand has a standard that is world class. I need free reign to implement those standards and to make sure everyone reaches those standards before they graduate."

Looking at her surroundings Priscilla had to agree with Randy. The Renaissance standard was off the charts. She supposed that was because he was a perfectionist.

"I feel like this would give those who can't afford it the opportunity to get the education and training they need to get into the work industry."

The rest of the lunch and day went by quickly. Priscilla was happy and not so happy about it. Not so happy that it was over because she enjoyed being with Randy and happy that it was over because she enjoyed being with Randy. It had been a long time since she had one on one time with someone of the opposite sex. She realized that she missed having that male perspective; Lord knows their minds worked differently. Randy was logical, analytical and methodical in his thinking. It was clear for her why he was so successful as a businessman.

She was passionate about opening a youth center, and she

believed God had given her the vision for it. However, she had not fleshed out all the details of what it would take to bring her vision to life. When Randy asked her how much would it cost to run the center in its first five years, she didn't have the answer. She hadn't even thought of the question before. She had worked out the cost to open it, but not to run it. She was relieved when Randy offered to help her work out those details as well.

Thanks to the conversation they had over lunch, her mind didn't have a chance to taunt her or make her feel self-conscious. She was glad that she hadn't let fear of not fitting in cause her to ask Randy to choose another restaurant.

When they walked outside Randy's SUV was waiting for him. As he was tipping the valet, a Mercedes AMG SL63 pulled up. Priscilla was so busy admiring the car and cataloguing every visible feature of it that she didn't notice the couple that got out of the car or that Randy was talking to them. She was startled when Randy called her name.

"Priscilla, this is the Minister of Youth, Sports and Culture, Deon Bethel. I was telling him a little about your youth center idea. The ministry does have some grant money."

Priscilla froze. She knew she needed to say something, but all she could do was nod. Deon Bethel. He extended his hand to her. She forced herself to accept his handshake. She couldn't believe this was happening.

"Nice to meet you." He handed her one of his cards. She smiled and managed to say thank you. She looked down at the card with the seal of the Commonwealth of the Bahamas. She read the name. Was this really happening? She heard the devil taunting her. *See, you don't belong.*

"We'll catch up later," he said to Randy before walking off.

Randy assisted her in the SUV. He tried to make conversation, but she was too shook to talk. She had just run into her father.

Ten

Priscilla had been excited about throwing the baby shower for Avery, but when the day came, she was not in the mood. It had been a week since she'd seen her father, and no matter how much she tried, she could not shake the shame she felt. She knew the circumstances of her conception were not her fault, but how could she feel anything other than shame being the product of an affair.

"Priscilla."

Hearing her name brought her out of head and back to the shower. Priscilla looked around the room that was decorated with a Lion King theme to see who was calling her. Reign stood at the candy bar, motioning for her to join.

"Girl, are you ok? You've been zoning out the whole day." Reign popped a handful of jelly beans into her mouth.

"I'm good." She lied.

Reign shrugged before eating another mouthful of jelly beans. "Let's do the last game then wrap things up. Avery looks like she's about to smack her mother-in-law."

Priscilla had noticed that Avery's mother-in-law had been by her side and in her ear almost the entire two hours she had been there. Avery's pasted on smile told her the conversation was not good. Just then Avery looked over to them and mouthed "help me." Priscilla shook her head and mentally noted to add to her husband prayer list: no crazy mama.

After leaving the Hilton where they had rented a banquet room for the shower, all Priscilla wanted to do was go back home and continue to process last week, but she had to help

Reign and Avery's husband take the shower stuff to their house. Vince helped her unload gifts from her car, then she went inside to say goodbye to Avery and Reign. Walking into Avery's foyer and through the living room to the kitchen, Priscilla felt like she often felt when she came to Avery's house — like she had walked into an episode of MTV cribs. When a contractor and a pretend interior designer got together to build their dream home the result was opulence. *Maybe one day.* Priscilla thought wistfully.

"Did you see Ms. Mortimer hiding plates of food in a shopping bag she had under the table?" Reign asked as soon as Priscilla walked into the kitchen where they were eating leftovers.

"What? Who is Ms. Mortimer?"

"The head usher lady from church." Avery answered.

"She was toting food?" Priscilla's family was notorious for toting so she would be the last to talk about anyone toting food. Last family function they had at the buffet at Atlantis, one of her cousins brought foil baking pans in her oversized purse to tote food from the buffet. Her family was in a league of its own when it came to toting.

"I stopped counting at seven plates." Reign shook her head.

"Well, you know she has all her grandchildren staying with her. She probably took it for them." Priscilla reasoned.

"That's true." Avery agreed. "But she could've asked instead of trying to do it on the low. We had more than enough. We would have been happy to give her all the food."

"What you mean all?" Reign's eyebrows shot up to her hairline.

"I said what I said. We should take some of this food to church tomorrow for her." Avery decided.

"In that case," Reign hopped off the stool and started

opening cabinets, "let me get my plates. Where's your Tupperware?"

"Probably at your house along with the ones you took from my house." Priscilla laughed before giving Avery a high five.

"You got jokes, aye," Reign pulled out a Pyrex dish from a cabinet.

Avery folded her arms. "Girl, put back my good dish. You better get the Glad out of the cabinet next to it."

Once Reign found the plastic Glad containers, she shifted the conversation back to Priscilla.

"So, what's up with you? You were kind of low key today."

"Yeah, you seemed not 100% present." Avery agreed with Reign.

"I'm good." Priscilla refused to give either of them eye contact because she knew that they knew she was lying.

"Lies! Heifer, how long have we known you? You can play that doing just fine track with someone else. We know when something is up, so spill it." Reign said as she retook her seat at the island.

Priscilla contemplated Reign's words. She'd known them since college and they knew almost everything about her. Almost. She'd never told anyone about her father. She'd told them she didn't know who her father was. In that moment she felt the Holy Spirit nudging her to release the burden. As clear as day He showed her a vision of herself walking around with an oversized backpack that was obviously too heavy for her. The backpack was the burden of shame. She felt like the Holy Spirit was asking her for the backpack. All she had to do was take it off.

"Remember when I told you guys that I don't know who my father is?" Reign and Avery nodded. "Well, I lied."

"What?" Avery almost choked on the mouthful of water

she'd just drank.

The surprise on Reign and Avery's faces would have been comical to Priscilla if what she was about to say wasn't so serious. They both always teased and called her Honest Abe for what they sometimes deemed unnecessary honesty.

"Why would you lie about that?" Avery asked.

"Because Deon Bethel is my father."

Avery leaned her body forward. "Hold up. The Minister of Youth, Sports and Culture is your father?"

Priscilla could see the journalistic wheels in Avery and Reign's heads spinning. "This is off the record."

"Come on, Lala. You know our conversations are always off the record. Right, Reign?"

Reign hesitated. "Yeah, but usually y'all talking about when y'all going to clean your bathroom. Boring stuff. This is a scandal!"

"Reign!" Avery reprimanded.

"Sorry. This is definitely off the record. So, what's the scoop?"

"My mom used to do day work for his parents. He was away at school when she started. He came home for break and they had a summer thing. When she found out she was pregnant, he was back at school. She waited until his next trip home to tell him, but he had news of his own. He was married."

"Yup," Reign nodded, "him and his wife got married two years before you were born. I did a story on him for the magazine. They got married right after high school because she was pregnant. He'n said that, but his oldest son was born five months after their wedding."

"Right. He gave Mummy some money and told her to go to the States to have an abortion. She took the money and moved to Exuma. When I was about two, we moved back to

Nassau and she ended up getting back with him. He was my mum's "friend." I'm sure he knew who I was, but he never acknowledged me.

"When I was in tenth grade, I found out who he was. I had a debate match at Lyford Cay School where his kids attended. His oldest daughter was on the debate team. We're actually the same age. People kept saying how much we looked alike and were asking if we were sisters. It made me excited because I wanted to know who my dad was and know his side of the family. So, I started asking her questions about her family. She was very standoffish with me. I could tell she thought I was beneath her."

"Man, this is better than a Lifetime Movie." Reign interrupted Priscilla. "You're talking about Stacia Bethel, right?"

"Yes, his princess Stacia."

"I know Stacia." Avery added. "We were debutantes the same year."

"Anyway, the next time we debated against Lyford Cay, she approached me. She told me she knew who I was and that her dad wanted nothing to do with the bastard child he had with the family maid." One lone tear dropped from Priscilla's right eye. Avery grabbed Priscilla's hand and Reign handed her a piece of tissue from her purse.

"I felt all of the air leave my lungs. It was like someone had punched me in the gut. After that, I think things between him and my mum were off. At least, I never saw him again. Then my senior year his wife confronted me and there was that word again. Bastard. I didn't know Mummy had asked him for money for my college tuition. I guess his wife found out about it. Mummy had taken a job in Abaco, and I was living with my grandmother at the time. His wife came to my grandmother's house. She was waiting outside for me when I left to go to school.

"She said she was tired of me and my whore of a mother effing with her marriage and her family. She said I wasn't getting any of their money. She accused me of being a gold digger like my mother. Then she called me a bastard, threw some money at me and spat in my face."

For years, Priscilla had forced herself not think about that memory. She had never before told anyone about that day. Not her mother. Not her grandmother. Not her best friends. It was hard to admit a truth as humiliating as this to anyone. She knew the Bible said that when you knew the truth the truth made you free, but the only thing this truth did was imprison her in shame for nearly twenty years.

"I never liked that trifling trick."

"Reign!" Avery shushed her.

"Sorry. Nah, I'm not sorry. That hooker is trifling. She mussy forget when Deon Bethel met her she was working in the numbers house, selling numbers. She dropped out of the College of the Bahamas because she was failing most of her classes. She should be the last person to be looking down her nose at anyone. She don't wan' me to put her on blast. Tell her your best frien' owns the most popular magazine in the country, and I will be happy to spill all her tea. She may be importing her tea straight from China now, but she used to drink Lipton just like the rest of us."

"Spilling tea will not be necessary because you can't spill hers without spilling mine." Priscilla said. Reign sucked her teeth.

"Look, La, you are not a bastard. God is your Father. It doesn't matter what the circumstances were concerning your conception. Before that, God knew you and called you daughter," Avery said.

"In theory I know that, but last Saturday when I was with Randy and saw my father, it all came back."

"I think God allowed that to happen so you can address it and heal it. I mean heal for real."

"I totally agree with what Avery just said, but you know I'm not just going to let you gloss over that you were with Randy Knight last Saturday." Reign took a sip of her water. "Spill it."

"He took me shopping." Priscilla shrugged.

Reign's eyes looked like they were about to pop out of her head. Before Reign could ask, Priscilla clarified what she meant. "Not like that. My car is still out of commission. I needed to run some errands, one of which was last minute shopping for the shower. You were MIA and Vince had put Avery on bedrest. Pedro was working, so Randy offered to take me on my errands. I didn't want to, but I didn't have an alternative. After we ran the errands, he suggested we go to The Palace for lunch."

"The Palace? Vince has been trying to get reservations for us forever. You'll have to tell us all about the dining experience another time. Right now, we want to hear about the Randy experience."

"After seeing my father, I can't tell you much about anything. Randy has been calling and texting me, but I haven't gotten back to him. I can't deal with him right now." In spite of her tears, Priscilla wanted to laugh because Reign was literally biting her tongue. She opened her mouth to say something, but Avery shot her a look that said shut it up.

"If you don't want to deal, that's what it is. I'm not going to give you a whole bunch of advice. I'm just going to say pray. God's advice is way better than mine." Avery said.

Priscilla nodded, but the truth was she hadn't prayed about it. She didn't want to. She was feeling like Jonah when God told him to go Nineveh to preach repentance to the city. He didn't want to go because he knew God would forgive the people of Nineveh. She didn't want to pray because she knew God would tell her to forgive her father and his wife. Like Jonah, she didn't feel like they deserved to be forgiven. *Like you deserved forgiveness?* Priscilla squirmed at the Holy Spirit's gentle rebuke.

Later Priscilla was happy to be home in her bed, sipping a cup of tea. She wished someone was there to give her a foot massage. She'd been standing since she got up at seven that morning, making sure everything was in place for the shower. Reign called it micromanaging. She might agree with her a little bit, but she just wanted everything to go as planned.

She was about to put on a Netflix movie when she noticed a notification on her phone. It was a text message from Randy asking how the shower went. Part of her wanted to melt into her pillows and part of her wanted to say, "like you really care about a baby shower." She put the phone on the nightstand without answering the message.

She'd almost completely bared her soul to her friends. What she didn't share was her decision not to have anything to do with Randy outside of dealing with him about Eden. Hopefully, Eden would stay out of trouble. That meant Priscilla would have no dealings with her father at all.

The truth was she couldn't shake the fact that Randy was rich and privileged. Just like her father. There was no way she was going to end up like her mother. Men like Randy Knight and Deon Bethel used women outside their social class as entertainment. She'd seen that play out too many times before. She refused to let it be her.

Eleven

It was nearly six o'clock when Randy pulled up into the driveway of Dave's lakefront home. He thought he would've missed the after-church crowd that usually congregated at his brother's house, but there were four cars in the driveway that he didn't recognize. He could do without being asked when was he coming back to church. He'd stopped going because of the incident with his dad and the overwhelming disappointment he'd felt because of it. As the years went by the more time he spent away from church, the less sense the whole church thing made to him.

Randy's phone rang interrupting his thoughts. He was hoping it was Priscilla. It'd been a week since they'd hung out. He thought they'd had a good time until she went ghost on him again. The screen on his car's console let him know it was not Priscilla. He cursed under his breath. It was Eden's mother. She stayed in touch with Eden, checking in with her once a week, but she rarely called him. When she did call him, it was always about money. Randy didn't feel like dealing with Kim's drama, but this was the mother of his child.

He answered the call. "Hey."

"Hey yourself," she cooed. Her once sexy voice now sounded like fingernails on a chalkboard.

"What's going on?"

"I'll be in Nassau for your dad's pastoral anniversary. I need a place to stay. Can you book me a suite at Atlantis or Baha Mar?"

Randy was silent. What was he? Her personal assistant? He didn't book rooms for himself. Plus, why was he paying for her room anyway? The more Randy thought about it, the more upset he felt himself getting. With the alimony he was paying her, she could afford to pay for her own suite.

"Unless you want me to stay at the house."

"Not at all." Randy quickly said. "I'll have my assistant take care of it. Is there anything else?"

"Yeah, I want Eden to stay with me while I'm there."

"She can if she wants to."

"Why wouldn't she want to?" Kim snapped. Randy wanted to say because you walked out of her life when she was two and didn't show up again until she was eight.

"See you when you get here," he said instead.

"I'm looking forward to it."

Randy released the breath he hadn't realized he was holding. Things were never as they appeared with Kim. She hadn't been to Nassau in two years. What was up with this trip? And who the heck invited her to his dad's thing? Eden probably. He felt an uneasiness settle in his stomach. He hoped she wasn't up to anything.

Randy shook his head as if wanting to shake thoughts of his ex away. Every time he spoke with her, he asked himself what did he ever see in her. Each time they spoke he saw how shallow and selfish she was. He used to tell himself she wasn't always like that, but that was a lie. The signs were there all along, but he chose to ignore them because she was his first.

He'd met her at a club in Nassau that Jason was DJ'ing at back in the day before he got "discovered." She approached him, and he was shocked a city girl like her was interested in an island boy like him. She looked like one of the girls in a Sean Paul music video, and he looked like he'd just come off the boat from Freeport. She saw potential in him, she'd always said that. That's how she hooked him. Well, that and sex. But when Renaissance hit a rough spot and they were losing money out the ying yang, she started cheating on him with some famous music producer. It was right up under his nose, but he didn't even notice. One night she didn't come home. It was late, like almost three in the morning so he called and asked when she was coming home. She flippantly replied that she wasn't and hung up. It didn't hurt now as much as it hurt then, but he still felt a little sting from her rejection and betrayal.

Randy was not surprised that he was able to walk right into the house. Dave never locked his doors. As soon as he entered the foyer, he heard Dave's big mouth arguing with someone. The foyer opened to a grand staircase, and to its left was the kitchen and dining room. To the right was the living room and study. Behind it was the man cave and that's where Dave's loud mouth was. Randy was shocked to see Dave arguing with Jason. He had no idea Jason was on the island.

"What are you doing here?"

"If you would answer your phone, you would know we were in town this weekend." Randy's youngest brother, Rome said, walking up behind him.

"What is going on? Why are you both in town?" Randy watched his brothers look at him like he was an alien lifeform, an ugly alien lifeform at that.

"Will someone say something instead of looking at me crazy?"

"Dad's fiftieth pastoral anniversary. The church is having a week of services. We were summoned by Mum." Randy turned around when he heard his twin's voice.

"You're here too." Randy hadn't noticed Storm sitting in the corner of the room. "The pastoral anniversary is next weekend. Why are you here a whole week early?"

"Mummy didn't call you and tell you the family is doing a whole week of stuff?" Jason raised an eyebrow at Randy.

He and his mother had been playing phone tag. She did leave a couple of messages, but he never checked his messages. Maybe he should have taken his assistant's offer to check his cell phone voicemail messages, but Randy felt like if you're too busy to check your own voicemail messages, you're too busy.

Jason smirked. "You know she did, and he probably sent her to voicemail same as he did all of us."

"I'm going to do better with that." Randy took a seat on the couch next to Jason before taking the Vitamalt Dave handed him. He frowned at the malted beverage.

"You can turn down ya lip all ya want. You know ain' no Kalik in this house." Dave settled into his recliner.

"You don't drink, but you smoke cigars." Randy mumbled.

"Occasionally," Dave said around the Cohiba.

Randy scoffed. "That's only because they're so daggone expensive, and you better not let Victoria catch you smoking that in here."

"This is my space. I can do whatever I want in here."

"Dave, stop. You know good and well you wouldn't dare light that thing up in here." Jason laughed. "Your peace is far more important than a good smoke."

"Amen to that," Rome said.

"Trouble in paradise already?" Dave raised an eyebrow at Rome, who was a few weeks away from his wedding.

"Nothing like that. Just learning that marriage has a lot to do with being willing to compromise. From what type of wedding we will have to where we live to whether we're having joint bank accounts or not. This two becoming one business is not easy."

"But it is worth it. There have been so many times in my life where my wife has been the one to pull me back from the brink of self-destruction. Me without her doesn't work." Jason said, shaking his head.

"Same here. I am a train wreck without Shiloh." Rome admitted.

"If this is going to be a husbands therapy session, I'm going to bounce." Randy stood to leave, and Storm nodded his head in agreement. They were the only two who weren't married and didn't have any prospects.

"You so dumb." Dave laughed. "Sit down. What you got going on with you besides work?"

"Nothing. You know it's all about work." Randy shrugged.

"Eden not setting houses on fire or stealing any more cars?" Rome joked.

"You're not funny. To answer your question, no. She's been on her best behavior. I thought you knew that. She says she wants to be more like Jesus."

Rome and Jason jumped out their seats and gave each other a high-five. Randy thought they were going to chest bump, but they didn't.

"Yo! God is amazing. Man, He is so good! We've been praying for her. I mean going in for her, especially me," Rome said. "I was where she was, and you saw the path that it took me down. I didn't want that for her."

"The only one left now is her knucklehead daddy." Storm mumbled.

"Don't start, Evangelist Storm." Randy warned.

"Anything else new and exciting happening in your life?" Dave smiled a bit too brightly for Randy.

"You're being weird, Dave. What are you talking about?"

"You really think you were going to take someone to The Palace and I not find out?" Dave smirked.

Randy was not thinking anything about Dave or the fact that he had eyes everywhere when he took Priscilla to the Palace.

"Who he took to the Palace? Jason inquired.

"Eden's school counselor." Rome quickly supplied the answer. Randy guessed he had been talking to Dave.

"Ms. Deveaux?"

"How'd you know her name?" Randy eyed Rome suspiciously.

"Eden mentioned her. Not that you're dating, but stuff she's said to her."

"We're not dating. Actually, she's gone ghost on me since The Palace."

"Might've been overkill, bro." Storm shrugged. "You shoulda took her to Bamboo Shak."

They all stared at Storm, trying to figure out if he was serious or joking. He was the cheap brother and was known to cut corners when it came to spending money. Granted he was the only one of them who had a "regular" job, but they made him invest in Renaissance when they first started, so he was actually part owner. Still he acted like the only money he had was from his nine to five. He lived in an apartment, drove a Ford F-250 and wore the same outfit every day. He told them it wasn't the same outfit, but they didn't believe him.

"Bruh, are you serious?" Randy wondered not for the first time if they were really twins, but then noticed the side of his mouth turn up and his lip twitch. Realizing that he was joking, they all sighed.

"Don't sweat it too much. You can talk to her when she comes to church on Sunday. Eden invited her and she said she'd be there." Rome informed him.

"Why would she do that? She's really involved at her

church."

"Because Eden is singing on Sunday." Rome cut his eyes at Randy, who wondered why Eden hadn't said anything to him.

"You haven't come to church any of the other five hundred times she asked you." Dave said answering his silent question.

Randy started to say that wasn't true, but the looks his brothers shot him didn't allow the words to leave his mouth. Besides, they were right. Eden had been pressing him a lot recently to come to church, and his answer was always no. Over the years he'd been to church for the occasional wedding or funeral, but it had been almost ten years since he'd been to his dad's church. He still felt so much hurt and disappointment. He felt stuck in a loop that always brought him back to the day he saw the headlines in the local paper.

"I know how you feel." Storm's words brought Randy back to the conversation. He moved from his seat and walked over to him.

"You have to let that crap go. Unforgiveness will kill you. It's poison. Forgive the old man. Forgive Kim." Storm rested a hand on his shoulder. Randy felt a lump form in his throat. Everything came back to him all at once. The scandal with his dad. His wife leaving him and Eden. How could he forgive that?

"I want to, but it's hard."

Storm nodded, and Randy knew that he got it. He understood. And although he joked that they acted nothing like twins, there were times throughout their lives when they would have that unexplainable twin connection. They would feel each other's emotion or know each other's thoughts. This was one of those times.

Storm gave him a hug. "I'll be praying for you, bro."

"We'll all be praying." Dave said.

***

Randy couldn't sleep. He tried to do some work, but he couldn't focus. He kept thinking about what Storm said about unforgiveness. He was right. So many things had died from the moment he read those headlines. Pastor of popular Freeport megachurch being investigated for his ties to gambling kingpin, Duppy Rose. The headlines hit him like a train he hadn't seen coming and it wrecked him. The story claimed his dad was using the church to launder money for Duppy. His dad and Duppy were once best friends whose lives took them in opposite directions. Randy still wasn't sure how it all came about, but when they needed money to complete the church facility building project, his dad went to Duppy for a loan. When it was time to repay the loan Duppy's terms were not what they originally agreed on. He wanted to use the church to make his dirty money clean. The church had bank accounts all over the world with millions of dollars made from drugs, gambling, prostitution and other illegal activities.

Randy wondered why his dad didn't ask him and his brothers for the money when it was time to repay the loan. By that time, they were all wealthy. Then he found out there was also blackmail involved. An affair. It all crushed him. He hadn't just admired or looked up to his dad, he had wanted to be him. Wanted to eventually be a pastor like him, have a marriage like his and have five wild boys just like he had. That all changed in what seemed like a moment.

His brothers each reacted differently. Dave wanted to help pick up the pieces for his parents and the church. Storm got lost in his work and the whole thing actually drew him closer to God because he felt like he had to be more vigilant about not being "attracted to the things of the world." Jason told his dad you reap what you sow and had no sympathy for him. But once he got back with God, he forgave his dad not just for what happened with the church, but everything that had been wrong in their relationship. Rome was the only one who didn't confront their dad right away. He was silent on it. It wasn't until years later that he confronted him, but they all forgave, moved on and now each had a pretty decent relationship with their dad. He wasn't sure if he could do the same.

The next morning when Randy came downstairs for breakfast, he could hear Eden in the kitchen singing. He wasn't familiar with the song, but the melody caused his fingers to yearn to feel the keys of the piano beneath them. He hadn't played or sung in almost as many years as he hadn't been to church.

"Good morning." Greeting Eden and Ms. Gloria, Randy took a seat at the kitchen table. Eden walked up to him and planted a sloppy kiss on his cheek just like she used to do when she was a little girl. It warmed his heart so much it almost made him shed a tear. She was happy. He hadn't seen her like this in a long time.

"Mornin', Mr. Knight. How you doin' dis mornin'?"

"I'm good, Ms. Gloria. Eden, what were you singing?"

""Way Maker" by this Nigerian gospel artist, Sinach."

"I like it."

"I'll be singing it at church on Sunday." Eden told him. Randy could tell Eden was trying to sound casual, but the hopeful look in her eyes told him otherwise.

"I'll be there." He said just as casually.

Eden's eyes lit up like Bay Street around Christmas time. She looked like she almost jumped out of her seat. "No, you're not."

"I am. You know my word is word."

"That's true. Cuz when you say you ain' coming, you don't come."

***

Eden had spent the night at Dave's house so Randy rode to

church alone. He tried to ignore the anxiousness he was feeling, but the closer he got to the church the more anxiety he felt. It had been over ten years since he'd heard his dad preach. Since they had any sort of relationship. His father was celebrating fifty years in the ministry. It was a major milestone, but he wondered if he would have decided to attend if Eden wasn't singing and if Priscilla wasn't going to be there. Probably not.

The church was a fraction of the size of the one they had built in Freeport so it was easy for him to find a parking space. After the scandal broke, his dad was forced to step down as senior pastor of Freeport Tabernacle. He stayed in Freeport for a little while before moving to Nassau. Then after a couple of years he opened the doors of Tabernacle of Love.

Randy had driven by the building lots of time, but each time he pretended like it wasn't there. Today he stood outside its doors taking in the simple rectangular structure. He wasn't impressed with the architecture. Would he be impressed with the service? A male usher in the standard black usher suit greeted him with a firm but warm handshake. The female usher standing opposite him smiled.

"Welcome home."

Her words puzzled him. He didn't recognize her, but obviously she recognized him. She led him straight to the front pew where Dave and his wife, Victoria, along with Jason and his wife, Jael, were already seated. He already knew Storm and Rome would be late. They always were. He greeted his sisters-in-law. Then his brothers both stood to greet him with hugs.

"Glad you made it." Jason grinned as he accepted a hundred-dollar bill from Dave.

"Y'all had a bet about me coming, and you have the nerve to be accepting a bet in the house of the Lord. And I can't believe you bet against me." Randy frowned at Dave.

"Can you blame me? Your track record speaks for you."

"But you should never bet against the Holy Spirit. I knew the Holy Spirit was going to bring you here today," Jason said, re-taking his seat.

As Randy sat also, he wondered if it was the Holy Spirit who got him there. He stared at the gigantic cross that hung on the wall in front of them. Could it be possible that the Holy Spirit used Eden and even his desire to see Priscilla to get him to church? His eyes moved from the cross to the pulpit directly beneath it. He remembered when he was a teenager, he would daydream about one day standing in a pulpit and delivering the Word to people. That seemed like several lifetimes ago. He chose another path or was it God's path for him all along? He couldn't imagine his life without Renaissance.

His thoughts were interrupted when the choir began to fill the pews behind the pulpit. Eden waved at him. He smiled, his heart swelling with pride, and waved back. She looked like she would drown in the large purple and gold robe. After the choir entered, his parents entered with the other pastors and elders of the church. Randy glanced behind him and noticed the church was now full. The band began to play and he immediately recognized it as the song Eden had been singing. Women and young girls dressed in gold leotards and long, flowing purple skirts started to fill the space in front of the pulpit and each of the three aisles in the church. Some had large gold flags that they began to wave in rhythm to the music. Then Eden stepped forward, "You are here moving in our midst..."

Her voice was clear, strong, confident, powerful and... anointed. He knew that right away because he felt it. Felt it in every part of his body. When her voice projected, it charged the air with electricity. All he could do was listen in awe. The choir joined in and Randy felt the Holy Spirit nudging him to stand, to surrender. When Eden sung You are here mending every heart, he felt those words in his soul.

He wasn't so far away that he didn't remember what the

presence of God felt like. He was there with them right then, and like He called the prodigal son, He was calling Randy out the mess of the pigpen back to the house of his father. Randy looked up on the stage at his father. There was just too much bad blood between them. Although God was calling him back home, he resisted.

Twelve

Priscilla accepted the tissue from the usher and wiped the tears that were freely streaming down her face. The song was moving, but what was even more moving was the person singing it. God had totally and completely transformed Eden from a rebellious teen who hated everyone and everything to the beautiful, loving young woman who was now singing praises to God. Priscilla was amazed by what God had done in Eden's life in a year and a half, and she knew that if He did such a miracle for Eden, He would do one for her. As Eden sung, He is a way maker.

The rest of the praise and worship was just as powerful as Eden's opening song. The church had several gifted singers. After "Way Maker," the choir sung Tasha Cobbs Leonard's "Your Spirit." The lead singer's voice was just as powerful and anointed as Tasha's. It was obvious this church was a house of praise and worship. After the choir sang another song, the guest speaker was introduced. Pastor Josiah Bridgewater spoke about faithfulness. Priscilla found it hard to pay attention to the message, though, because unlike in worship when her focus was totally on God, her attention kept wandering to Randy who was sitting in the front row with his family.

"Brothers and sisters as we honor Reverend Knight today, I want to pray over him and his family. Would you join me up here?" Pastor Bridgewater motioned for the Knight family to come on stage with him. "You know what, why don't you sing something for your dad?"

Randy and his brothers looked as stunned as Priscilla felt. The quintet reluctantly stood and made their way to the stage. Randy slid behind the piano while his twin, Storm, got on the drums. Rome picked up a guitar and stood in front of a mic stand. Dave and Jason also took mics. Dave said something off mic, and his brothers nodded.

"Good afternoon, church," Dave said. "I was glad when they said unto me come, let us go into the house of the Lord. I always count it a privilege and joy to be in God's house. Today especially as we celebrate my dad and his service to the work of the Kingdom. We're going to take it back a bit, but we're going to need the choir's help."

When he said this the choir stood. Randy called the choir director to him and whispered something. The director nodded and took his position. Randy began to play the first few notes of a song Priscilla recalled from back in the day when her grandmother used to have to drag her to church. She smiled as the congregation applauded their approval of the song selection. Then the choir began to sing about a sweet and beautiful joy. When Dave started the first verse, the smoothness of his voice caused her to close her eyes and let the words he sang wash over her. As the song transitioned from the first verse to the second, the voice switched from smoothness to power.

"When I get weak..."

Priscilla's eyes popped open. It was Randy singing, and it was apparent where Eden got her voice from. There was not just power in his singing, but passion that stirred her soul. She knew he was not just singing about hopelessness and being devoid of joy, he was testifying about it. She felt his emotion in every word he sang and so did everyone else.

After the song the speaker gave an invitation to the congregation for salvation and prayer. One by one, people made their way to the altar where people were waiting to pray with them. Dave and Jason went back to their seat, while Randy, Storm and Rome remained playing their instruments softly.

Once the prayers were done service was dismissed. Priscilla watched as people swarmed Randy and his brothers. She was trying to decide if she should greet Randy or not when Eden came barreling into her. The teen, who was almost a half a foot taller than Priscilla, almost toppled her over with the force of her hug.

"Ms. Deveaux! I'm so happy you made it. Come. I want you to meet my mom."

Before Priscilla could reply, Eden had taken her by the hand and dragged her across the church until they were standing in front of a woman who looked like she could be Vanessa William's twin.

"Mummy, I want you to meet my counselor from school, Ms. Deveaux."

Priscilla looked from daughter to mother. Standing next to her mother, Eden seemed even more striking than she usually did. The two were gorgeous.

"It's a pleasure to meet you." Eden's mom extended a perfectly manicured hand.

"Likewise," Priscilla gave a fake smile.

So, this is what Randy Knight likes. She and this woman were night and day. Eden's mom was tall, light skinned, pencil thin and polished. She looked like a real life, perfectly airbrushed magazine ad. Next to her, Priscilla felt awkward in her maxi dress, cardigan and sandals. Her hair, hid underneath her headwrap, was a complete mess. She looked like India Arie and this lady looked like the Duchess of Sussex. There was nothing wrong with looking like India Arie, except it seemed like Randy preferred a demure black princess instead of a warrior queen.

"I'm Ms. Knight." Eden's mom was saying. Priscilla wondered why she still used her married name. From what she'd read in the Bahamian tabloids, she and Randy had been divorced since Eden was three.

"You have a very smart and talented daughter. It has been a pleasure to get to know her."

Eden's mom smiled and hugged Eden whose matching smile was a mile wide. Priscilla was getting ready to excuse herself when Randy walked up.

"Randolph, you were excellent. It brought back good memories."

Priscilla wanted to roll her eyes when Eden's mom lowered her voice and batted her fake lashes at Randy. Ms. Knight was probably used to using her good looks to get her way with men, but Randy seemed unbothered by his ex-wife.

"Thanks," Randy said before turning his attention to Priscilla.

"I'm glad to see you here." He smiled at her, and she felt herself shiver under his gaze and the soft caress of his voice. She also felt Eden's mom staring at them.

"I'm glad I could make it to hear one of my favorite students sing. I'm sorry some of my other colleagues couldn't make it." Priscilla was going to keep this professional in front of Eden's mom. It was obvious the woman felt like she still had some kind of claim to Randy, and she didn't want no foolishness.

"Yeah, she was amazing. She sings around the house all the time, but I had no idea she had that in her."

"Come on, Dad. Stop it. You were pretty awesome too. We should do a duet!"

"Eden, you would sing circles around me." Randy laughed.

Priscilla wanted to interject that his voice was just as powerful as Eden's if not more so, but she wasn't trying to comment on nothing about this man in front of his ex.

"No, we would complement each other so well. Ask Uncle Dave. He'll agree."

"Eden, thank you for inviting me." Priscilla was about to excuse herself. "I think I'm going to go now—"

"Ok. Bye." Eden's mom responded before Priscilla could

finish her complete thought.

"Can I talk to you before you go?"

Priscilla had expected Randy's request. She had been ducking and dodging him for a couple weeks now. She knew he wouldn't let this opportunity pass to talk to her privately. Before answering she glanced at his ex. The lady looked like she wanted to snatch her. Randy was not getting her jumped in the church parking lot.

"If you want to discuss Eden's progress this term, we can make an appointment for this week. I'm not sure how long you'll be here, Ms. Knight, but I'd love to meet with you both." Priscilla watched Randy physically recoil, receiving her words like a gut blow. He was hurt, and even though it took seconds for him to recover, he was not deterred.

"We can definitely do that, but the conversation I want to have with you now is personal."

Priscilla felt heat rise all the way to the tip of her ears. She was glad for her dark skin; she was blushing hard. She had forgotten this man did not become who he was by being passive when he wanted something. She could tell he had stopped playing games with her and was coming for her hard. But then what happened when he got her? Would he check off another accomplishment and dismiss her?

"We don't have anything personal to discuss." Priscilla gasped when he took two steps towards her and stepped into her personal space.

"We can either have this conversation here or we can have it in private, but you owe me at least that after ghosting me."

Again, heat rushed to Priscilla's face, and she could see that Eden's mom looked like she wanted to spit fire at her. Eden looked like she wanted to give her dad a high five. She was definitely a fan of them being a couple.

"Mummy, you haven't said hello to Grandpa yet. Let's go

rescue him from Sister Anderson and her husband." Eden took her mom by the hand and led her away from Priscilla and Randy.

"Priscilla, what happened? I thought the time we spent together that Saturday, especially at lunch, would take us to the next level."

Priscilla wanted to tell him that he was wrong. Tell him that Saturday was uneventful for her, but she couldn't fix her mouth to lie, especially not in church. The only alternative was to tell him the truth. She felt little butterflies dancing in her stomach at the thought of being that honest and vulnerable with him.

"Never mind. Don't answer that now. We're having something for my dad at Dave's house. Please be my guest."

Priscilla was grateful that his request for her to join him forestalled her answer, but she wasn't so grateful that she would agree to be his guest at a family function.

"It's not just family." He seemingly read her thoughts. "It won't be an intimate, sit down at the dinner table, get interrogated by mom type of thing. Will you come?"

"Please say yes to this boy so we can leave. I'm hungry and these shoes are not kind to my feet."

Randy's mother stepped from behind Randy.

"Ms. Deveaux, it is a pleasure to see you again. Gratefully, it's been a while since I've had to come down to the school. We want to keep it that way."

"Pleasure to see you again also, Mrs. Knight, and congratulations to you and your husband on this anniversary." Priscilla hugged her instead of shaking her hand and wondered what in the world had gotten into her. Suppose this woman didn't like to be hugged or touched.

"I like her, Randy. I'll see you at the house, Priscilla. Come on, son. Flats and food are needed. In that order." She walked off.

"You can't say no to her. I'll text you the directions. See you at the house." Randy laughed as he followed his mom.

Priscilla sat in her car staring at the text from Randy with directions to his brother's house. She wanted to drive off and go straight home, but something wouldn't let her. Could it be the Holy Spirit prompting her to go?

"Father, your word says to guard my heart. That's what I'm trying to do." Priscilla prayed out loud. Before she could finish her prayer, the Holy Spirit reminded her of a sermon her pastor had preached on Proverbs 4:23. He said there was a difference between guarding your heart and putting up a wall. A guard stands watch at a gate and uses discernment to decide who to let in the gate. When you put up a wall, you're saying to yourself and others that no one can enter.

Realization dawned on her that she had erected a wall around her heart, and Priscilla felt uneasy. It had been there so long she didn't even realize it. Reign and Avery always complained that she was sometimes aloof with them and never shared when she was going through something until after the fact. She even kept them at arm's length, especially Avery because of her "status" and money. She'd admit that after all their years of friendship, there were still times when she felt like she did when they first met as freshmen in college. Avery came traipsing into their dorm room with her designer luggage, designer clothes and designer attitude, and Priscilla had felt so inadequate with her everyday ordinary self. She'd felt like she wasn't enough, and that's how Randy made her feel. Compared to him, she felt like a major underachiever.

Priscilla's last thought made her pause. She didn't like the path her thoughts were leading her on and decided to redirect them. She knew what Galatians 6:4 said. She shouldn't be comparing herself to anyone else. She dismissed all the doubts in her mind and decided to go to the celebration.

As Priscilla followed the directions Randy gave her and

drove through Dave's neighborhood, she found herself moving at a snail's pace admiring the elegant homes. Randy lived in an exclusive neighborhood, but these homes were not only in an exclusive neighborhood, they were breathtakingly extravagant. For years she drove by Lake Killarney on the way to Sir Lynden Pindling International Airport wondering what the homes on the lake looked like from the front. Now she knew they looked like something from an episode of *Lifestyles of the Rich and Famous.*

She pulled up to a mammoth gate that was monogramed with a K. After speaking with someone through the call box, the gates swung open. She knew better than to expect a long, winding road that led to a main house. Nassau didn't have enough land for properties to have long, winding roads. Instead she drove to a huge circular driveway where a valet attendant greeted her. He assisted her out of her car. Gawking at the luxury cars that were already parked, she tried not feel inadequate in her Prius.

"Don will escort you inside." The valet attendant nodded to a suited man who had stealthy walked up on them.

"Right this way, Ms. Deveaux."

She shouldn't have been surprised that he knew her name. It was just like when Randy took her to The Palace. They entered a grand foyer. Everything seemed to be glistening and gleaming. She found herself walking carefully like she was afraid to mess anything up. Everything looked perfect and unlived in. That was until a little boy whizzed by followed by a group of laughing children who almost ran her over. She was just getting her balance when a straggler running by bumped into her. She felt herself tittering. *Jesus, please don't let me embarrass myself by falling in these people's house.* Priscilla felt a strong hand steadying her. She thought it was her escort, but when she turned to offer thanks, she saw that it was Randy. She felt herself blushing under his gaze. *Get yourself together, girl.*

"Thank you," Priscilla said in a soft voice that she didn't recognize as her own, and maybe she even batted her eyelashes. *Oh lord, what was on Randy's ex must've gotten on me.*

"No problem. You have to be careful around here. These kids run everywhere."

"No harm done."

"Don, I'll escort Ms. Deveaux from here. Thank you."

The young man nodded and left.

"You found it okay?"

"Yup. No streets names, north, south, east or west, but your directions got me here." She quipped.

Randy let out a hearty laugh. "You must think you're in the States. Girl, you know how we do. Drive straight 'til you get to the big jumper church on the corner then make a right. Keep going 'til you get to the corner where Manny and dem is be. Turn right there. It's the fourth house on the left. It yellow and brown."

It was now Priscilla's turn to laugh. Attending college in the States had gotten her used to directions with street addresses. She never got lost when someone gave her an address in the States. With Bahamian directions she got lost almost every time.

"Well, I didn't get lost, so your directions did the job."

Priscilla took in the grandeur of the home as Randy led her though the house. From the grand staircase to the formal dining room that looked like it seated twenty to the family room that she was sure she'd seen on MTV's *Cribs,* each element of the home had Priscilla's jaw dropping. Randy led her to the backyard that was much bigger than she imagined. Round tables were draped in ivory tablecloths with white, gold and green floral arrangements at the center. Various floral arrangements on pillars were arrayed throughout the backyard. Servers with trays walked about offering appetizers and cocktails. *Probably mocktails.* Priscilla thought.

"You didn't say it would be fancy."

"I didn't know, but I should've. Dave is over the top like this. We said a small gathering after service for family and friends. This looks like someone's wedding reception. It's a good thing you have on your Sunday best."

"Ha ha... You got jokes."

"Come. There's someone I want you to meet." Randy grabbed Priscilla's hand, and she tried to ignore the tingle she felt.

Priscilla was glad she had accepted Randy's, really his mother's invitation to the party. It allowed her to see people with money differently than her past experiences. Randy's brothers, their wives and Rome's fiancée were some of the realest people she had met in a while. There was no pretentiousness at all. They didn't name drop. They didn't flaunt their clout. They didn't show off their wealth. Although their stories were of people and places she only imagined to meet and go, they told them for the story's sake and not to let her know where they vacationed or who their celebrity friends were. They made sure she enjoyed herself. They didn't let her be a wallflower and included her in their conversations.

"Randy's been trying to make his way over here for the last fifteen minutes, but he keeps getting stopped. Look at Aunt Dorothy trying to set him up with Sister Gardiner's daughter." Jason's wife, Jael laughed. Priscilla turned to see who she was talking about.

"You better go rescue him, Priscilla. Aunt Dorothy just made them hold hands. Next she'll try to get Dad to marry them." Victoria, Dave's wife, took the drink Priscilla was nursing out of her hand and shooed with a head nod in Randy's direction. "Go."

Priscilla was a bit hesitant, but it did look like he needed some help. Aunt Dorothy had indeed forced him to hold hands with the young woman they were talking to, and her eyes were searching the crowd for somebody, possibly Reverend Knight. She stood to go and extract Randy from the situation.

"Hey, babe, there you are." Priscilla put her arm around Randy's waist. He caught on immediately.

"Hey," he said wrapping her in his arms and kissing her lightly on the lips. Priscilla didn't expect the kiss, and in that moment she forgot Ms. Dorothy and Sister Gardiner's daughter were standing there.

"Who dis?" Aunt Dorothy's nose scrunched up like she smelled something foul.

"Aunty, this is my fiancée." Priscilla gawked at Randy's outrageous lie. She wanted to elbow him, but she didn't when Aunt Dorothy and Sister Gardiner's daughter's mouths dropped to the floor. They looked like something out of a cartoon.

"David and Jackie didn't mention that you had a fiancée. Come on, Jonquelisha, let's go find Storm. He's single."

"What kind of name is Jonquelisha?" Priscilla asked after they walked off.

"She's named after her dad."

"If you have any more girl children, please do not follow that trend."

"That's an idea. What could I call them? Randia, Randolphia and Randonya?" Randy mused. Priscilla laughed at Randy's silliness.

"You having a good time?" Randy draped an arm around Priscilla's shoulder.

"I am. I'll admit that I had some preconceived opinions about rich people that were not favorable. That's why I didn't want to come here today. That's why I didn't want to be involved with you. My experiences with people with money have not been good. My dad has money and he's ignored me all my life." Priscilla admitted. Randy led her to spot where they could have some privacy.

"I don't know your dad, but I promise I'm not like him. I want you to be a part of my life."

"I know that. I guess I always knew that, but I didn't want to take the risk, roll the dice, lose and end up getting hurt."

"This is a risk for me too. You met my ex-wife. She cheated on me and bounced. I promised myself I would not be played like that again, so all of my relationships since have been superficial. You are the first woman I've met that I wanted to take that risk and open up to in order to see if this thing my parents and my brothers have with their wives is for me too. That's where I'm at. That's what I want to explore with you."

Priscilla was speechless. She knew Randy was intentional. With all of his successes there was no other way that he could not be. However, she never before considered that he would be just as intentional in his pursuit of her. She thought his pursuit was about conquest, but it was more purposeful than that. He was looking for a wife. Not a conquest. This revelation left her speechless.

"I don't know what to say to that, Randy."

"Say you want to explore the possibility of us too."

Us. She hadn't been a part of an "us" since 2010. For so long, it had been me, my and I; she wasn't sure she even knew how to be us, ours and we anymore. She wanted to try, though.

"I do want to explore the possibility of us."

Thirteen

Randy couldn't concentrate on what Dave was saying in their meeting. He was too busy thinking about how he and Priscilla could make dating work with Eden being at her school. He said he could move Eden to another school, but he was joking.

He could call their thing friendship, but he had already kissed her twice. He wanted to take her to Blue Lagoon Island because when they went on the field trip, she mentioned she thought it would be cool to swim with dolphins (in a controlled environment with supervision, she had added). If Eden went with them it wouldn't technically be a date. Right? He didn't want Eden with them, though. He wanted more one on one time Priscilla. Maybe if Eden brought along her friends she would be preoccupied and he could spend time with Priscilla.

Randy texted Eden to ask if she down with his idea. She quickly responded that she was, and asked if she could invite Dakari. He immediately responded: **Heck no.** Eden replied: ☺ **I had to try. I'll ask Kaley and Alex.** Later that afternoon Eden texted that her friends' parents had given them permission. He called Priscilla when he got home from the office.

"Hey, beautiful."

"I'm feeling anything but beautiful right now.

"Why? What's the matter?"

"My car broke down again, and I had to walk home from the Prince Charles Shopping Center. Then halfway home it started raining."

"I'm on my way."

"You don't have to do—"

Randy had hung up and didn't hear the rest of Priscilla's protest. She needed a new car. He noticed how much she admired the Range Rover when they'd gone shopping. He grabbed the keys to the Range. He had the drive to her place to figure out how he'd convince her to take the car. He stuck his head in Eden's room to let her know he was going out. She was lost in some show on Netflix and waved him off.

When Priscilla opened the door, she did look a bit startling. Her hair was a tangled mess.

"Don't you say one mumbling word about my hair." She stepped aside, and he walked in. He knew enough to keep his mouth pinned on the hair subject. She plopped onto the couch and he took a seat next to her.

"I had my hair blown out yesterday."

"So, it was straight?"

She nodded and handed him her cell phone. Her straightened her was long. She looked good with it straight, but it wasn't her. At least, he didn't think it was her. She was afro and headwraps to him. To him it translated as a challenge to the status quo, especially in Bahamian culture where women would spend their whole week's pay getting a weave in or a wig made. He overheard the young ladies he employed talking about it all the time, and every time he was astonished by how much they spent on getting their hair done.

"Nice."

"Right. Then this." She threw her head back and closed her eyes. Even with crazy hair she was beautiful. He took the moment to catalogue every part of her face. The mole on the side of her left eye. The shape of her brows. The dip of her lip.

"Are you just going to stare at me?" Priscilla's eyes were still closed.

"How did you know I was staring at you?"

"I feel you staring at me." She opened her eyes and their eyes met.

"May I ask what a stare feels like?"

"It feels like warmth with no sun. A chill with no breeze. A caress with no touch. It feels like a hug without an embrace. A whisper with no words. That's what it feels like when you stare at me."

Priscilla's voice did to him what his stare did to her. He was feeling like he wanted more than a kiss, but from her posts on social media he knew she was on that sex after marriage kick. In his past experiences even with the ones who said no ring, no t'ing, if he pushed, he'd get it, but he felt like Priscilla still wouldn't budge if he pushed.

"Are you trying to seduce me, Ms. Deveaux?"

"What would make you ask that?" She looked genuinely puzzled.

"You really have no idea what your voice and those words could do to a man?"

"Oh," she lowered her eyes, "I really wasn't trying to; the words just came to me."

"I'm honored to be your muse."

"I didn't say all that." She hit him with a throw pillow.

"Anyway, let me get up out of here before I get us in trouble."

"I'm not even gonna comment on that."

"I think that's best for all parties concerned."

"Me too."

"I'm going to leave my car here for you to use until you get your car situation sorted out."

"What?"

"You heard me."

"I can't take your car."

"You're borrowing it until you get a new car."

"Randy, I don't plan on getting a new car any time soon."

"It doesn't matter. You can use my car until then. You wan' walk in the rain again?" He folded his arms across his chest. Priscilla sucked her teeth. He knew he had her then.

"Give me the keys." She said with attitude. He smiled and fished the keys out of his pocket. When he handed them to her, she stared at them for a while before saying anything.

"The Range. You're loaning me your Range Rover?"

"You want the Maybach or Aston Martin?"

"It's a Range Rover. I can't borrow that."

"It's a car."

"An expensive one."

"So?"

"Dis what I was talkin' 'bout right here. People don't wan' loan you dey Civic and you tryin' to len' me ya $100,000 plus SUV." Priscilla slipped into full Bahamian dialect.

Randy surmised that she was upset, but didn't know why. "I'm loaning it to you because I don't want you out on the streets in a car that breaks down every other day. I care about your safety. Why is that upsetting you? Because it's an expensive car? I can go buy you a cheap car if you want, but you're not riding around in that piece of crap anymore."

"You shame a me driving a piece of crap?"

"Don't twist my words, Priscilla. You know your car is a piece of crap." Randy snorted. She was silent for a moment. She must have been contemplating if she should take the SUV. She didn't realize that she didn't have a choice. He had no plans on leaving until she agreed to take it.

"It is a piece of crap." She admitted reluctantly.

"You're going to take the Range?"

"As long as you don't go buying me a car."

"That is an option."

"That is not an option." Priscilla warned him.

Randy shrugged his shoulders. "Well, good night. Oh yeah, we're going to Blue Lagoon tomorrow."

"Eden told me."

Randy shook his head. That girl couldn't hold water. Her mouth ran like a faucet. "My ride's been waiting for a minute. Let me go for real. See you in the morning."

Randy sang and hummed all the way home. He was very much looking forward to Blue Lagoon. He pulled up to his house and saw a strange car in the driveway. He didn't want to jump to conclusions, but Eden had better not have anyone in the house. He quickly got out of the car and into the house. He heard voices coming from the kitchen and when he entered, he was shocked to see Kim there. He counted silently to ten and willed his temper not to rise, hoping she didn't come to ask him for money.

"Hey," he said, trying to sound casual.

"Daddy, Mummy stopped by unexpectedly to see you." Eden emphasized unexpectedly. Randy guessed it was so he could know that she didn't have anything to do with her mother being there. Randy didn't like unexpected anything.

"I hope you don't mind, Randolph. I needed to talk to you before I left in the morning." Kim started to walk toward him. He suppressed a groan. *Here we go.* He thought.

"I think that's my cue to go to bed." Eden darted pass them and out of the kitchen.

"What's this about?" Randy cut the niceties.

"Straight to business as always. I wanted to ask you if

Eden could spend the summer with me."

"She's going on a missions trip this summer."

"I know, but that's in July. I meant before that, until she left for her trip. I've already discussed it with her and she said I had to ask you. So, what do you say?" Kim smiled and crossed her fingers for him to see.

"Why now?" Randy asked with a frown. He knew Kim was up to something, he just couldn't figure out what.

"Why not now? I think I've been gone too much already."

"You think?" Randy was sarcastic. "What are you up to? What game are you trying to run?"

"I know you may find this hard to believe because of the past, but I'm not up to anything. I don't have an agenda. I'm not trying to get money from you. I just want to spend time with my only child."

Randy mulled over Kim's words. He didn't want to deny Eden spending time with her mother, but he also didn't want her to get hurt. He couldn't let her get hurt. He was about to tell Kim no, but she spoke before him.

"I had no intention of sharing this with you, but I... I had a miscarriage last year, and I really wanted that baby. I think maybe I thought I could make up for all the mistakes I made with Eden. After the miscarriage and the grief and the depression and blaming myself, I realized I have a child, and I needed to make things right with her. I didn't need a second chance with another child. I needed a second chance with her."

"I'm sorry to hear that." Randy thought about what she had said. He looked at her. Looked into her eyes and saw that she meant what she said. "When your conscious is assuaged you won't bail again, will you?"

"It's not like that. I'm really sorry for leaving the way I did and not being a part of Eden's life. I was selfish. I'm working on me, and I want to work on my relationship with my daughter."

"OK." Randy said after a long silence. For some reason he believed Kim and he believed she wouldn't abandon Eden again.

"OK?"

"She can spend the summer with you."

"Thank you," Kim said quietly. "I owe you an apology as well. You were better to me than any man I've ever been with. I didn't deserve you. I'm sorry for hurting you. I hope one day you'll believe that and accept my apology.

Long after Kim left, he replayed their conversation in his head. He couldn't believe she had apologized. He refused to believe she was sincere even though she had no need to lie. Maybe she was sorry she had missed out on having joint bank accounts with him and not because she had hurt him. He sighed and hoped too that one day he would be able to accept her apology.

Despite staying up late thinking about the whole Kim thing, Randy was up early the next morning. He stood in his room looking at the swim trunks Eden chose for him. They were a nice shade of blue. He liked it, but she'd paired them with a t-shirt that read HUNK. Eden thought it was cute and funny. He didn't like it; he didn't consider himself to be a hunk. He'd feel more comfortable if the tee said THE BRAIN.

"Eden!" Randy went to his bedroom door and yelled for his daughter. She came running into the room in less than a minute.

"Yes, sir?"

"Are you ready?"

"I sure am. This is going to be so much fun. I can't wait to swim with dolphins, seals and stingrays."

"I'm having second thoughts about this t-shirt. I would like it better if it said THE BRAIN."

Instead of answering, Eden ran into his walk-in closet. She came back with another t-shirt with word "Nerd" across the chest.

"Where did that come from?"

"Uncle Rome got it for you for obvious reasons."

Randy laughed. Yup, this is definitely something his little brother would buy for him, and he now remembered that he also bought him a pair of Clark Kent glasses to complete the look.

"Are *you* ready now?"

"I was born ready."

"Super corny, Dad."

After getting Kaley and Alex, Randy picked up Priscilla. Her eyes danced with excitement and her smile made him smile.

"Good morning," she greeted as she got into the car.

"Morning," Randy said, resisting the desire to kiss her hello.

"Morning!" The trio in the back seat sang.

"Ms. Deveaux, I'm so glad you're coming with us," Kaley said.

Eden smirked. Randy shot her a look through the rearview mirror. "Sorry," she mouthed and drew her friends into a conversation about music.

It was about a twenty-five-minute drive from Priscilla's to Paradise Island where they would get on the boat to Blue Lagoon Island. Priscilla was uncharacteristically talkative, chatting the whole time about a trip her senior class in high school had made to Blue Lagoon. It was the last time she had been there.

Once on the ferry, Randy led Priscilla to the railing and

away from the girls. The sun's rays danced off the sea, causing it to shimmer. Randy smiled as he closed his eyes and inhaled the fresh air. He looked at the ocean. The wind wrapped around him, and he felt at peace.

"Every time I see this I can't help but think how amazing God is," Priscilla commented.

"It is beautiful." Randy smiled down at her. He hoped he could convince her that he wasn't like her dad or whoever the "rich people" were who hurt her.

Once the ferry docked on the small island, the passengers of mostly tourists made their way off the boat. Randy had upgraded their trip to the VIP package, and a private tour guide greeted them when they arrived. Sandra, their guide, led them to a private beach area and advised them that they could leave their beach bags on their beach chairs. She said they had forty-five minutes until the Segway Safari of the island and after that would be their dolphin encounter. She suggested they hit the water until then. Eden and her friends didn't have to be told twice. They ran off before Randy could give them his spiel about being safe.

"I guess it's just you and me."

Priscilla turned to him. "I'm sure that's exactly the way you planned it."

"Maybe," Randy smiled and nodded toward the recreational equipment. "Let's grab a water trike."

"Looks like fun, I'll race you to it." Priscilla discarded the wrap dress she was wearing to reveal an African print one-piece swimsuit. Unveiling the swimsuit and revealing her curves had Randy distracted. Priscilla was off and running, and he was still standing with his bag in his hand.

"You cheated," Randy said when he caught up with her.

"Priscilla 1 – Randy 0." She winked and patted the space next to her on the trike.

"Oh, it's like that. You know I am highly competitive."

"We'll see about that today. Start pedaling and stop talking."

Randy was happy that Priscilla was relaxed and having fun with him. Unlike her usually reserved self, she seemed to have thrown caution to the wind. Maybe not all caution because she didn't seem like that type, but enough of it to allow them to be silly and giddy and real with each other.

Forty-five minutes felt like ten and before they knew it, it was time for the Segway tour. Eden, Kaley and Alex were waiting for them with Sandra, who walked them a short distance to the Segways. She introduced them to their Segway tour guide, John. He gave them some instructions and they hopped on the Segways.

They all caught on to how to operate the Segway immediately. Eden was completely into the tour, which offered a view of the island's animal rescue initiatives. Rescued sea animals from around the world were brought there. Randy and Priscilla were not so interested in that. They hung back a little from the group and talked.

"You said swimming with the dolphins is on your bucket list. You get to check that off today. You want to travel the world. Hopefully, we'll get to do that together too."

"I see you're planning for the future."

"I already told you what I'm about. Why wouldn't I be making future plans?"

"Seems too soon to be thinking like that. We haven't even been on an official date."

"You know the reason for that. It's October. Eden graduates in seven months, and I can't wait for two reasons. First, there were times I didn't think she'd make it to her senior year. Second, I'll be able to spoil you like I want."

"You think so?"

"I know so. Get ready to visit the real Buckingham Palace."

"I could be down for that."

"Could be? You are 100% down for your dream trip to England. Stop tripping. What else is on your bucket list?"

"I'm not telling you nothing else before you start trying to make those happen too."

"I might, but still tell me. I want to know. I'll tell you one that's on mine."

"What is it?"

"I want to go to Africa. Ghana, Kenya, Rwanda, Nigeria and South Africa are on my list. I don't want it to be a week or two, though. I want to go for a few months."

"Whoa."

"It would have to be after Eden finished school. Plus taking off for several months is something I have to mentally prepare myself for. I can't imagine being away from work for that long."

"I want to go to Jerusalem. That's close to the top. Be where Jesus was when He was here on earth. That would be awesome. You already know about the center, and I want to skydive."

"Skydive? You were scared to snorkel."

"I was not afraid. I was cautious. This would be throwing caution to the wind and liberating myself from my fears."

"Rome said the same thing to me when he tried to convince me to go skydiving with him. I'll admit I passed out." Randy revealed.

Priscilla hollered with laughter. She almost ran her Segway into a palm tree. "You passed out?"

"Yes, when we were getting ready to jump out the plane. My heart was already in my throat so when I looked down from 13,000 feet in the air, I blacked out. Rome teases me about it to this day."

"How was it growing up with Rome Knight? You two seem completely opposite. I mean from what I've heard or read of him in the media."

"You're a fan?"

"I'm not really into sports, but he's a Bahamian who made it to the NBA. He's a legend."

"I'm not into sports either. I like to watch, but I never got into playing much. All my brothers played sports, though. Rome was the typical little brother. We picked on him. He got us in trouble."

"If you didn't play sports, what did you do?"

"Jason and I were heavy into music."

"I used to buy Jason's mixed tapes!" Priscilla giggled.

"Yeah, we sold those things all over, from Mayaguana to Grand Bahama and every island in between. Mummy made sure we all learned an instrument. We each started with piano when we were about two. I picked it up quickly, faster than my brothers did. Then she taught me guitar. I learned how to play the drums and sax on my own. I feel connected to music and instruments. I think I would have mastered any instrument I picked up."

"Why didn't you go into a music career?"

"My dad hated secular music. As archaic as this sounds, he called it devil music. He kicked Jason out of the house when he found out he was DJ'ing. Jason didn't tell Dad about my involvement. I wanted to be like my dad. I didn't want to disappoint him. So, I left the music alone. I played and sang in church, of course. But it wasn't the same."

"Why not? There are a lot of successful gospel artists."

He hesitated. "You're right, but I saw that I could be more successful as an entrepreneur. It worked out; spreading the gospel is not important to me anymore."

For the first time that day, a frown marred Priscilla's beautiful face. He knew she assumed based on his family that he loved God like she did. Priscilla was quiet, and he knew she was deep in thought. A few moments passed before she spoke.

"I know you love God. There's no way you could sing the way you sang at church the other day and not love God. My prayer is that you let go and let God heal you."

Her words echoed what Dave had told him about letting go. He took note, but wasn't ready for that yet. Before he could respond their guide called for them to catch up. They had reached the end of the safari. Sandra rejoined them to take them to the dolphin encounter area.

"We'll continue this conversation later." Priscilla whispered just before Eden squeezed in between them, looping arms with both of them.

"This is going to be epic." She squealed.

A family of three from Norway were the only other people in their group. The eight of them joined the trainer in the enclosed area of water where the dolphins trained. Randy stood in between Priscilla and Eden. The excited energy that bounced off the two of them was palpable. He was happy to make this experience happen for his two favorite girls.

The trainer, Conrad, told them they were going to start off with some hugs and kisses from Neil. Randy wondered who named the dolphin Neil. Neil was a name that should only be given to humans. Conrad asked them to kneel. He asked Priscilla who was first in line to open up her arms wide. When Conrad blew his whistle, Neil swam up to Priscilla and rested his head on her shoulder. Randy laughed when Priscilla closed her eyes and gave the dolphin a squeeze like he was a person. The trainer blew his whistle again and Neil touched his mouth to Priscilla's lips. Randy was so busy enjoying Priscilla's reaction to the dolphin's hug and kiss that he was caught off guard when the dolphin started splashing water on him, which gave everyone a good laugh. Neil skipped giving him a hug and kiss and went to Eden, who got two hugs and two kisses. The five of them worked up an appetite during their time with Neil and were glad for lunch time.

Fourteen

After lunch Priscilla lay reclining in a beach chair. She gazed out at the lagoon. She spotted Eden and her friends running around, spraying each other and some guy friends they had made with water guns. She looked at Randy in the chair next to her. He had his eyes on those boys like an eagle watching his prey.

"Stop giving those boys the evil eye."

"I don't trust teenage boys."

"But you trust your daughter, right?"

"If you would have asked me that same question a year and a half ago, I would have given you a quick no. Today, I can say yes I trust her."

"Then trust her, she knows how to handle herself."

Randy took his eyes off of the kids and looked at Priscilla. Their eyes connected and the warmth of his gaze washed over her.

"Thank you. I needed to hear that." He smiled.

Priscilla felt heat that didn't come from the sun flush her face. His earnest thanks melted her heart.

"You have made a great impact on my daughter's life." He continued.

"She wasn't easy."

"Who you telling? I know that, and I wasn't easy. I was so done at the time, but I'm grateful that you weren't done." Randy's words echoed the depth of his gratitude. "You didn't give up on her when I had." He looked away, but not before Priscilla noticed unshed tears in his eyes. "You saw in Eden what I was blind to. You helped my little girl heal from the pain of rejection. For a long time I blamed that on her mother, not realizing that I was doing the same thing."

"I was just doing my job."

"You went beyond doing your job." Randy turned back to her, reached over and took her hand in his to convey his sincerity.

A jolt shot up her arm. She had never felt this type of energy from someone. She knew she was attracted to him, but this was something else, something more. She could tell by the way his eyes dropped to her lips that he felt it too.

"This is the part of the day where I wish I hadn't brought Eden along. There's no way I could get away with kissing you and her not seeing."

"I can't believe you just said that." Priscilla playfully swatted Randy on the shoulder.

"Which part? That I wish Eden wasn't here or that I want to kiss you?"

"All of the above." Priscilla laughed. "And how'd the conversation go from deep and serious to this?"

"I started staring at your lips and thought dang I want to kiss her right now, but my nosy behind daughter is right over there."

"Randy!"

"You asked. Okay, let's get back to deep and serious. What led you to become a counselor?"

"You expect me to be serious now?"

"You can do it. Refocus." Randy wiped the smile off his face and put on a serious expression, which caused Priscilla to giggle. "Stop laughing and answer my serious question, seriously."

"Boy, you are a mess." She paused to gather her thoughts. "I've always been intrigued with what makes people do the things they do, the way they think, and the way they process information. That led me to psychology." She paused again because although she'd had the conversation of why she chose her career with herself, she'd not had it with anyone else. Not even Reign and Avery.

"I have a huge family with lots of cousins with kids. When I was in high school, I was always spending time with the kids. As an older cousin, they talked to me when they didn't feel like they could talk to their parents. But, I could not give them the help they needed. Of course, I told my grandmother and she counselled them in the right direction. I was like I want to do that. That's what I want to do when I grow up."

"That's admirable."

"There's so much more to do, though." Priscilla looked away. She didn't know how admirable it really was when there was so much more that needed to be done. She felt like she wasn't living her life to the fullest potential of what God had planned for her. She'd wanted to open a youth mentoring center on every major island in the country. Her goal was to open the first one by thirty. Here she was five years later still trying to get it done. *Not by might nor by power but by my Spirit says the Lord.* She heard Zechariah 4:6 in her spirit. She knew it wasn't by her own efforts alone but by and through God that it would get done.

She looked over at Randy. He too was lost in his thoughts. She leaned back against the beach chair and closed her eyes. The combination of sun and wind was the perfect lullaby for the couple, and before they knew it they had drifted off to sleep. Then Priscilla felt someone watching her. Her eyes fluttered open to see Randy staring at her again with a look of admiration.

"You know you're beautiful even when you're asleep." Randy's compliment caused Priscilla to blush. "But just as much as I am like dang she's fine, I am like man, her heart is full of love and compassion. You're different from other women I've dated. You have a career, but you aren't career driven. Most of the professional women I know seem to be chasing a title or a salary. You're chasing your passion."

Randy grew quiet and Priscilla didn't mind because she was wrapping her mind around what he'd said. She wondered where he was going with the conversation. It sounded like the beginning of a "let's get serious" conversation. Yes, she liked him. He wasn't the rich, self-centered, neglectful father as she first pegged him. He'd been hurt, so he was guarded and pretended to be aloof. That wasn't the real him, though. The real Randy was smart, thoughtful, helpful, kind and fun. He was also all the things that made him successful like driven, focused and strategic. Plus, he was handsome and had a great body. She let her eyes sweep over his shirtless chest and then quickly looked away. Yes, the Lord made this man and then declared that it was good. If he was all that and a bag of chips, why was she resistant to the gravitational pull into Randy's stratosphere? Was it because he was Eden's dad? Was it because he was wealthy?

"I like you." Randy's words drew Priscilla out of her contemplation. Despite her hesitation, Randy's admission warmed her heart. She hadn't known how much she wanted to hear him say those words. She didn't realize how much she wanted him to like her.

"I like you too." Priscilla admitted.

"Good." Randy leaned forward to kiss Priscilla.

"What about Eden?" Priscilla blurted out, stopping Randy in tracks. He frowned at her.

"What about her?"

"Didn't you just say you don't want her—"

"They ran off two minutes ago to the food pavilion." He leaned in, his lips imploring her to let him in.

She still wasn't sure if she should, but she did.

***

Priscilla woke up still on cloud nine from her Blue Lagoon experience with Randy. She stretched and smiled as she thought about his kiss. It had been a long time since she'd been close enough to a man for him to even try to kiss her. Her last serious relationship felt like it was a millennium ago.

Bryan Saunders was one of Pedro's friends. They'd gone to the same high school, and Bryan had been trying to get with her from high school days. She'd never been interested in him; she thought he was a little rough around the edges like Pedro. Then he left for college and returned refined. The sagging jeans and tennis shoes were replaced with suits and ties.

She liked the refined version of Bryan. He was a CPA at one of the major accounting firms on the island. He was smart, ambitious, handsome, and treated her like a lady. He was everything she could want, until she was introduced to another man, Jesus. She accepted Jesus Christ as her Lord and Savior, and that changed a lot about what she wanted in a man. At the top of her list was saved, sanctified and filled with the Holy Ghost.

After she got saved Bryan went to church with her every Sunday, but he never accepted Jesus Christ for himself. She loved him and prayed that he would fall in love with Jesus. The more her relationship with God grew, the more she realized how wrong Bryan was for her. He did not understand and refused to accept that the old Priscilla had died and in Christ she was a new creation. He actually wanted them to move in together and could not fathom why she didn't drink any more or didn't want to party with him. She'd lived the unequally yoked scripture and never wanted to go through that again. Eventually she built up the courage to end their five-year relationship. Of course, their break-up didn't make sense to him. He thought they were good.

Priscilla was happy with God in her life. She didn't have

to waste another five years with the wrong man. She could just pray and ask God to reveal His perfect will to her about the relationship. These thoughts brought her full circle back to her questions about Randy. Priscilla shook her head. She didn't know.

"Father, I was not in the market for a relationship. If this is Your will, please show me." Priscilla got out of bed and prepared to read her Bible before praying and then getting ready for church.

Priscilla was not surprised that Avery was not in church. She was due in a couple of days. She was kind of disappointed that Avery was not there, though. She wanted to tell her and Reign about her Blue Lagoon adventure with Randy. She had tried both of them when they returned from their outing and got their voicemails. Reign sent her a WhatsApp message letting her know that she was working on a story. She immediately prayed a prayer of protection over Reign because working on story for her could mean anything from sitting in front of her computer to sitting in front of some drug dealer's house. Priscilla hoped Reign would stop by her grandmother's after church.

When church ended, Priscilla did what she always did, headed to her grandmother's house. She was a little later than usual; it seemed like everyone and their mama stopped her after service to talk. After talking with Sister Stanley for twenty minutes about her grandson, who was acting out at school, Priscilla kept her eyes straight ahead and made a beeline for the car. When she got to her grandmother's house she was pleased to see Reign's Jeep Wrangler haphazardly parked on the street.

"Girl, I fixed you a plate." Reign said as soon as Priscilla opened the door.

"Why are you standing at the front door with a plate of food in your hand?" Priscilla asked.

"I was waiting on you. I need to know what went down yesterday." Reign grabbed Priscilla by the hand and practically dragged her to her grandmother's sitting room.

"You know Mama doesn't allow anyone in here."

"I know," Reign smiled. "But she's busy so it's perfect. No one will come in here and interrupt us."

Priscilla took a seat and took the plate of food Reign had prepared for her. Her grandmother had cooked curry chicken. It was her favorite dish. She was just about to dig her fork into the food when Reign snatched the fork out of her hand.

"What is your problem?"

"I'm not about to sit and watch you eat. That is not what I'm here for. I'm here to hear about you and Randy Knight."

Priscilla rolled her eyes at Reign and then proceeded to tell her about yesterday.

"He kissed you!" Reign jumped up from her seat and started to do a mini praise dance.

Priscilla laughed, "Girl, sit your tail down. It was just a kiss."

"Just a kiss? When is the last time you just kissed any-body?"

"A couple of weeks ago." Priscilla chuckled at Reign's stunned silence. "I thought that would stop you from running on. A girl can't always kiss and tell."

"Not all the time, just the first time. How you had a first kiss with Randy... The kiss a couple weeks ago was with Randy right?"

"Really, Reign?"

"I'n know. I gotta be sure. You keeping secrets and what not."

"Yes, with Randy."

"Interesting. As the title of that great song by Mrs. Pots says, "There's Something There.""

"Who's Mrs. Pots?"

"You know from *Beauty and Beast*. Mrs. Pots sings that song about Belle and the Beast. There's something there that wasn't there before."

"Are you really quoting lyrics to a song from a cartoon?"

"*Beauty and the Beast* is not a cartoon, it's a full-length feature film. But that's not the point. The point is there's something happening between you and Mr. Knight just like there was something happening between Belle and the Beast."

"Reign, please stop talking about the cartoon characters like they're real people."

"You get my point though, Priscilla. You can't deny this is something, if not special, different."

"I agree. I have to pray about it, though. You know he has money."

"You the only heffa on this island who mad cuz a man have money. Girl, go somewhere with that."

"I told you about my dad."

"That ni—"

"Reign!"

"Sorry. You can't compare Randy to the sperm donor. Just like all men aren't alike, all rich people aren't alike."

"Logically, I know you're right. But emotionally, I'm skittish."

As Priscilla was about to comment further her cell phone rang. Not recognizing the number, she sent the call to voicemail. Then Reign's phone began to ring. Never knowing when a call could be "the story," Reign never sent her calls to voicemail.

"Reign Bryant."

Priscilla watched Reign jump up out of her seat and bolt for the door. She was used to Reign leaving without any explanation so she wasn't stunned. However, she was stunned when Reign bolted back into the room and grabbed her by the arm.

"Girl, Avery is having the baby. Put that food down. We've gotta go!"

"I can't leave it in here. Mama would have my head."

"Go run put it in the kitchen. Then meet me in the Jeep."

At the hospital, Priscilla and Reign met Avery's family in the waiting area.

"Thank you for coming." Avery's mom said as she hugged Priscilla and Reign. Priscilla knew the grandmother of six boys was excited to meet her first granddaughter.

Priscilla had always wanted children. When she was a teenager, before she realized how much responsibility children were, she'd wanted six. She still wanted a fairly large family, but she'd be satisfied with three or four children. Priscilla found herself wondering if Randy wanted any more children.

They had been in the waiting room for four hours. Truthfully, she was ready to leave, but she prayed for patience and stayed. She had been to see Avery a couple of times during the wait. Avery was Avery, a diva even in labor. She had actually wanted to document the labor for her radio show, but Vince shut that idea down quick, fast and in a hurry. Reign was fast asleep, probably because she was out chasing a story all night. Vince and Mrs. Grant were in the room with Avery. Avery's dad and brothers were huddled in front of the TV watching football. Priscilla was about to join Reign in dreamland when she got a text message from Randy.

Hey beautiful. Just checking in to see how your day is going.

At the hospital with Avery. She's having the baby!

Hope she has a safe delivery. How long have you been there?

Since after church.

That's a while. Have you eaten?

Had something from the vending machine.

I'll send something by from one of the restaurants. How many of you are there?

You don't have to do that.

I know I don't have to but I want to. How many?

Eight. Thank you. ☺

My pleasure. ☺

Priscilla was surprised when Randy accompanied his staff to deliver the food. She couldn't help the wide smile Randy's presence put on her face. He tried to put on this nonchalant front, but she saw his heart. She saw the capacity he had for kindness, a fruit of the Spirit.

"I wasn't expecting you," she said as she stepped into his embrace. He smiled down at her and placed a sweet hello kiss on her lips. It seemed like the most natural thing in the world.

"An excuse to see you," he winked. Priscilla felt all eyes in the room shift to her. Reign cleared her throat loudly. Never one to miss any type of news, there was no way Reign would have slept through this.

"Everyone this is Randy. Randy meet Avery's family."

"Chief Justice Ashton Grant, pleasure to meet you, sir." Randy approached Avery's father, the first black Chief Justice of the Bahamas, and shook his hand vigorously. Priscilla could tell Randy was excited to meet him.

"The pleasure is mine. What you and your brother have done for Bay Street has been incredible." Chief Justice Grant said.

"Thank you, sir. I appreciate you saying that."

Priscilla stepped back and watched as Randy chatted with Avery's dad and the rest of Avery's family. They all seemed enamored by him. Each were successful in their own right, but the way they responded to Randy you would think they had met a celebrity. In a way, Priscilla supposed Randy was a homegrown celebrity. Despite the many compliments and "atta-boys," he appeared humble, even almost embarrassed by the attention. After fifteen minutes with the men and Reign, Randy excused himself to join her.

"Thank you so much for doing this."

"Really, this is nothing. Let's go for a walk." Randy suggested. "You look like you're ready to get out of here."

"Is it that obvious? We've been here going on six hours now. This baby needs to hurry and come on. I want to leave, but I don't know labor etiquette. Is it rude to leave before the baby arrives?"

"If it is, you might need an overnight bag. Kim was in labor with Eden for nearly two days."

"What? That's still happening? They need to find a drug to make labor shorter. I think the world's science is advanced enough for them to figure out how to make this childbearing thing more bearable."

Priscilla excused herself before she and Randy left the room. The two walked down the hall for a few moments in silence before Randy spoke.

"Did you ever connect with the Minister of Youth, Sports and Culture about your youth center?"

Priscilla had been hoping Randy would not bring the subject up again. She didn't know how to tell him, but she looked over at him and saw in his eyes that she could trust him with the truth of her messy past.

"Deon Bethel is my father."

"I beg your pardon?"

"My mom used to do day work for his family and they had an affair. I'm the product of that relationship. That's why I tripped after lunch at The Palace. When I saw him, it threw me off kilter."

"He didn't say anything to you that day. I'm assuming he doesn't know he's your father."

"I'm not sure. He came around until I was a teenager. Because of that, I've always thought he's known. But he has never acknowledged me."

"Wow. I would have tripped a little too if I ran into the father who's never been a father to me. That's rough. Do you want him to be a part of your life?"

"At this point in my life I feel that everything he could possibly have to offer me as a father has already passed. I feel like I needed him when I was Eden's age, not now. And I thought I had released all the resentment and bitterness I felt towards him to God, but when I saw him that day, I felt this twinge of something I couldn't identify at first. Then I realized it was rejection."

"I know that feeling." Randy sighed. Priscilla knew he was talking about his ex-wife. She appreciated his transparency.

"Did Eden's mom leave?

"That is a good question. I'm not sure. She says that she wants a relationship with Eden, but her popping up doesn't sit well with me. We haven't seen her in years."

"Years?"

"You heard me. She's always had an excuse about why she couldn't come see Eden or why Eden couldn't see her. Last time she was living somewhere in Asia and lost her passport."

"That's a pretty good excuse."

"She'n had no business being in Asia in the first place. Running behind man." He sucked his teeth. "Now she wants to be in Eden's life. I should believe her, but she hasn't given me a lot of reasons to trust her."

Priscilla noted that like her when Randy got mad he threw the Queen's English out the window and went into full Bahamian dialect. For her it made him more relatable. Listening to him just now made her feel like she was outside her grandmother's house talking to one of the neighbors and not a man who was probably worth several million US dollars.

"Well, she's here now and hopefully her desire to be a part of Eden's life is genuine." Priscilla tried to put a positive spin on things. Randy stared at Priscilla for a long while. Priscilla feared she had said something wrong.

"I hope so too." He sighed. "As much as we don't see eye to eye, I can't deny that Eden needs her mom."

Fifteen

Randy's phone chimed, indicating a voicemail. The sound brought him out of his thoughts and back to his computer screen. A year later and they were still dealing with the aftershocks of Hurricane Dorian, and would be dealing with it for years to come. With 185 mile per hour winds, Hurricane Dorian was the deadliest cyclone to make landfall in the Bahamas. Luckily, for their new project, Paradise Island was not hit directly by the storm. Randy was thankful the structure had not sustained any major damage. Some windows had to be replaced, but there was no water damage, the roof was unscathed and there was minimal work delay. He had breathed a sigh of relief after inspecting the property with the construction manager after the storm. It looked like the project would remain on schedule for a late summer opening the following year.

The celebration for him was short lived when reports surfaced of the destruction on Abaco and his native Grand Bahama. Hundreds of people were missing, homes and businesses were totally wiped out like they had never existed. The official death toll was seventy, but with all the undocumented people on Abaco, they would never know the real number. The damages from the hurricane on both islands rang to the tune of $3.4 billion US dollars.

Renaissance was one of the first companies to respond to the needs of the people on the islands, lending their company jet to get people off the islands and sending relief items. Despite their efforts Randy felt helpless. Life for Abaconians and Grand Bahamians would never be the same and there was nothing he could do about it. He went to visit Grand Bahama shortly after the storm to assess the damage at Renaissance Mall. While there he went to check on the house he'd grown up in. The house was gone, only the foundation remained. The neighborhood was completely devasted. He promised then to help rebuild and that's what he was supposed to be working on. Not daydreaming about Priscilla. Their Blue Lagoon "date" had gone better than he expected with Eden and her friends chaperoning them. He was going to ask her on a real date and planning the perfect date for them had distracted him from his work.

He sighed. He was going to have to go to Grand Bahama. They were building a new housing development where their old neighborhood was and were way behind schedule. He had no desire to go to anywhere. It would have to be this week, but Eden had a thing at school he wanted to go to and he wanted to see Priscilla again. Maybe he could convince Dave to go. Randy got up from his desk to make the short trek down the hall to Dave's corner office.

Not bothering to knock, Randy walked into Dave's office and was surprised to see that he was not sitting behind his desk. The buzz of a clipper caused Randy to look to his left at the sitting area in Dave's office. With a sofa, love seat, coffee table, large flat screen tv and mini kitchen right in front of a view of the beach that was across the street from Renaissance Towers, the sitting area was considerably larger than Dave's work area. But he had argued that since he spent so much time at work, he might as well make it comfortable.

Neither Randy nor Dave had a normal enough schedule to walk into a barber shop, and Mo, one of Dave's friends from high school, owned one of the top barber shops on the island and had no problem coming to the office or the house at any insane hour they asked him. Of course, it cost more than if they'd went to the shop, but paying the extra was worth the convenience of fitting a haircut into their schedule without having to look like a woolly mammoth.

"What up, Randy?"

"Erry t'ing cool." Randy greeted Mo with a handshake and man hug. "What's up with you, bro?"

"Erry t'ing cool on this end too. Looks like you need a shape up."

"I could use one if you have time when you're done with Dave."

Mo nodded, indicating that he did. Dave had his head buried in his phone. He was probably checking his emails. Their phones practically ran their lives. Most times, Randy felt like running across the street to Goodman's Bay and throwing it into the ocean.

Dave looked up at Randy. "How was your weekend?"

"Good, you know." Randy couldn't help the smile on his face, which caused his brother to frown at him.

"Is that goofy look about Ms. Deveaux?"

"I don't have a goofy look."

"Mo, didn't he look like the heart eye emoji just now?"

"Yeah, you did." Mo chuckled.

"Whatever."

"So, where'd you and Ms. Deveaux go this time?"

"We are not talking about this." Randy took the seat opposite Dave.

"Fine, but just so you know Eden already told me." Dave laughed.

"That little blabber. What did she say?"

"She mentioned in conversation that you all went to Blue Lagoon. You know I have to ask since you never bring anyone around Eden. What's the deal with you and Ms. Priscilla Deveaux? You feeling her?" Dave raised an eyebrow at Randy.

Randy frowned at Dave's question. He was way past 'feeling her,' but he wasn't ready to admit that to Dave.

"Thank God she's not your usual M.O." Dave continued when Randy didn't answer him. "I've been praying that you'd grow tired of looking for the female version of yourself, which you've been doing for the last fifteen years. If I had to endure another double date with you and some ladder climber who incessantly talked about herself, I'd already promised myself that me and Vikki would walk out on you."

"The female version of me? Really, Dave?"

"Yes, really. That last one, Donna, Dinah, Debra...whatever her name was. She brought her resume to your date. Dude, she gave you her resume."

"That wasn't for you to repeat, David."

"Well, you shouldn't have told me then. You know I talk. I'm happy to see your taste has matured."

"I'm not having this conversation with you."

"Mo is leaving right now. Come back tomorrow and shape him up, bro. I've been waiting to have this conversation with him, and he is not getting out of it."

"Text me and let me know what time you want me to stop by tomorrow, Randy." Mo packed his stuff.

"Will do."

"Next week, Dave."

"A'ight." Dave said as Mo close the door behind him. "So, as I was saying," Dave hopped right back into the conversation as soon as the door clicked. "It's fine if you don't want to talk about it. I can respect that, but I will tell you this. This is a woman who loves God. Mom and Victoria know her. She's prayed with them. She's been praying for Eden. If you're still on your 'I don't need God' trip, you need to tell her that."

As usual, Dave got right to the point. Randy wanted to side eye him. As the oldest, he took telling them all what to do seriously, even in romance.

"I have hinted it to her."

"Hinted? Hmph. You gotta be as straight as you can with her and let her know where you're coming from. I'm praying God just shows up one day in your office like He did with Saul."

"A Damascus Road experience?"

"Glad you still know your Bible."

"Ha! Now let me ask what I came in here to ask in the first place. I need you to go to Freeport to check on things at Renaissance Mall."

"Why can't you go?"

"Eden has this thing—"

"You don't have to say anything else. If it's something you need to do with E, I'll go."

Randy was happy he didn't have to make a trip to Grand Bahama, but his conversation with Dave left him feeling pensive about his plans for a real date with Priscilla. He leaned back in his chair and ran his hand over his face. He tried to rationalize things. It wasn't like he didn't believe in God. He believed God existed. It wasn't like she'd be with an atheist. It could work between them. He knew he was lying to himself. He wasn't going to go to church. He sure as heck wasn't giving no church ten percent of his money. He wasn't praying, studying the word or trying to "hear God's voice" on nothing. He wasn't checking for God, His Son or the Holy Spirit, and none of that would fly with Priscilla. A notification popped up on his cell phone, Priscilla.

All went well with Carl and his parents today. God worked it out.

It would be easy for him to reply "amen," but that would be misleading. He didn't think God had anything to do with this kid not getting expelled from school. Priscilla is the one who worked things out. Not God.

Where does her ability to counsel come from?

Randy heard the question whispered in his ear. It felt like a thought, but he wondered why he would think this to himself. Of course, it was a skill, an ability she had developed through education and experience.

When I formed her before she was in her mother's womb, I equipped her for this.

Randy sat up in his chair and glanced around the room. He knew the "I" speaking wasn't him. He would not refer to himself that way in his thoughts. Was he losing his mind? It was not his conscience. It was... Randy did not want to admit it, but it seemed very familiar to what Rome had shared with him about how God spoke to him. *But God doesn't speak to people.* He wanted to ignore what he had heard, but instead of ignoring the thought, he went to the Google app on his phone to search for the words he'd heard. He was certain it was in the Bible but didn't know where. Google led him to Jeremiah 1:5.

"Before I formed you in the womb, I knew you, before you were born I set you apart; I appointed you as a prophet to the nations." The scripture echoed what he had heard. How was that possible?

"I need some rest." Randy shook his head as he spoke the words aloud.

He looked down at his phone again. He'd been successful in his professional life for a long time. Now it was time to have the same in his personal life. He chose not to entertain Priscilla's comment. Instead, he responded with a dinner invitation. He pumped his fist when she replied: **I would love to.** Maybe Dave was wrong.

Later that evening when Randy arrived at her house, Priscilla opened the door and greeted him with a smile that warmed his heart. She hugged him. Held him. He heard Dave's voice again in his head. He chose to ignore it again and hugged her back. Held her. He thought *I could get use to this kind of greeting.* Having someone to come home to was not something he thought about, but now not only did he think about it, he craved it. Someone to hold, hug and kiss, but also to share his day with.

"How was your day?" Priscilla asked when they were seated in her living room, and Randy wondered if she could read his mind. He gave her the rundown of his day and she did the same.

"I read that Renaissance bought another island."

"I can't believe the media got ahold of that already. We just finalized the acquisition late last week." Randy shook his head. They hoped to keep the plans under wraps, at least until they secured all the funding they needed for their next venture.

"Come on, you can't keep that under wraps. You bought Norman's Cay. With all the craziness from that Fyre Festival, that spot is on everyone's radar. Why'd you buy it? You're not trying to recreate the Fyre Festival, are you?"

"You got jokes, I see. We weren't even thinking about that hoax when we looked at it. Originally, I was looking for a spot for the waterpark idea I had and we still may incorporate it, but the development is a retreat spot. A real getaway for individuals, businesses, and families. A place to 100% unplug from life."

"That idea is fire. See what I did?" Priscilla laughed and Randy groaned at her pun.

"As Eden would say, that was super corny."

Randy had never experienced this kind of genuine happiness for him from someone outside of his family. Most people were anything but happy for him. Some were jealous. Some people judged him, labelling him as bourgeois. Others wanted to use him. None were happy for his success.

"Which shoe? I couldn't decide. That's why I'm not ready."

Priscilla asked changing subjects. Randy looked at the shoes Priscilla held up. She held a combat boot in one hand and a purple ballerina slipper in the other. He laughed at the contrast between the two shoes.

"How in the world are they the options?" He studied Priscilla's cropped blouse that was a deep purple and complimented her skin perfectly. She'd paired the blouse with a knee length African print balloon skirt. She wore her hair in an afro that reminded him of the first night he met her at Renaissance Lounge. If she wore the ballerina flats, the look would not be a signature Priscilla look, which was always edgy and funky.

"The boots."

"Yeah, that was my choice, but I didn't know if it would be too much for you." She put on a pair of socks and slipped her feet into the boots.

"What do you mean too much for me?"

"I mean look at you."

Randy looked down at his gray Brooks Brothers suit. His blue and white striped shirt was matched with a yellow tie. The tie was kind of too much for him, but Eden had insisted that it made more of a statement than the blue tie he wanted to wear. His dress was ultra conservative, while Priscilla's style was daring. Her style broke the rules.

"Okay, I'm more on the conservative side."

Priscilla laughed. "No, boo, you are the poster child for conservatism. A picture of you is in the dictionary next to the word conservative."

"More jokes? For your information I've been trying to be a little more daring in my fashion. I've worn skinny jeans."

Priscilla looked appalled. "Don't ever do that again."

Randy and Priscilla continued to joke with each other as they drove to Renaissance Cove. Like The Palace, Renaissance

Cove was also a five-star fine dining restaurant that had received international recognition. Randy was proudest of this restaurant because it was their first try at a fine dining establishment. It cost a pretty penny to dine there. Guests could spend up to $500 on a meal, but the restaurant had been wildly successful since it first opened. It was posh and intended for people who lived a posh lifestyle. Lots of celebrities and foreign dignitaries dined there when they visited the island.

"I didn't even know this place existed. How many restaurants do you have?"

"Most people on the island don't. It's exclusive. That's why I'm glad I know the owner." Randy winked at Priscilla as she smiled and linked arms with him. "To answer your question, we have four – Renaissance Café, Renaissance Lounge, Renaissance Cove and The Palace."

"It seems like more."

"Good evening, Mr. Knight." The maître d greeted, interrupting their conversation. "It's a pleasure to have you dining with us this evening. Ma'am, welcome to Renaissance Cove."

"Thank you."

"Ken, this is Priscilla."

"Pleasure." Ken offered Priscilla his hand for a handshake, which she took. "We haven't seen you here in a while." He said to Randy.

"I know. I've been busy. How have you been? How's Gertrude and the family?"

"Everyone is well. Thank you for asking. How is Eden?"

"She is good."

"Tell her I said hi. She should come by and hang out with the girls."

"Definitely, I'll tell her."

"Right this way," Ken led them to their seats in a private room.

"Look at this room," Priscilla looked around the room, which was set up like a dining room in someone's mansion.

"The restaurant has fourteen private rooms like this. We wanted it to feel like dinner at home."

"Whose home?"

"Someone very rich."

"I'd have to agree with that." Priscilla laughed. "What's good?"

"Everything is good, and I'm not just saying that. We designed it that way. We wanted everything to be good."

"I guess there are no burgers and fries on this menu."

"No burgers but fries yes, to go with the cracked conch. We wanted to be exclusive and allow guests the opportunity to experience some authentic Bahamian dishes."

"Nice." Priscilla said as the server walked up to place their appetizers on the table. She asked Randy to bless the food.

"No, you go ahead." Randy shook his head, ignoring the quizzical look Priscilla gave him. It had been the second or maybe even third time he had declined to pray when they were together. She was probably wondering what was up with that.

"Father, we thank You for this time of fellowship. I thank You for allowing me to meet Randy. I pray that You would continue to bless Him. Speak to him," Priscilla prayed. Randy's head shot up when Priscilla said this. He wondered what she meant. "Show up for him in a real way. Touch him so he can know you are real. I thank you for restoring and strengthening his relationship with Eden. You are so faithful, Father. I pray that You bless this food and bless the hands that prepared it. In Jesus name we pray. Amen."

Priscilla squeezed Randy's hand and then smiled at him.

He forced a smile in return. Speak to him? Touch him so he could know that God is real? Randy felt like Priscilla had stolen his diary and read it. Was it possible that God was speaking to her about him? That couldn't be; God didn't speak to anyone any more.

Sixteen

Priscilla discreetly glanced at her watch as she sat opposite Dakari. The track phenom had qualified for the Bahamas National Track Team and had won gold medals in the 100-meter, 200-meter, 400-meter and 4x100 meter relay at the Carifta Games. He was being touted as the Bahamas' new golden boy. He would more than likely qualify for the next Summer Olympics and had received over a dozen athletic scholarships to schools in the US, Canada and England. But he wanted to start his athletic career, and Priscilla did not agree with his game plan. She thought he needed to take advantage of a free education and get his degree.

"It has been done before." Dakari argued. He was right. It had been done by student athletes who lived in the US, the land of opportunity. "Usain Bolt didn't go college," he continued. "He was an anomaly."

"He's my standard. That's where my bar is set. I can beat his times. I can be greater than him." Dakari's passion was almost palpable. Priscilla was sure her eyes were bulging. He believed he could run faster than the fastest man to ever run. She could see in his eyes that he didn't just believe it, it was like he knew it. He knew that he would do it.

"Ms. Deveaux, I've prayed about this. I know this is the direction God is moving me in. I have a coach who has coached some of the world's elite track athletes. I'm going to the World Athletics Championship, and then I'm going to the Olympics. And I'm winning everything." His faith blew Priscilla away. She needed to get on his level if she wanted to win the Commonwealth Spoken Word Competition.

"Well, then I look forward to watching you win it all." Priscilla had to concede. The young man was exercising the faith God required.

After Dakari left her office Priscilla kicked off her shoes and leaned back in her chair. It was time for a mental break. She picked up her phone to indulge in the frivolity of social media. She frowned when she noted that Randy never replied to her text message from the day before. She reminded herself that he was probably really busy with all he had to do running Renaissance; but then she remembered that when she'd told him she understood the busyness of his life and didn't need to see him every day, he told her that he made time for what was priority. She had melted when he said it. Now she was frowning thinking about it. *Girl, stop tripping. It's just one unreturned text. Just text him gain.* So, she texted: **Just saying hi** ☺ and opened her Facebook app.

She liked a picture of herself at one of her cousin's engagement party. Toya's wedding was in six months. She loved weddings, but she was going to start saying no to people when they asked her to be in theirs. She didn't want to buy one more expensive ball gown or wear shoes that were so high they needed a warning label on the shoe box. She already told Avery and Reign that if she decided on a traditional ceremony, they could wear whatever they wanted as long as it was teal.

Priscilla's thoughts drifted back to Randy. She could imagine spending forever with someone like him. No, that wasn't true. It wasn't someone like him. It was him. She could imagine spending forever with him. She didn't want to admit this because it was premature for her to be thinking about forever with someone she had only known a couple of months.

She'd fallen for him, and that scared her. Scared her because it wasn't supposed to be a guy like him. It was supposed to be the around the way, boy next door type of dude. But she knew that type of dude wouldn't challenge and champion her the way Randy did. He had encouraged her to pursue her dream of opening the youth center, and when he saw she wasn't really on it the way she should be, he challenged her. Just do it, he said. She told him that was easier said than done, but quickly realized that's not an argument you want to present to someone like Randy who always just did it.

Knowing she didn't want to talk to the sperm donor about getting a grant for the center, Randy came up with a list of potential donors to invest in her idea. He was at the top of the list. He offered to help her develop a business plan and advised her to invest the money she was going to win from the spoken word competition instead of using it on the center. "Use other people's money to start the center. Invest your money. Let it make money for you." That blew her away. He blew her away. He not only engaged her heart but also her mind. She picked up her poetry journal to capture in words what she was feeling.

Later that evening, during open mic night at Studio Café, Priscilla decided to share the piece she had written earlier that day. Randy still hadn't hit her back. She'd wanted to invite him out, but was glad now that he wasn't there. She wasn't ready to make this confession to him yet. Priscilla took the mic from the MC and took a seat on the stool that was center stage.

"I wish I could stop the hands of time. Set back the clock to the day, the time, that

moment when I sat next to you. My eyes fixed on you. Watching you. Taking you in. And in that moment, I was so confused because there was no thump of my heart. No shivers down my spine. The hairs on the back of my neck didn't stand up. A 90s love song wasn't the soundtrack. That's what I used to think that love should feel like. Then I realized it doesn't. It feels like your favorite pair of socks on a cold day. Like the strength of a hand that catches you when you're falling. It feels like hours of conversation about everything and nothing. Like the silence of listening to you think. It's safety in vulnerability. Trust in uncertainty. It's the peace and freedom to just be me. I wish I could stop the hands of time. Set back the clock to the day, the time, the second, the very moment when I knew that I love you." Priscilla's eyes fluttered open at the sound of fingers snapping. She didn't know at what point she closed her eyes, but she had. With her eyes closed, she imagined that her audience was just Randy. She walked off the stage with a smile in heart, looking forward to one day having the courage to tell him how she felt.

***

The next day Priscilla was in her office when Eden burst in out of breath like she'd run a couple of miles.

"Ms. Deveaux, they're fighting in Mr. Cameron's classroom. He stepped out to go to the restroom."

Priscilla picked up her radio and called security to Mr. Cameron's classroom before dashing out behind Eden. When she walked into the classroom, she had to push her way through the crowd of students to find Jaret Dixon repeatedly punching Avante Brown in the face. Priscilla wanted to turn around and go back to her office. Jaret was always being picked on by the other boys because he was shy and not good at sports. She guessed he'd had enough of their bullying.

After a few seconds Priscilla pulled Jaret off of Avante. By that time security had arrived and pulled Avante up off the ground. His nose was bleeding and he had a gash over his right eye. That didn't stop him from yelling the F word at Jaret before lunging at him. Before the security guard could grab him, he swung a punch at Jaret. Avante missed Jaret and caught Priscilla on the side of her face instead. The room went still and everyone let out a collective dramatic gasp. Lightheaded, Priscilla stumbled back a little. She felt herself falling, but Eden and Dakari caught her.

It was almost six o'clock, and Priscilla was finally leaving the hospital. She had a clean bill of health except for an unattractively swollen face. With all the commotion, speculation and rumors flying around the school (among the faculty and staff), someone was texting her every five minutes, talking 'bout: **How you doing, Ms. Deveaux? You alright?** She knew most of them were not concerned about her wellbeing. They just wanted to know what went down in Mr. Cameron's classroom. So, she turned off her phone.

Some were genuine in their concern, like Mr. Johnson who was always checking on her anyway. Mrs. Thompson, the Home Ec. teacher was also cool. She and Priscilla hung out outside of school. Of course, Mrs. Lowe, who taught biology, was genuine in her concern. The rest just wanted the scoop. She shook her head as she started the Range Rover.

When Priscilla got home, she was surprised to see an unfamiliar car parked in front of her yard. As Priscilla neared the car, she noticed someone getting out of the car. Randy. She felt her heart beat a little faster when she recognized him. She was happy to see him. Matter of fact, she was so happy she forgot all about her swollen, aching face.

"What are you doing here?" Priscilla asked as she got out of her car. Randy didn't respond and the serious expression on his face caused her to stop in her tracks. "Is something wrong?"

While he still did not respond, his steps toward her were quick and powerful. When he was standing in front of her, he wrapped her in his arms. Then he drew back and looked at her face, releasing a few expletives. Her hands shot up to cover her swollen face, but he removed them from her face and held them in his.

"I've been calling you since two o'clock. Eden texted me that there was a fight and you were in the hospital. She told me you were okay, but I kept texting and calling and you didn't reply. I didn't know what to think."

"I turned my phone off. The amount of texts and calls I was getting was overwhelming."

He nodded before taking her purse, work bag and keys from her. He led her to the front door, and she told him which key unlocked the door. "You don't have an alarm system?" He asked as they entered the house.

"Those systems are pricey." As soon as she said it, she wished she hadn't. She could already see he was trying to figure out a way to get her to let him get her one. "Don't even think about it. I'm good."

"Fine." He shrugged. "What did the doctor say about your face?"

"Nothing's broken. Thank God. Keep ice on it." She took a seat on the sofa in the living room. He headed to the kitchen. Priscilla guessed to get ice.

"You must have thought I was crazy how I came at you just now." He handed her the ice pack he'd made.

"Weird but not crazy."

"Yeah, I was freaked out. It made me think about what would I do, how would I act if something happened to you. I didn't like the thought. I felt like my air supply had been cut off."

"I think I would feel the same way." Priscilla admitted.

"I feel like this thing is moving way too fast."

"It's God." Priscilla watched Randy cringe.

"What?" She tried to assess his emotions. He seemed uneasy. She wondered why her mentioning God would make him feel uncomfortable.

"When we met, I wasn't looking for a relationship, but as soon as I saw you, I knew I wanted to be a part of your life in whatever way you would let me." Randy scooted toward the edge of the seat he had taken and looked Priscilla in the eyes. "Since I've known you, I've felt more alive than I've felt in a long time. I'd become so consumed with building a legacy that I never had time for anything else, not even Eden. You reminded me that life is to be enjoyed. Laugh. Have fun. Swim with the dolphins." They both smiled at the memory of their visit to Blue Lagoon Island.

"I've already told you that I can't imagine a life without you in it, but..."

Priscilla's breath caught in her throat. There was a but. There was always a but in her life. Couldn't it just be happily ever after with no buts in the way.

He continued, "I know your faith in God is extremely important to you. I admire your devotion, but I cannot say that I share the same beliefs that you do." Randy's words caused Priscilla's world to spin off its axis. Her head began to throb again. She didn't know if it was because of the punch she'd received earlier from Avante or the punch from Randy's words.

"How?" Priscilla couldn't manage to say another word.

"There are a lot of reasons. Things that have happened, that are happening that make me question God. So many things in the Bible that just do not make sense to me. That to me don't show a merciful, loving God. Things about how church is done that make me question preachers' sincerity. Blind faith and blind sheep. There hasn't been one prayer that I've prayed that God has answered. I'm not saying that He doesn't exist. He's there, but it's obvious He isn't concerned about me. Why should I concern myself with him?"

All types of thoughts, Bible verses, arguments swarmed through Priscilla's head, but she didn't voice any of them. It was as if the Holy Spirit had silenced her tongue. She closed her eyes. She inhaled and exhaled. After a few moments, she spoke.

"What exactly are you saying, Randy? I need you to be clear, so there is no misunderstanding."

"I'm not going to pray with you. I'm not doing Bible study with you. You want someone who's going to do those things with you. I'm not that someone."

"I see." Priscilla willed her tears not to fall, but they did anyway.

"I'm sorry. I thought I could…"

"Don't." Priscilla held her hand up to stop his words of apology. "Just go." She grabbed her keys off the coffee table and removed the key to his car.

"Keep it."

"Is that how you usually assuage your guilt when you hurt people? You give them expensive stuff? You're just like the rest of them."

"I want you to keep it because I care about you."

"Really?" Her words were sarcastic and biting, laced with Priscilla's hurt.

"Just because I don't think we should be together doesn't mean that I don't care about you." He implored.

Priscilla couldn't think of a reply for Randy. Logically, she knew he was right, but her heart didn't want to hear it.

"Bye, Randy." She held out the keys for him. He slowly took them from her and turned to walk toward the door.

Seventeen

When the door closed behind Randy, Priscilla hurled a bottle of water that had been sitting on the coffee table across the room. Hot, angry tears poured down her face. How did she get here again? Falling for a man she was unequally yoked with. She'd done this with Bryan and promised herself that she would never do it again. At least Randy didn't expect her to compromise her relationship with God the way Bryan did.

How did this happen? Priscilla replayed every moment she had spent with Randy from their first encounter at Renaissance Lounge to their last a few moments ago. Despite her reservations about him because of his wealth, he proved to be a good, kind, caring, considerate guy. He was a good man. *But not a Kingdom man.* Priscilla thought bitterly. He wasn't a man that could love her like Christ loved the church because although Christ loved him, he didn't love Him back.

All his "good" qualities made her ignore the elephant in the room. It made her pretend like he was going to change his mind. It made her prayers a little selfish. She prayed he would come back to God not because he needed God, but because she needed him to need God. When he sang at his dad's pastoral anniversary she celebrated selfishly, thinking, *yes, he's coming back to God, and we'll have a real shot.* Not rejoicing because he was back in his heavenly and earthly father's house.

She could admit now that she wanted the fantasy. She wanted the fairy tale, happily ever after, rich guy/regular girl story. She wanted that love story. The one she'd read about in romance novels, the ones she watched on the Hallmark Channel. Real life didn't work like that.

She went through the next few days in a daze. Thankfully the week went by quickly and without any more incidents. Instead of going home after work on Friday, she decided to stop by the Fish Fry, a group of small eateries on Arawak Cay. She wanted some conch salad and a good fried snapper. Renaissance Lounge had the best she'd tasted, but there was no way she was going there ever again in life. So, the Fry it was. She found a table in the corner away from the other patrons at Twin Brothers. She placed her order for a conch salad, a fish dinner and a virgin strawberry daiquiri.

While waiting Priscilla fished her cell phone out of her oversized purse to see missed calls from Reign and Avery. Reign had been hitting her up all day, but she hadn't replied to any of her messages. She knew she would accidentally spill the beans about Randy. She wasn't ready to talk about Randy with anyone yet. When she looked up, her breath caught in her throat. Randy had walked in. She quickly put her head back down and kept as still as possible, like that would make her invisible. When she looked back up, she was thankful he had taken a seat on the opposite side of the room. She quickly began to gather her stuff, but stopped when a woman joined Randy at his table.

Priscilla recognized her from TV. She was the evening news anchor. She wondered if Channel 12 was doing a story on Randy or Renaissance. Randy stood to greet her, but instead of a handshake or a hug, he kissed her. On the lips. It was short and quick, but it was definitely a kiss on the lips. Priscilla dropped back into her seat. She felt her blood pressure rising. It hadn't been a week. Was he seeing this Ms. Newscaster Chick while he was seeing her or whatever it is they were doing? *You have to keep your options open.* It was advice he had given her about securing funding for the youth center. Did this advice apply to women too? Anger propelled Priscilla out of her seat and across the room.

"Priscilla!" Randy's voice sounded an octave higher than usual.

"Good evening, Mr. Knight." Priscilla was amazed that she was so calm. When she was walking over to his table, she imagined throwing his glass of water on him, but knew she wouldn't ever do anything like that.

"Good evening. This is Natalie."

"Natalia." The news anchor lady corrected and extended her hand to Priscilla. Randy cringed. Priscilla smirked. Everyone knew her name. She was on the news Monday through Saturday at seven p.m.

"I won't interrupt long. I just wanted to thank you for the advice. I now understand what you meant when you said to always keep your options open. Enjoy the rest of your evening. Pleasure meeting you, Natalia." She noticed Randy's lips had parted like he wanted to say something, but he quickly pursed them together. He had no rebuttal, so Priscilla quickly turned and walked away.

Priscilla couldn't escape fast enough. She refused to cry. How could she think that he was any different? She pounded her hands against the steering wheel of another borrowed car. This one was her cousin's. Her tantrum was interrupted when her phone rang. It was Reign again. She wasn't ready talk, but now she felt like if she didn't talk to someone she might explode in anger, heartbreak and disappointment. She blurted out the whole pitiful story to Reign all in one breath.

"Hold up. Stay right where you are. I'm around the corner. Is he still in there? I've got my gun on me." Although Priscilla was angry with Randy, she didn't want Reign catching a case on her behalf. She knew her girl wouldn't shoot anybody, but she wouldn't hesitate in pistol whipping a negro.

"You don't need to come over here. I'm fine."

"Lies. I'm calling Avery."

"Don't call her with this nonsense. She just had a baby. She has enough on her plate."

"Let me decided what's enough on her plate." If Reign was near, Priscilla would've mushed her in the head. She'd merged Avery into the call, which meant she'd been talking to herself when she said don't call Avery.

"What's going on?"

"That Randy Knight is a f—"

"Reign!" Priscilla and Avery belted out the reprimand in unison.

"Freaking. I was going to say freaking dog."

"This sounds like a conversation that requires ice cream," Avery noted.

"And liquor."

"Have you already had a drink?" Priscilla asked Reign, half joking but half serious.

"Never mind her, Priscilla. Y'all come over here."

"We can't do that."

"Why not? I'm inviting you. Vince is more than capable of watching the baby while we talk. Plus, my mom is here."

"We're on our way." Reign spoke for Priscilla.

Avery opened the door and greeted Priscilla with a warm hug. She went to give Reign a hug, but the sequined shirt dress Reign was wearing distracted her.

Priscilla shook her head. "I gave her the exact same what the heck are you wearing look."

"This emergency friend intervention meeting is not about my attire. This is about Priscilla. So, let's proceed to the kitchen where there is food." Reign walked pass Avery. Priscilla and Avery exchanged questioning glances, shrugged their shoulders and followed Reign to the kitchen.

Priscilla joined Reign at the island while Avery took plates out and set them in front of her friends before slicing a chocolate cake that was sitting on the counter. She put a thick slice of cake and heaping spoonful on ice cream on a plate and placed it in front of Priscilla.

"Thanks," Priscilla said stuffing a forkful of the delectable dessert in her mouth.

"What's the deal? What happened?" Avery took a seat, and Priscilla sighed.

"I saw Randy at the Fry with that news anchor chick from Channel 12."

"What?" Avery jumped up off her stool so fast she almost tumbled over. "Wait. Hold up. I must've missed something. Before I get in my car to drive over to Randy's house and slap the black off him, I need you to start from the beginning."

"I'm with you, Ave. I'n even slapping. I gern in dere gun blazin'." Reign was up out of her seat too.

"Both of you sit down. There's no need for slapping or blazing guns. You guys serve gossip. You should not be the gossip."

"Gossip?" Reign and Avery raised their eyebrows at Priscilla.

"We report legitimate news to the Bahamian public."

Priscilla wanted to laugh at Avery's statement. Her show was strictly for the entertainment of the Bahamian public. Reign's magazine covered more serious topics, but it had its fair share of gossip too.

"I'm sorry. I stand corrected. You report the news. You don't want to be the news. How's that? Now sit down and let me tell my story. Y'all get on my nerves with your extra-ness." Priscilla waited for them to sit back down before she continued.

"After the whole thing the other day at school Randy came over to check on me and then broke up with me because I'm a Christian and he's not."

"Wait... Huh? Randy Knight, son Rev. Dr. David Knight, Sr., is not a Christian?" Confusion was etched on Avery's face.

"That's what he says. He believes in God, but doesn't believe in having relationship with God or something like that. He got hurt really badly by the church and his dad when that scandal went down a couple of years back."

"A couple of years? Wasn't that like 2005?" Reign frowned.

"Whenever it was. He stopped going to church. Cut his Dad off. Cut God off."

"How you do that?" Reign mused. "I mean are you like 'I'n checking for You no more, God'? Wow. I can't do that. Not after knowing Him and His love. He wasn't saved for real in the first place."

"Girl, you don't know what that man's relationship was like with God. Only God knows the hearts of man." Avery reminded Reign who shrugged.

"Whatever it was or wasn't, it's no more. He said I need a man who loves God as much as I do. Then I see him tonight at the Fry with that chick. Was he with her the whole time he was with me?"

"She's the fall back chick. It's not like he was pursuing her like he was you, but he stayed in touch. Sent a check in text every once in a while to keep her on the radar just in case it didn't work out with you." Avery broke it down for Priscilla, and Reign nodded her agreement.

"I don't care. It's too soon. It's not been a week and he's out sitting up with someone."

"I agree." Reign said around a mouthful of cake.

"Let me ask you something, though. Were you dating? I'm asking because I remember you being adamant about not dating a student's dad." Avery asked.

Priscilla was silent for a while. Were they dating? Not officially. She had a rule not to date a student's parent, although it was her self-imposed policy not a school policy.

"We weren't officially dating, but he made me feel like we were. He asked me all the time. He suggested switching Eden to another school."

"But you weren't dating?"

"No," Priscilla frowned. "What are you getting at, Avery?"

"You refused to be with the man, but then you get mad when he does what you've been asking him to do, which is not date you. And did you know how he felt about God?"

"I picked up on it, but when he came to his dad's church anniversary, I thought he was on his way back to God. What? Why are you looking at me like I should know better?"

"Because you should know better," Reign replied for Avery. "When people show you who they are believe them."

Priscilla felt her stomach take a dive. Reign was right.

"We've all done it before. We know something ain't right, but we want to make it right so bad that we ignore all that's wrong. That was me in every single relationship before Vince."

"Yes, chile, you ain' lying 'bout that. Remember Lamont? Plain as day he was a gold digger. He was like Tommy on Martin. Where do you work, bruh?" Reign said, referring to one of Avery's most notorious exes.

Despite the despair she was feeling, Priscilla couldn't help the laugh that spilled from her lips as she thought about Lamont. He was fine, drove a nice car and wore nice clothes, but he never had any money. The first time Avery went out with him, he "forgot" his wallet at home so she had to pay for dinner. Yes, the truth was obvious, but Avery didn't admit it until he asked to borrow ten thousand dollars.

"I'm glad you can find something amusing, but you get our point?" Avery asked.

"I get your point. To be one hundred with you, I liked the attention. But then we connected. I liked him. Then I realized I didn't just like this man. I love this man, and obviously, he doesn't feel... he never felt the same way."

"That's not true. This man came to see you when you were at the hospital for Ava's birth and brought a catered meal for my family. He doesn't even know my family. He gave you a car, and before you try to discredit that by saying that he has money, let me tell you that wasn't the reason. It was because he cares about you. And the very fact that he walked away because he knows how much you love God says clearly how much he cares about you."

"I don't know, Avery. He was with that Natalia chick. I just feel like I fell for the okey doke just like my mom did with Deon Bethel."

"You did not." Avery reached across the island to take Priscilla's hand in hers. "Don't think that. I don't think in any shape or form that Randy was using you for his entertainment and enjoyment. That's what Deon Bethel did with your mom. I know you don't think so or you don't want to hear it, but Randy cares about you. Whether you're supposed to be with him or not, I think the most important thing is his soul. Keep praying for him."

Eighteen

Randy stood on his bedroom balcony. It was Rome and Shiloh's wedding day, and he needed to hurry up and get dressed. He was dragging, though. Had been dragging for days. A frown creased his lips as he stared out the sliding door at the ocean. Its waves looked as ominous as his thoughts. He was trying desperately to be happy for his brother, but it was hard when he'd lost his chance at love. Honestly, he didn't even feel like going to wedding. He felt within that Priscilla could've been it. His one.

After their run in at the Fry, he'd called, texted and did a drive by her house, but was unable to get in contact with her. He contemplated showing up at her job, claiming he was there for Eden, but decided against it. That was her job; there were some lines he wouldn't cross.

He thrust himself into work, so he had something other than Priscilla to occupy his mind. Both Eden and Dave had noticed his extended work hours and his funky attitude. He'd snapped at Eden for no reason on more than one occasion. Her response to him told him that she was truly a changed child. In the past, Eden would have come out the side of her mouth at him with a disrespectful clapback, but all she did now was purse her lips together before leaving him to himself.

He wanted to kick himself. He needed to apologize and went to her room. Her room was uncharacteristically clean, which caused him to stop in the doorway.

"It's okay, Daddy. I know you're going through something right now, and it has nothing to do with me." Eden sat perched on her bed.

Randy stepped back and stared at his daughter in disbelief, wondering when and how she had become so mature and... wise.

"You know, E, you've really done a total 180, and I want you to know I'm proud of you." He leaned against the doorframe.

"I didn't do it, Daddy. Jesus did it." Randy stared at Eden in disbelief for the second time.

"Jesus?" He stood up straight and took a step back.

"Yes, Jesus, the Son of God. You do know Him right? He created me to be so much more than who I was being. He didn't make me to be always getting in trouble, fooling around with boys I didn't even like."

"We don't have to rehash that part."

"Sorry," she shrugged. "I'm just saying He made me in His image to be like Him."

"Like Him?"

"Yeah." Although it was one word, the way Eden said it made Randy feel like the class dunce. "While Jesus lived here on earth, he was our example on how to live life the way God intended it to be lived. Paul said he pressed toward the mark. Being like Jesus is the mark that I want to reach. Jesus said love those who hate you. Pray for those who despitefully use you. Be angry and don't sin. Love. Those are the marks."

"Going to church with Uncle Dave did all this?"

"Going to church didn't, but knowing that I am a child of God and a disciple of Christ has. You know, Daddy, at first, I was kind of skeptical about God. I wasn't sure about Him, but He has shown me how much He loves me by totally transforming my life. I couldn't be this person without God. There is no way. All I knew how to be was angry, rude and out of control. I am so happy God's love changed me." Eden's eyes held unshed tears, and Randy walked over to her.

"I don't say this often enough, and I promise to say it more. I love you and I'm happy that you're not angry, rude and out of control any more. But for the record, I loved you even then." He bent down and placed a kiss on top of her head before giving her a hug.

"I love you too, Daddy, and I hope that whatever you did to upset Ms. Deveaux you fix quickly."

"How do you know—" Eden gave him a "come on, Dad" look that didn't allow him to finish his sentence.

"Fix it quick, Daddy."

Randy would have never guessed the reason for his daughter's transformation was Jesus. He should have guessed, though. Rome credited his own transformation to Jesus too. Randy shook his head as he thought of all the fights his brother had gotten into, the women he had run through, the time he had spent in jail and all the suspensions the NBA had to give him. Bad boy did not begin to describe Rome. He was a time bomb waiting to self-destruct. Rome said he had accepted Jesus as his Lord and Savior and became a new creation. It was the same thing Eden said. Randy could not deny that both of them had transformed, and if they gave the credit to God, he guessed he had to believe them.

Randy dropped Eden off at Dave's house so she could ride to the wedding with her cousins then headed to Baha Mar where Rome and his other brothers were getting ready. Storm opened the door to the suite and Randy froze. He was not used to seeing his twin brother in a suit. They were fraternal twins and looked nothing alike, but in a suit if you closed one eye and squinted, they looked like twins.

"Boy, you're looking like you could be my twin today."

"Shut up and get in here."

Randy embraced him before giving him a playful pat on the back.

"Randy, what the he... heck took you so long to get here?" Rome yelled. He might be saved, but his mouth wasn't. He still cussed and was loud as always. Randy walked over to where his brother sat getting his hair cut. Rome had worn his hair long and wild for years. It was his signature. His cutting his hair was symbolic of the fact that he had put that wild life behind him.

"I'm sorry. I got up late."

The room went completely silent. The only thing that could be heard was the buzz of barber's clippers.

"Late?" Jason frowned. "Don't you get up before the crack of dawn?"

"Is it because you still haven't heard from Priscilla?" Dave asked.

"Probably," Randy admitted.

"Storm and I have been praying about this."

"You told Storm?" Randy asked, giving Dave a hard stare.

"Sleeping in and memory loss. Must be your age." Storm smirked.

"Negro, you never answer your phone, and I haven't seen you in weeks. I know we haven't talked about this." Randy gave Storm a pointed look.

Busted, Storm shrugged, "Eden told me."

"I can't believe she sold me out."

"Who sold you out?" Jason joined the conversation as he entered from the adjoining suite. "Are we talking about Priscilla?"

"Yeah." Dave, Storm and Rome said in unison.

"So, what happened?" Jason asked and Dave brought him up to speed on everything related to Randy and Priscilla.

"Ah, help me understand why you took the reporter chick out?" Jason had a puzzled look on his face.

"Help me understand why you took her to the Fry." Rome's disgust caused the brothers to laugh. "That's someplace Storm would take a date, where we took girls when we were broke. You're a daggone millionaire, buying someone a five dollar conch snack. But yeah why you took the h... tri... whatever, you know what I'm trying to say."

"Are you trying to say woman?" Jason asked sarcastically.

Rome turned to Jason. "Don't you start. God is delivering my tongue daily.'"

"What you mean why? You out of all of us know why." Randy was a little frustrated with his brother's question.

Rome placed a hand on his chest. "I don't know what you're trying to imply, Randolph. I've been celibate for two years."

"And look at God. You lived to tell the tale." Dave teased.

"It did almost kill me, though. So, you took the woman to the Fry because you wanted... How do saved people say this?" Rome looked at Dave, Randy, Storm and Jason. "Are we even supposed to be talking about premarital sex?"

"You know what, Rome, you are an utter and complete mess." Dave shook his head.

"I guess I didn't want to think about Priscilla and needed a distraction." Randy shrugged. "Today is not supposed to be about me and my issues. This is Rome's day. Let's drop the subject."

"Yes, it is." Rome stood to look in the mirror to admire his new haircut.

"Dang! Your head is big." Jason frowned.

"His head has always been big." Randy pointed out.

"I do have a big head, but big head or not, I am fine. Believe that."

"I guess along with delivering your tongue, God is also working on your conceitedness." Dave laughed.

Randy grew serious while his brothers laughed, "Real talk, Rome, we are proud of you. You had the best season of your career. You won an NBA championship. Got both the regular season and finals MVP awards. You didn't get suspended one time last season. I don't even think you fouled out of a game. You've got your mentoring program. You're about to walk down that aisle and pledge your life to the woman of your dreams. You did good. You're doing good." Randy walked over to Rome and embraced him. Randy knew there was a time when the family didn't think Rome would ever get to the place where he was today, but he was there.

"Thank God for being patient with me because y'all weren't so patient." Rome reached under the lapels of his tuxedo jacket, stretched his suspenders, and let them go with a loud pop. "Now let's get this wedding started, so I can get to the honeymoon."

Randy, Storm, Jason and Dave followed Rome downstairs to the waiting limousine. Dave, Jason and Storm prayed over Rome as they drove to the church. Randy had to admit he felt something in that limo that he had never felt before when his brothers began to pray. Something was stirring on the inside of him, in his gut. He felt like shouting hallelujah along with his brothers, but he suppressed it. Then he heard a whisper in his ear, *I AM*.

Before Randy could analyze what he thought he heard, if he had heard anything at all, the limo came to a stop in front of the church. They got out of the limo and made their way inside to wait for the bride and her party.

Randy watched Rome gaze at Shiloh at the entrance of the church's sanctuary as she walked toward him serenaded by K-Ci and Jo Jo's "All My Life." He saw in Shiloh's eyes the same love reflected in his brother's eyes. He glanced over at their dad who stood behind them ready to preside over the ceremony. Pride beamed on his face. Randy knew it was the look that Rome had craved from their father for most of his life. Their mother was crying joyous tears, as were a lot of people in the congregation. Many of them did not think Rome would ever get to this point in his life where someone meant more to him than himself.

Randy looked down the line at his brothers, each of them had the same gleam of pride on their faces their father had. Shiloh now stood in front of Rome. Her parents gave her away, and she joined hands with her groom. Randy listened to the exchange of the vows, and their pledge of forever to each other. He wanted that. He wanted to be standing where Rome was standing, and he wanted Priscilla to be standing where Shiloh stood. It seemed like it was too soon. They had only known each other a short time, but some things didn't take time. They took knowing. Knowing within your heart and soul, and he knew.

The wedding was great as far as weddings went. Randy didn't consider himself an expert. He had only been to a handful, including Dave and Jason's. He supposed if he was a woman he would have gushed over the décor, the dresses and the food. He wasn't a woman, though. For him what made the wedding great was seeing the look of love in his brother's and his new sister's eyes. It gave him the feeling that this would last. They would work to make it work.

Eden dragged him onto the dance floor, and after doing his best to keep up with his daughter, he returned to his seat. It wasn't long before he wished he was still concentrating on keeping step to the music. Sitting brought his mind full circle back to his problems. The festivities did nothing to stop the thoughts that swirled around in his head.

Randy went home, grateful that Eden was spending the night at Dave's house. Restlessness led him to his music room. He walked over to the piano. After opening it, he ran his fingers over the keys and sat down. He intended to play a song he knew by heart but heard something else in his spirit. He closed his eyes and started to play from that spirit place. Words bubbled out of his spirit and tumbled out of his mouth.

"Sometimes I don't know what to think or how to be. I fight and fight. Now I realize my enemy is me. So, I surrender. I lay it all down. I surrender to Your will and Your plan. I give all to You so You can use me. This is my battle plan. This is my war cry. This is how I fight. I lay it all down. This is my battle plan. This is my war cry. This is how I fight. I lay it all down. I surrender. I surrender. I surrender all to you. I surrender. I surrender. I surrender all to You. This is my battle plan. This is my war cry. This is my armor, sword and shield, and I claim victory. I have won. I claim victory. I have won."

Randy was amazed by the lyrics that flowed from his lips so freely. He had never been a composer. Ever. He didn't know what to make of what he had just experienced, but he knew if it wasn't him, it could only be God. And if it was God giving him these lyrics and the melody and the music, did that mean God cared? And if He cared, should he care back?

He went into the music room to escape his thoughts, but he was leaving with more on his mind than he had walked in with. On top of thinking about Priscilla, now he was thinking about God. Maybe his brothers' prayers were indeed having some kind of effect on him.

Nineteen

Every sad love song ever written ran through Priscilla's head. Of course, there was Toni's "Another Sad Love Song," Babyface's "When Will I See You Again," which took her back to Toni Braxton and her trying to "Breathe Again," Boyz II Men's "End of the Road," Mariah's "Love Takes Time," Usher's "Burn" and her all-time favorite, Whitney's "I Will Always Love You."

Two weeks had passed since the "incident" with Randy at the Fry, but it felt much longer. He'd called several times and sent text messages, and she could've sworn she saw his Range Rover drive through her neighborhood. She was still mad and humiliated and heartbroken, but she was also curious. Why was he calling, texting and driving by when he didn't want anything to do with her? She decided to satisfy her curiosity.

Priscilla picked up her phone and put it back down. Her stomach felt like a million butterflies were swimming around inside. She groaned. She didn't understand why she was so nervous about calling Randy. Maybe it had something to do with the fact that she hadn't received a text from him in the last three days when before he had been texting her every day. Maybe she should have replied to one of his messages, but she was too busy wishing he would disappear like he never existed in her life.

She admitted to herself she was chicken and decided to make dinner. Maybe she'd have more courage on a full stomach. Priscilla took almost everything out of her refrigerator. She took out the leftover spaghetti and popped it in the microwave. She noticed there was some leftover cake from Sunday when she went to her grandmother's house. She couldn't have spaghetti without a nice salad and garlic bread. And there were frozen chicken wings in the freezer. When she was taking out the wings, she saw the ice cream. What was cake without ice cream?

She sat at her kitchen table with a proverbial feast sitting in front of her. Her conscience nagged her about all the calories, but she ignored her conscience. She always felt insatiably hungry when she was nervous. Butterflies made some people queasy; they made her hungry. She was on her second helping of ice cream when she heard her cell phone chime indicating she had a text message. The cell phone was in the living room, so she jumped out of her seat and made a mad dash for the living room hoping it was Randy. She grabbed the phone and plopped down on the couch. Randy.

Call me.
Please.

Priscilla picked up her phone and dialed Randy's number. Her heart almost leaped out of her chest when she heard his voice on the other end. Like the mellow sound of Coltrane during the rain, his voice chased away her fears and apprehensions. Regrets and tears faded as his refreshing voice washed over her like a cool shower on a hot summer day. A change from the basing baritones and booming tenors, his voice was absent of the hardness, the roughness. It was soft like a feather grazing her skin.

"I'm sorry I haven't been responsive," she said.

"I understand. I'm not your most favorite person in the world right now. Are you free though? I want to talk to you in person, if that's okay with you."

Priscilla's eyes grew large. She didn't know if she was ready to see him. *What to do? What to do? What to do?* "Ah… Sure."

"Where? It's your call." Priscilla could hear the smile in Randy's voice.

"If you're still at work, we can go for a walk across the street on the beach."

"That works."

"I'll see you in thirty minutes then." Priscilla hopped up from her seat wondering why in the world she said thirty minutes. Forgetting about the feast on the table Priscilla went to make herself look cute, but not like she was trying to look cute.

When Priscilla reached Goodman's Bay she saw Randy's car parked, and then noticed him near the seashore. She got out of her cousin's car and made her way to where he was standing. He was facing the sea with his back to her. She noticed he had discarded his shoes along with his suit jacket. His shirtsleeves were rolled up, exposing muscular forearms.

As she approached him, he turned around. His smile was slow in coming but it was worth the wait, lighting his eyes with something she was afraid to label. It was crooked. Not perfect, but on him it was perfection. His smile made her smile. She took off her sandals and walked into the embrace his smile invited.

"I missed you," he whispered.

"I missed you too." She took a step back, stepped out of the comfort of his arms. She needed the space between them. They weren't anything to each other. Never had been. Right?

Randy led her a little way up the shore to where his discarded shoes and suit jacket were. He had spread a blanket down on the sand.

"You just drive around with blankets in your car?" Priscilla raised an eyebrow at the set up.

"I have an assistant who is like a genie. I could ask her if she has the sun, the moon and stars, and I promise you she would pull them out of her purse."

The two took their seats on the blanket and stared out at the ocean. Priscilla closed her eyes and enjoyed the sounds and scents of the ocean. She listened to the gentle lull of the waves as the scent of salt tickled her nose. The laughter of children was carried to her ears by a cool breeze, which caused her to shiver slightly. She felt Randy drape something over her shoulders, and she opened her eyes. Grateful for the warmth of his jacket, she pulled it close. This guy really had her heart. Why couldn't he just love God and that be it? It seemed real life never went as smoothly as make believe.

"I really like you. I might even love you, and I should have gotten the facts about what you believe and do not believe before I let my feelings get that far gone. I never want to be in a relationship with a person who does not feel the same as I do about God." Priscilla turned her gaze away from the ocean to look at Randy. "I've been there, done that. Don't ever want to do it again." She watched the tension crease Randy's brow as he nodded.

"I sensed that. That's why I decided to leave you alone." Randy paused. He appeared to be gathering his thoughts. "I'm sorry for hurting you, and I'm sorry for that run in with Natalia. You probably thought I was messing with her while I was talking to you. I wasn't. I've never been that guy."

"You don't have to apologize." Priscilla held up her hands, like they would stop his words and her thoughts from wondering if he was lying. He had always been truthful, though.

"I should and I need to. I should've fallen back as soon as I figured out what type of woman you were, but the type of woman you are is what made me want to fall in instead of falling back."

"You wanted to see me to apologize?" Priscilla threw another seashell.

"I wanted to see you because I wanted to see you." A slow smile found its way on his lips as his eyes danced with what looked to Priscilla like something that could be labelled as love. He drew her close to him, wrapping her in his arms. He slowly let his lips meet hers.

"I needed to see you." He whispered against her lips before kissing her again. Priscilla felt like her heart had dissolved into a puddle of mushiness.

"Wait," Priscilla pulled herself out of the Randy induced brain fog she was experiencing. "We're not doing this. We're not together. We're not trying to be together." Randy turned away from her, bowed his head and exhaled.

"I apologize. I shouldn't have kissed you. I shouldn't have even asked you to meet me. I am working out some stuff between me and God. I need to be sure it's for me and not because I want to be with you."

"Ok," Priscilla said, but she really wanted to do a praise run up and down Goodman's Bay while shouting hallelujah. *Calm your tail down.* Priscilla admonished herself. Like him, she needed to make sure her excitement was because he was coming back to God and not because him coming back to God meant he could come back to her. "I'll be praying for you."

Twenty

Randy whistled as he stepped off the elevator onto the executive floor at Renaissance Tower. It was a tune that had been stuck in his head since the day before, but he couldn't remember where he picked it up from. It was seven a.m. and the floor was quiet. Most folks didn't get in until nine o'clock. Thankfully, Eden was on end of term break and he didn't have to take her to school. He popped his head into Dave's office to say good morning. From his seat behind his desk Dave held up his coffee cup as a gesture of hello. Randy didn't bother to enter; Dave was on a phone call. He continued down the hall to his office and was surprised to find Storm sitting at his desk.

"Why are you sitting in my office in the dark?" Randy flipped the lights on.

"You didn't get my text?"

Randy slipped his phone out of his pocket, and sure enough he had an unread text message from Storm.

"Sorry, I missed it." Randy was training himself to check his phone for messages when he got into the office instead of checking when he first woke up.

"No problem. Was that you that was whistling "Nobody Greater" a little while ago?"

"That's what that was? I've been trying to figure out what song it was. I must've heard Eden playing it."

"Yeah, she killed that song in church last Sunday. She's good. She has your singing skills when you were her age and my preacher swag."

"What is preacher swag?" Randy asked curiously. Storm

stood.

"Come on. I need everyone in this building to get on their feet right now and give God some praise. If you woke up this morning, you have reason to praise Him. If you're in your right mind when you know you should have lost it a long time ago, you have reason to praise. If your creditors have stopped calling for no apparent reason, you have reason to praise Him. Praise Him because He is Jehovah Jireh. Praise Him because He is Jehovah Rophe. Praise Him because He is Jehovah Shalom. Praise Him because He is God!"

"That's what you call that?" Randy asked once Storm had finished his demonstration and retaken his seat.

"Preacher swag, Holy Ghost boldness, anointing. Whatever you want to call it, the girl has it."

"Whatever 'it' is, she probably got 'it' from hanging with you and Dave."

"Nah, we didn't have anything to do with 'it.' It came from God."

"I won't argue with that, but I know you didn't come over this early in the morning to talk about Eden."

"Actually, that is what I came to talk about. Are you going to be at the concert tonight?"

"What concert?"

"I figured Eden didn't mention it to you. I'm surprised motormouth Dave didn't say anything. Eden has organized a concert to raise money for the missions trip with Jael to Rwanda."

"Why would she need to raise money for the trip?" A confused frown sat on Randy's face. "I already gave her the money for the trip."

"Not for her. For the other kids who can't afford it. Unless you're writing a check for them too."

"She didn't say one mumbling word. Why?"

"Because she thinks you hate church and wouldn't want to hear anything about it. But it's a big deal for her. I think you need to be there."

"Of course, I'll be there. Why wouldn't I be there?"

"Are you really asking that question or are you just talking to hear how you sound? We had to coerce you into going to the parents' pastoral anniversary thing. And that was the first time you've been inside a church building in years. You think she didn't notice that?"

"I would go to support her. Besides, I'm not so adverse to going to church as I used to be."

"Rewind. Come again."

"Ever since we sang that day, the Holy Spirit has been speaking to my heart. I believe He's been knocking at my heart all these years. He never stopped. Storm, He never stopped loving me. When we sang... when I sang, it opened my heart."

"Hallelujah!" Storm was out of his seat again; this time with his hands raised. "Thank you, Jesus!"

"Will you be quiet before Dave hears you?" The words were not all the way out of Randy's mouth before Dave burst into the office.

"What's going on?"

"Nothing," Randy said quickly.

"Randy said that he's not adverse to coming to church anymore, and the Holy Spirit has been speaking to his heart."

"All y'all talk too much." Randy grumbled. He watched his brothers slap high-fives and do chest bumps like Rome had just won another NBA championship.

"The prayers of the righteous avails much." Dave beamed.

Twenty-One

Priscilla was daydreaming about the evening she and Randy spent on the beach. They sat out there until Eden texted asking Randy where he was like she was the parent and he was the child. They had talked about everything. It was a beautiful night that had her wishing, hoping and praying Randy would surrender to God. Not because she wanted to be able to love him, but because she wanted him to experience the love of God. The light knock on her office door drew her attention away from her thoughts. She smiled when Eden walked into her office.

"Ms. Deveaux, I wanted to remind you about the concert at my church tonight."

Priscilla had forgotten that the youth ministry at Eden's church was having a concert to raise money for their summer missions trip to Rwanda. Jason's wife, Jael, had lived in the East African country for several years and took a group on a missions trip to Kigali and Butare once a year in the summer time. It would be the first time for Eden to go and she was way past excited. She had single-handedly organized the whole concert.

"I did forget, but I'll be there." Priscilla assured Eden.

"Good. I'm so excited." Eden did a little jig out of Priscilla's office, causing Priscilla to smile. Her smile brightened a bit as she thought of the possibility of seeing Randy again.

***

Priscilla was really missing Randy's ride. Her bubbler was acting up again, and she was contemplating using some of the money she'd saved for the youth center to buy a new to her car. Instead, she was bouncing around the streets of Nassau with

Reign, who seemed to think because she drove a Jeep she could drive through every pothole in the road.

"Did you see that pothole?"

"The Jeep can take the potholes."

"Yeah, but I can't!"

"Sorry," Reign sounded sheepish. "We're almost there, but I have to make a stop first." Priscilla threw her head back against the headrest. There was no way they were going to be on time for the concert.

Priscilla's eyes grew large when Reign pulled up in front of the numbers house. "You are not still playing numbers."

"Girl, I ain' play numbers since I got saved. I'm here for a lead."

"I hope you're not writing a story about Lucky."

"Why not? The guy is a multimillionaire."

"Off of cheating people with his rigged gambling houses."

Reign shrugged her shoulders and hopped out of the Jeep. "You coming in?"

"Are you crazy? I'm not going from the numbers house to the church house."

"Fine, I'll be right back."

"If you're not back in five minutes, I'm leaving your raggedy behind here and going to the concert."

"You bet' not go anywhere."

"You better be back here in five minutes."

Priscilla took out her phone and opened Instagram to pass the time while waiting on Reign. After a couple of minutes, she looked up to see if Reign was coming and a cherry red Mustang Shelby GT350 caught her eye. If she wasn't as sensible as she was, this would be her dream car. She was expecting a handsome, young, muscled guy to step out of the car but a woman stepped out instead. Priscilla gasped, not because it was a woman. It was her sister.

Back in high school she had recognized the resemblance between the two of them, and over the years, time had made them look even more alike, almost like twins. Of course, she'd heard the rumors like everyone else on the island. The politician's daughter was dating the numbers man.

Priscilla's eyes locked with Stacia's, and Priscilla watched them turn ominous. Stacia slammed the car door shut with such force, it caused Priscilla to jump. She watched the woman's long, angry strides as Stacia advanced toward her.

"What are you doing here?" she hissed.

Priscilla cocked her head to the side. This chick had some nerve talking to her out the side of her mouth. She was about to tell her exactly what she was doing there when the Holy Spirit reminded her that the fruit of the Spirit included love, kindness, gentleness, and self-control.

"Waiting on a friend," Priscilla fake smiled.

"I thought I made it clear the last time our paths crossed that you should make it your business that they don't cross again."

Priscilla's eyes moved from her sister to Reign who was speed walking to her Jeep.

"Excuse me," Reign feigned like she accidently bumped into Stacia before Priscilla could respond. "Could you move out my way so I can get in my car?"

"You must not know who I am." Stacia craned her neck and put her hands on her hips.

"You must've mistaken me for someone who gives two cents who you are. I'm going to need you to move from in front of my car door before I move you."

The two stared at each other for a minute, and Priscilla prayed Stacia moved. She didn't want to have to go jail on account of Reign getting in a fight. Stacia slowly took a few steps back, and Reign hopped into the Jeep.

"Thanks," Reign smiled sweetly as she started the vehicle.

"I don't want to see you around here ever again, Priscilla Deveaux." Stacia yelled after them.

"That girl is cuckoo for cocoa puffs. Why was she carrying on like that?"

"I don't know." Priscilla shook her head. "Maybe she thinks I'm going to hit her family up for money."

"If you haven't bothered them for money in all these years, why would you now?"

"Exactly. I don't want anything to do with any of them. They're a bunch of greedy, selfish, evil hypocrites. Just like all rich people. I hope her relationship ruins her father's political career." Priscilla didn't realize she was yelling until there was silence. Feeling guilty for her outburst, she apologized to Reign.

"No need to apologize. You were venting." Reign pulled into a parking spot at the church. "And all rich people aren't like the Bethels." She put the car in park. "Avery isn't like that. Okay... she used to be like that, but God changed her. Randy and his brothers aren't like that."

"I know. It's just... I feel resentful when I see Stacia or her brothers driving around in their fancy cars, living in nice houses and I'm driving a bubbler. They haven't had to struggle for a thing and all I've had to do is struggle. Even if he never acknowledged me, why couldn't he at least provide for me like he did for them? Things would have been so much easier."

"You know I know what you feel better than anyone. I know what it's like to be the outside child. When my dad died, they didn't even include me in the obituary."

"But at least your dad checked for you." Priscilla's comment made Reign suck her teeth.

"Check for me? He never took care of me financially. His wife wouldn't let him. I assume it's the same with your dad. It's easier for them to make it like we don't exist. Otherwise, it's a constant reminder of their husbands' indiscretion."

"It's become so normalized in our culture. I pray I don't end up with a man like my dad."

"You might if you don't forgive your dad. Didn't Bishop say you end up with what you don't forgive?"

"He said you become what you don't forgive."

"Same thing. The point is forgiveness. I can't explain how grateful I am that I had the chance to forgive my dad before he died. If I hadn't, that would've been one of my biggest regrets, I think. I'm not saying your dad is going to die any time soon, but he is old so you never know."

"Really, Reign?"

"Sorry, but you get my point."

"I do." Priscilla sighed. *Can I forgive my father?* As Priscilla asked herself the question, she heard the Holy Spirit whisper, *yes*.

Twenty-Two

Randy didn't tell Eden that he would be at the concert. He wanted to surprise her. A smile tugged at his lips as he thought about her reaction when she saw him. He was startled out of his thoughts when he heard someone call his name.

"Randy Knight, I know you're not going to walk by me without speaking." Randy turned around and quickly put his public smile in place. His eyes widened when he saw Priscilla's friend, Reign. He wondered what she was doing there.

"Of course not." His smile became genuine, and he gave her a friendly hug. He liked Reign. "I was lost in my thoughts. What brings you here?"

"Your girl needed a ride. She had to take a call. I came to grab us some seats, based on the parking lot it looks pretty full."

Randy's heart skipped a beat. He looked around and saw Priscilla walking from the parking lot. He could tell when she realized it was him talking to Reign. There was a slight hesitation in her steps, but then she smiled and picked up her pace a bit.

"I'm so glad you came. Eden must be ecstatic." Priscilla said as soon as she walked up to them.

"She doesn't know. It's a surprise."

"She will be overjoyed."

"We will be out of seats if we don't hurry and get inside." Reign interrupted.

"The front row is always reserved for the family."

"Well, all of us ain't a part of the first family." Reign teased, but Randy didn't realize she was joking.

"What I meant is that you ladies can sit with me. I'm sure there's space." He clarified.

The three walked around to the rear of the church where they entered through the entrance Randy's father used. It led to his office and a backstage area. It reminded Randy so much of the church where he had grown up. The wall color was the same and so was the carpet. He stopped when he heard Eden barking orders like a drill sergeant. Well, a drill sergeant if the drill sergeant was him. His heart swelled with pride.

Everything appeared to be going smoothly. Eden was in conference with the stage manager, informing her that the sound people, tech team and talent were all in place. Sound check had been completed. The food for afterward was already set up in the fellowship hall, and there were snacks in the back. Everything was a go except the MC had not arrived yet. Randy waited for his baby girl to react. She nodded her head calmly and slipped her phone out of her pocket. She called who he assumed must have been the MC.

When she didn't get a response she said, "Okay. We're going with the contingency plan." The stage manager nodded.

Randy and Priscilla exchanged impressed looks. She had a contingency plan. Eden was a natural at this. He felt his eyes moisten.

"You okay?" Priscilla whispered. He nodded. "God did that," she added.

Randy was silent, but he agreed that only God could totally change a person the way Eden had changed. Eden looked away from the stage manager and noticed Randy. She shrieked, startling everyone backstage.

"Daddy!" Eden came at Randy full speed and leaped on him. Closing his eyes, he hugged her tightly and savored the moment of having his little girl in his arms.

"What are you doing here? Ms. Deveaux, did you tell him?"

"It wasn't me."

"Why didn't you tell me?" Randy searched her eyes. She dropped her gaze to the ground.

"I thought you'd say no because you don't like to come to church." She admitted.

Storm was right. Randy lifted Eden's chin and looked into her eyes. "I want to be present for whatever you're involved in. I don't care where it is. I've spent too many years trying to escape my issues with work and not being involved in your life. Not anymore. You got that?"

Eden nodded her head, and Randy kissed her on the forehead.

He, Priscilla and Reign made their way into the sanctuary. An usher appeared at their side when they came through the door that was to the side of the stage. She escorted them to seats at the very front of the church.

"We must be important. Front row seats," Reign joked as they took their seats.

His mom and dad were escorted in. He watched his mom's eyes light up when she spotted him. She elbowed his dad. The reverend started to walk toward him.

"Son!" He greeted him. Randy stood to hug his dad and then his mom.

"Hi, Dad. You remember Priscilla?"

"Of course," He embraced Priscilla.

"Thank you for coming, Priscilla." His mom hugged Priscilla and gave her a wink.

"I'm so glad you're here, Randy," his dad said. "We'll talk afterwards?"

"Yes, sir." Randy wondered what his dad wanted to talk about.

"Great," He smiled and his eyes held a gentleness that Randy hadn't remembered seeing before. "Well, let us go on and get up there. We're the contingency plan."

Randy roared with laughter. He would have never guessed.

His parents opened the night with prayer, and to his amazement they were funny. They told many anecdotes about raising a family of five boys, which meant a lot of his embarrassing childhood stories were shared. He was impressed by all of the local talent, but not as he impressed as he was with Eden. She came out with a group of dancers, but held a mic in her hand. From the first note she sang, he was entranced. It was Kirk Franklin's "Now Behold the Lamb." Randy remembered that song. Tamela Mann sang lead on that track. She was hard to imitate, but instead of imitating Tamela Mann, Eden made the song her own. You felt every single word she sang. Randy looked behind him at the audience. Many were crying. She had one of those voices that moved you, and Storm was right. She was anointed.

When the song was done, the entire room was on their feet in applause. Randy was so caught up in his parental pride, he missed the first time his dad called his name. He looked at Priscilla questioningly.

"I think he is calling you up there." She gave him a slight push.

Randy reluctantly stood. He should be used to this. His father was forever and a day doing this to them. He had no clue what his father was calling him up on stage for, as they often had no clue when they were growing up. Once on the stage Randy could fully see the crowd. He was shocked to see Jason in the sound booth. Dave and Storm were sitting in the balcony, and Rome was standing in the entrance to the backstage. They were all there.

"You know they say the apple doesn't fall far from the tree." His father was saying. "This is Eden's dad. Why don't you play something for us, son?"

It was posed as a question, but Randy knew it was not a question. He saw all of his brothers' smirks. Randy had never been one to get nervous. As Dave often said, he and Storm had nerves of steel. But for some reason, right at this moment something felt different from the last time he was on the stage at the anniversary. He remembered the song he had written the other day and felt inclined to play it. His stomach took a dive. It was the first time he'd ever written and composed something. *It's time.* Randy wasn't sure if it was his thoughts or God's voice. Whichever it was, the words propelled him towards the keyboard and the room burst into applause.

He remembered the melody and just played the piano for a while. Soon the drum and guitar joined in. Then he started to sing from that place he had never known he could sing from. From his soul. He felt it and even though everyone in the church felt it, he was not playing for them or singing to them. He was playing and singing for an audience of one.

***

Randy stood outside the church with his arm around Eden's shoulder. They were chatting with Priscilla and Reign. The concert had been a success, raising enough money for ten teens to go on the missions trip. Eden's face beamed with excitement.

"I'm so happy you were all able to make it. This has been the best night of my life."

"We're happy we were able to bear witness to this moment with you, Eden." Priscilla smiled. Randy wished that he had more time to talk with Priscilla, but his dad had beckoned to him. Again, he wondered why he wanted to talk him.

"Ladies, I'll have to excuse myself. Eden, I'm not sure how long I'm going to take with Dad."

"Don't worry about it, I'll get a ride." She pointed at the black Challenger with red stripes and matching red rims.

"Whose car is that?" Randy involuntarily scowled. Any boy that drove a car like that could not be up to any good, and he knew for sure a car like that belonged to a boy.

"It's Dakari."

"That punk you've been chatting on the phone with?"

"You don't even know him, Daddy." Eden rolled her eyes.

"I can vouch for him as I did before. I guarantee you that he is not a punk. He's a really good kid." Priscilla said in Dakari's defense.

Randy skeptically eyed the tall, lanky teenager who stepped out of the car. He was dressed, ironically very similarly to him, in a pair of black jeans with a black blazer and a black t-shirt. On his feet he wore a pair of Chucks. They had on almost the exact same outfit. At least he didn't dress like a thug.

"Good evening. I'm Dakari Taylor." He extended his hand to Randy. Randy stared at it for a few seconds before accepting his handshake.

"I remember you from the field trip."

"Oh... Ah... Um..." Dakari stammered. "I'd... I'd like permission to take Eden home."

"And what else?"

"Daddy!" Eden's fair skin had taken on a tinge of red.

Priscilla elbowed Randy and Reign snorted a laugh.

"What else?" Randy repeated.

"Nothing else. I just want to make sure she gets home safely. I'm taking her straight home. I'm not going to stop any place else. I have to be home by ten myself, and my mummy will kick my butt up down the street if I'm late." Dakari said with a hint of fear in his voice.

Randy grinned. He didn't know the boy's mama, but he liked her. He sensed she had put some fear in him.

"Eden speaks of you quite often, and Ms. Deveaux seems to be very impressed by you. They like you. I don't. I'm going to allow you to take my only daughter home. I don't know you and I don't trust you, but I trust her. But if I ever have any inclination that you have hurt or disrespected my daughter in any way, I will break your jaw." Randy heard Eden gasp and felt Priscilla staring at him, but didn't dare look in their direction. "Is that understood?" He asked pointedly.

Dakari swallowed before nodding his head. "Ye...Yes, sir. Understood."

"Good. I'll see you when I get home, Eden." Randy wrapped Eden in a hug and kissed her.

"Break his jaw. Really, Daddy?" Eden whispered.

"I love you too." Shrugging his shoulders, Randy smiled.

"Bye," Eden rolled her eyes before walking off.

"Ladies," Randy turned to Priscilla and Reign, "my dad is waiting on me. It was good to see you."

"You mean it was good to see Priscilla. You could care less about seeing me." Reign laughed and Randy laughed with her.

"It was good seeing you, Priscilla." He corrected. "I hope to see you again soon."

"He said soon." Reign almost squealed.

"Same here," Priscilla smiled.

"Good night." Randy walked off.

Randy entered his father's office. It was an office he'd never been in before, but like the backstage it reminded him a lot of the office his father had when he was growing up. His dad's back was to him as he was hanging his coat on the back of his desk chair. There was a droop in his shoulders that Randy didn't remember being there. When his father turned around, he examined his face. The wrinkles were more defined and his mustache and beard were completely white. He was seventy-five, but looked much older to Randy.

"Have a seat, son." He motioned for Randy to take the judgment seat. That's what Randy and his brothers had called it when they were kids and were called into their dad's office.

"What's up, Dad?' The word felt foreign coming from his lips. He hadn't addressed his dad like that in fifteen years. A great sense of regret washed over Randy. Looking at how his dad had aged, he realized he had more years behind him than in front of him. Randy also realized he'd wasted fifteen years being mad at his father. Years he could never get back.

"I never said this to you. I guess I was too full of pride back then or it could've been shame, but I am sorry for hurting you. I betrayed your trust. You were the only one of my boys that wanted anything to do with church and ministry. I envisioned passing the baton on to you. If I had imagined that what I did would drive you away from God, I wouldn't have done it." Tears moistened the reverend's eyes.

"Why didn't you just come to us?"

"Like I said it probably was pride. I couldn't admit that I had taken loan from a known thug and was laundering his money through the church. We grew up together. We were friends at one point. I thought I could trust him."

"Is it true that you bought the house you and mom moved to with the money? And got mom that Mercedes with it?"

"No, that was the rumor mill working overtime. The money didn't fund "my lavish lifestyle" as the papers put it. You know I worked outside the church. We didn't have much, but I was smart enough to save. Then later I learned how to invest what I had saved. Where do you think you and your brothers' smarts came from?"

Randy always wondered why his dad kept his full-time job when the ministry had grown enough to provide him with a decent salary. Randy realized that he not only inherited his smarts from his dad, he had definitely also inherited his work-aholic tendencies from him as well.

"I needed the money for the church we built. After we did the building fund drive, we had enough money for a down pay-ment, but still couldn't get any bank to loan us the money to start the building. So, I went to Duppy. It was stupid. I almost went to jail, lost the church and lost you and your brothers. Jason followed in my footsteps doing something just as stupid when he got mixed up doing business with that drug dealer."

"What about the affair?" Randy asked. He figured if dad was coming clean, he might as come clean about everything.

"Affair?"

"Duppy was blackmailing you because you were having an affair."

"Duppy was blackmailing me because when we were younger, I worked for him." The reverend's shoulders drooped even more with his admission.

Randy was sure his eyes were as large as saucers. He would never have guessed that in a million years.

His dad continued, "I've done some things I am not proud of, and I didn't want anyone to know about those things. Again, it was pride. I just wanted to tell you that I'm sorry for all of it."

He had been waiting all these years for an apology, but had never given his father an opportunity to apologize. He wished he had given his father the chance to tell him his truth a long time ago, but every time his dad reached out, Randy's hurt, anger, disappointment and feelings of betrayal pushed him away. His father's actions were not justifiable, but knowing the truth did something for him. It set him free.

"I'm sorry too. I should have let you explain."

"You don't need to apologize. Nothing about any of this was your fault."

"No, Dad, at the very least I should've listened to you when you tried to explain."

"God has been restoring so many things in my life. My relationship with Romeo. The church and ministry. I've been praying for Him to open a door for restoration for us too. We can rehearse the shoulda, woulda, couldas or we can work on the right now and the henceforth. Can we do that?"

Randy studied his father for a moment. Tears still shone in his eyes, and Randy saw something else along with them. He saw a desire to make things right. He saw love, the love of the Father.

"Yeah, we can do that, Dad."

Twenty-Three

It was Tuesday and Priscilla was still on cloud nine from Friday night's concert. From the moment Randy sat down at the piano, the entire atmosphere in the church changed. There was an expectation that something extraordinary was about to take place and something extraordinary did take place. From the first note to the last, there was no doubt in Priscilla's mind that Randy had God's attention. The glory of His presence filled the place.

That was the difference between being a good singer and being a worshipper. With his eyes closed Randy did not sing for a church full of people. His worship granted Him access to God's throne room, and they all followed him in. There they experienced heaven on earth.

"Father, I pray for Randy's soul. I pray that he completely trusts You and receives Your love. I pray that he begins to walk with You again. And if a relationship between us is not what You want for me, I trust You. I know that you are a good Father and the man You have for me is a man after Your heart."

After praying, Priscilla quickly dressed for work. Glancing at the time on her phone, she forewent breakfast and headed to her car so she wouldn't be late. As she drove to the school, she continued talking with God. She got out of her car feeling like she had just won the National Spoken Word Competition and felt like running all around the school praising Jesus in a victory lap. But she was certain if she did that, they would have her committed to Sandilands. So, instead she was content humming Hillsong's "Shout Unto God."

Priscilla looked up from her work. The time on her computer screen said it was only ten o'clock. But it felt like she had been at work a full day already. It seemed like the entire senior class had asked her to either review their college applications or write an admissions recommendation. It was something she encouraged them to do since it was November and application deadlines were in January. She was expecting everyone to wait until January like students usually did, but this class was different.

Her ringing phone brought her out of her musings. She frowned. The number's prefix told her it was someone calling from a governmental office. Maybe it was someone from the National Spoken Word Competition, but why would they be calling?

"Good Morning, Priscilla Deveaux."

"Good Morning, Ms. Deveaux, this is Ms. Bartlett from the Ministry of Youth, Sports and Culture," the woman said cheerfully.

Priscilla felt her heartbeat accelerate. This was the ministry that Randy had encouraged her to partner with for the youth center. It was also the ministry her father presided over. "Yes, ma'am, how may I help you?"

"I wanted to talk to you about your youth center initiative. We would like to give you a grant through the Urban Renewal Program."

Shock rendered Priscilla temporarily speechless. They wanted to give her a grant.

"Ms. Deveaux, are you still there?"

"Yes, Ms. Bartlett, I'm still here, but I am little confused. I didn't apply for a grant."

"No, you didn't. I'll explain when we meet. Are you available at eleven o'clock?"

To Priscilla, the lady sounded hopeful. She glanced at the

clock and shot out of her seat. Eleven o'clock! That was in fifty minutes, and she was at work. She could take an early lunch. She didn't have any counseling sessions, study halls or parent conferences.

"Yes, I'm available."

"Perfect. I will see you when you get here."

"Yes, see you when I get there."

Priscilla disconnected the call and sat for a while in stunned amazement. It had to be Randy's doing, but what did he do? She resisted the urge to call him. It would only take her about fifteen minutes to get the ministry, but she wanted to leave now because you never knew what Nassau traffic would be like. She quickly stopped into the principal's office to let them know she was leaving early. By 10:25, she was in her car thinking that was more than enough time to get to her destination. But when she turned her key in the ignition, her car would not start.

Priscilla pounded her fist against the steering wheel and said a quick prayer asking God to please let her car start. She tried again. Still nothing. She picked up her phone and the first person she thought to call was Randy. So, she did.

***

Randy glared at the president of the Bahamas Development Bank. He had just turned Renaissance down for a loan and Randy could not fathom why. He was about to jump out of his seat and give the man a piece of his mind, but Dave rested a restraining hand on his arm. He turned his glare on his brother who simply shook his head. Randy relented, sighed and sat back in his seat, giving the floor to Dave.

"Thank you for your time, Mr. Moultrie." Dave stood.

Randy remained seated, wondering what Dave was doing. They needed the loan to finance their next development.

"Let's go." Dave whispered to him and Randy stood.

Alone with Dave outside, he was about to ask what was he doing in there but his phone vibrated in his pocket. He took it out and saw that it was Priscilla. She could be calling about Eden, but he hoped she was calling for him.

He answered quickly answered, "Hey, what's up?"

"The Ministry of Youth, Sports and Culture called and wants to meet with me, but my car won't start." Priscilla's words ran into each other. Randy could barely understand what she said, but he heard Ministry of Youth and car broke down.

"Are you at school? I'll be right there." Randy hung up the phone before she could respond. "I gotta go." He said over his shoulder as he headed for his car. Thankfully, he and Dave didn't ride together like they usually did.

When Randy arrived at the school's parking lot, he quickly got out of his car to assist Priscilla in getting in. Once they were on their way, he asked Priscilla why was she going to the Ministry of Youth, Sports and Culture.

"Wait. You don't have anything to do with this?" she questioned.

"Me? No, definitely not."

"I thought you pulled some strings or something."

"Maybe it was your dad."

"Who?"

"Your dad, the Minister of Youth, Sports and Culture. Maybe he pulled some strings."

"Why would he do that?" Priscilla asked after an extended silence. "He's never done anything for me in my entire life."

"Didn't he pay for college?"

"His wife paid for college and it was a payoff to make me

disappear."

"Payoff? Isn't that a little bit extreme?"

"Even if it wasn't, that's what it felt like to me. If this has anything to do with him, I don't want it."

Randy shook his head. "You never turn down free money. It's a grant, not a loan."

"I don't want him saying he helped me start the youth center."

"Really, Priscilla?" Randy sounded like Eden. "Think about what you just said. This is a man who hasn't claimed you in thirty-five years. I don't think he's going to start broadcasting any affiliation with you. He may be feeling guilty for all the years he didn't take care of you and wants to help you now, but he wouldn't want the cat out of the bag."

"If that's the case, he's a day late and a dollar short. I don't want anything from him." Priscilla folded her arms across her chest and turned to look out the window.

"Look, I can't say I know what is was like for you growing up without a father, but I do know unforgiveness is a burden you want to let go. I carried that thing around with me for years and didn't realize until I let it go how much it weighed me down. It caused me to be estranged from my father for fifteen years because he hurt me. I was disappointed in him and reveled in the satisfaction of being angry with him, even hating him. I was mad at the world, acting like a kid, sitting in corner, sulking, upset with the world and refusing to go outside to play while the world is outside playing, running around laughing, having a good time. The only one on punishment was me." Randy reached over and took Priscilla's hand in his. "Forgive him." He glanced over at her and she turned to face him.

"I don't know if I can do that." A tear slid from Priscilla's eye and she quickly wiped it away. "I was the bastard child who never had enough. The one in my cousin's hand me downs. The one who always got teased in school because my mom cleaned the houses of my classmates." Priscilla wiped away another tear.

"Never could afford to go on field trips. Never could afford to go to parties. Just as well because we couldn't even afford to buy birthday gifts or Christmas gifts. I was angry when my mom moved to the island and sent me to live with my grandmother. I felt like she abandoned me, but she was only doing the best she knew how to do in the situation he put her in." Priscilla spat out the last part with vehemence.

"It's possible for you to forgive him." Randy squeezed her hand as he arrived at the ministry. "Not only is it possible, it is necessary."

Randy parked the car. She opened her door, but his remained closed. "You're not coming in?"

"No, I'll stay here and pray."

So many thoughts swam through Priscilla's mind, each vying for attention. She knew what Randy said was true. It was the same thing Reign had said to her. Forgiveness. The words of the Lord's prayer tugged at her heart, "Forgive us our trespasses as we forgive those who trespass against us." She paused in front of the door of the building before entering.

"Holy Spirit, I need your help. I need you to help me to forgive my father." She exhaled and pushed the door open to go inside. She signed in with the security guard and received a visitor's pass before going to the fourth floor as Ms. Bartlett had instructed. The fourth floor also housed the honorable Minister Deon Bethel's office. Priscilla's stomach quivered at the thought of running into her father.

"Ms. Deveaux, I am so pleased that you were able to make it." Ms. Bartlett extended her hand. Priscilla shook the older woman's hand more aggressively than she intended.

"I'm sorry." Priscilla apologized, embarrassed. "I'm nervous."

"No need to be nervous," Ms. Bartlett motioned for Priscilla to take the seat in front of her desk. When she was seated, Ms. Bartlett handed her a folder. "Please sign the agreement inside."

"Agreement? I haven't even completed the grant application."

"It has been completed for you."

"What?" Priscilla sputtered. She eyed Ms. Bartlett suspiciously as she rounded the desk and took her seat.

"Let me formally introduce myself." Ms. Bartlett sat back in her seat. "My name is Hattie Mae Bartlett Bethel. I'm your grandmother." She smiled slightly.

Priscilla felt like someone had sucker punched her. She slumped back in her seat and stared at the older woman, shaking her head in disbelief.

"This grant is not from the ministry. It's from the BET-FAMI Foundation. I knew if I called you and told you that you would've never given me the time of day. My apologies for deceiving you."

"Wait..." Priscilla exhaled, trying to grasp what she was hearing. She wanted to pinch herself to make sure she wasn't dreaming or having a nightmare. "You're my grandmother?"

"Yes, Deon is my youngest son. I hired your mother. I wouldn't have if I thought she would have gotten involved with my son." Ms. Bartlett held up her hands when she saw the flash of anger in Priscilla's eyes. "That was not a slight to your mother. I liked Katherine. I meant that I wouldn't have hired her if I knew Deon would do what he did. I would have definitely warned Kat if I knew that he was engaged. I was just as surprised as she when he came home for Christmas break married."

"Why are you trying to make yourself out to be the good one? My mother told me about you." Priscilla wanted to jump out of her seat. Her right leg shook as anger coursed through her body. "You gave your son the money to abort me."

"I did." Ms. Bartlett admitted and dropped her head in shame. "I thought it would be the best option for them. My son was not going to take responsibility for the child, for you. My husband wouldn't allow me to assist in any way. It was too scandalous. He fired Kat as soon as he found out what was going on. I thought, how is she going to survive as a single parent? What kind of life will the child have? I thought it was what would be best. I'm sorry." Ms. Bartlett reached for her purse that sat on the edge of the desk and removed a handkerchief. She dabbed at the moisture in her eyes.

"I don't believe you." Priscilla fought back her own tears. "You wanted her to have an abortion because your family didn't want a bastard child to tarnish your lineage."

"That's not true. At least, it's not my truth. You are my oldest grandchild. Once I realized Kat didn't have the abortion, I've watched you from afar. I was at your kindergarten graduation. You were the old woman who lived in the shoe in the skit your class did. I was at your college graduation and every graduation in between. I started BETFAMI on your first birthday and every year I put ten thousand dollars into the foundation to fund this grant." Ms. Bartlett spoke quickly like she wanted to get everything out before Priscilla got up and walked out. Priscilla's eyes had widened. She had funded the grant with $10,000 every year since she was a year old. That meant there was at least $340,000.

"When I started the fund, it was more in honor of you than for you, but as the years went by and it became apparent that Deon would never do right by you, I decided I would give it you. I didn't know how until a couple of weeks ago when Randy Knight called the office."

"Randy said he never talked to Mr. Bethel." Priscilla interrupted. Even though Ms. Bartlett's story was touching and had her crying, she still didn't want to believe it.

"He didn't. He left a message with Deon's assistant, which I overheard and intercepted. As soon as I heard your name and the youth center, I knew that's what the money was for."

"Why didn't you approach me before this?"

"I don't know. I guess I was mostly afraid of you rejecting me. You're right to be suspicious of me. I'm not entirely innocent. I could've... I should've done something more to help you and your mother." Ms. Bartlett stood and walked around to stand next to Priscilla. She rested a hand on her shoulder.

"I'm sorry we didn't have a relationship when you were growing up, but I am hoping we can have one now."

Priscilla was silent. She didn't know how to respond. She realized she had spent her whole life hating this family. The word hate felt like a punch to her gut. It was the opposite of what God called her to do. He had called her to love. Love did not count up wrongs. Love forgave without an apology. She felt the wall around her heart begin to crack.

"I think I'd like that." The words came out slowly, surprising Priscilla even though she was saying them.

"Thank you," Ms. Bartlett bent and hugged Priscilla. The wall around Priscilla's heart crumbled as her tears flowed freely. She wasn't less than them. She was enough. Not because of Ms. Bartlett, her grandmother accepting her. She had always been enough just as she was. The little girl in the hand me downs who never had what the other kids had but was smart, kind and generous was enough. The woman with the afro who dressed in Bahamian Boho and drove a bubbler was enough for the millionaire business man who wore suits and drove luxury cars. As is, she was exactly enough.

Twenty-Four

Randy glanced at the clock on the dashboard for what seemed like the hundredth time. Priscilla had been inside for almost forty minutes. He didn't think it would take longer than twenty minutes, especially since Priscilla was hoping not to run into her father. Randy felt a bit of panic rise in chest. Supposed she had ran into her father and that's why she was taking so long.

Without thinking about it, Randy hopped out of the car and headed towards the building. *God, please be with Priscilla. Please be with me, so I don't go off if this man is acting up.* Randy didn't even realize he was talking to God as he entered the building. As he approached the security desk, he heard Priscilla's voice. He turned to see her and an older lady walking off of the elevator. He hurried toward them ignoring the security guard yelling at him.

"He's ok." The lady told the security guard who apparently had left his station and was walking up behind Randy.

"Is everything ok?" Randy eyed Priscilla suspiciously. Even though she was smiling, her eyes were red like she had been crying.

"Yes, everything is ok. This is Ms. Bartlett."

"Well, actually it's Mrs. Bethel."

"Oh yes, you had to say Bartlett to get me to come."

"And who are you?" Randy didn't like being out of the loop and with the last name Bethel, he was on guard.

"I'll explain in the car. Mrs. Bethel, I will be in touch." Priscilla smiled and waved before taking Randy by the hand and leading him out of the building.

"She's my grandmother." Priscilla said as soon as they'd walked out of the building.

"Your grandmother?" Randy questioned. Walking to the car, Priscilla brought Randy up to speed on everything that had happened in her "meeting".

"I didn't realize how much hate I had in my heart toward them, and I felt justified in it because my father had discarded me. I would never think that I hated anybody. Hate. It's such an ugly thing. As soon as I realized it while I was sitting there, I had to repent." Priscilla leaned against the car. "Once I did that it was like the scales fell from my eyes, and I could see what God was trying to tell me all along. That people were telling me all along. Who I am… who God made me is enough."

They were both silent for a while lost in their own thoughts. Randy wondered if Minister Bethel would ever come around. He hoped that he did because he was missing out on knowing a really amazing person.

"My feelings for the Bethels even affected how I felt about you." Priscilla's comment interrupted Randy's thoughts.

"What do you mean?"

"I thought you were like my dad. Entertaining yourself with a "commoner" until someone more qualified came along."

"I hope by now you know that I'm not like that. Like you said, you are enough. Matter of fact, you are more than enough for me."

"I don't know about more than enough."

"More than enough. You have more than enough love, wisdom, kindness and beauty."

"I thought I was the wordsmith in this duo."

"Duo, huh?" Randy pulled Priscilla towards him. "Is that a synonym for couple?"

"Ugh," Priscilla groaned. "That was really corny."

"You love my corniness." Randy pulled Priscilla even closer.

"I do love your corniness among other things."

"What other things?"

"I love the way you worship God."

Randy considered Priscilla's words. The time he had begun to spend with God felt like water to his dry soul. Like Priscilla hadn't realized the hate in her heart, he hadn't realized how empty he was of feeling. It was why he couldn't connect with Eden. It was why he had stopped his music. All that required him to feel. Feel God's love. Feel His joy. Feel His fire. Feel Him.

"Thank you for saying that." Randy smiled. They stood holding each other for a long while before Randy spoke again.

"I love you. I don't know the protocol for making that confession since we weren't technically dating and Eden is still one of your students. I don't know if I'm supposed to say that, but it is what it is. You make me feel like me. If that makes any sense. Other than Dave, you're the only person I feel free to be me. The corny me. The nerdy me. The smart me. The businessman me. The dad me. Hopefully, eventually the husband me."

"The husband me, huh?" Priscilla smiled. "I think the husband you would be just as corny as the single you, but like I said I love your corniness. I love you all of you, Randy Knight." She reached up and let her lips meet his.

He savored her kiss and was thankful they were about to get this relationship party started for real.

**

On Sunday, Priscilla and Randy walked hand in hand into church with Eden and Dakari trailing behind them. Randy glanced over his shoulder to make sure they weren't holding hands. They were. Randy scowled at Dakari, who immediately dropped Eden's hand.

"Leave that boy alone." Priscilla scolded. "I'm sure when you were his age you weren't trying to be walking up in church holding a girl's hand."

"You're right about that. I was the girls dem suga."

Priscilla laughed at Randy's retort, imagining a younger version of him who thought that he was "GQ." Before he began his sermon, Randy's dad called him up to sing a song. By now Randy expected this from him. He stood and walked to the stage. He borrowed a guitar from one of the guitarists and stood behind his mic.

"My daughter, Eden, loves music. She keeps the house filled with it. Like most teenagers, she likes to listen to the latest songs that young people listen to, but she also knows when to turn it off and tune into songs that give Him glory." Randy adjusted the guitar strap before strumming a chord.

"One of those songs is "You Still Love Me" by Tasha Cobbs Leonard. Every time she played it, I stopped whatever I was doing and listened to it. I didn't know then what attracted me to the song, but I do now. The song tells the story of a prodigal child who finds his way back to God. I'm that child. No matter how far how I ran from God, His message was consistently the same. He loves me." Randy began to play.

"Why do we do the things we do when it hurts You..."

From the first strum of the borrowed guitar to the very last word he sang, the room was captivated and moved to tears. Without anyone giving an altar call, as Randy sang, people made their way to the front of the church and fell on their knees before God. The music, the song and the singer ministered to them just as any sermon would. Randy went back to his seat. He draped an arm around Priscilla and she leaned into him.

"You think if I prayed God would anoint me to be able

to sing like you?" Priscilla whispered with a smile. The look in Randy's eyes turned her joking into a serious moment.

"The anointing comes with a price."

"I know." Priscilla tenderly touched his cheek. "Thank you for paying it forward."

Randy followed her eyes toward the altar that was still filled with people.

"I love you," she whispered.

He leaned over and whispered in her ear, "I love you too."

About The Author

Kendy Ward

Author and speaker, Kendy Ward first garnered recognition as a winner of BET's First Time Writer's Competition when her short story, The Perfect Story, was published in the BET Books anthology All That and Then Some. Later her first non-fiction work was published in the inspirational and empowering compilation, No Glory without a Story. In 2012 she took her a writing career to another level when she authored her first self-published work, God-Esteem: Seeing the God in You. Her first full length work of fiction, Oh Romeo, Romeo, the first book in The Knight in Shining Armor series, was released in October 2015. She was also a featured columnist for Essence Bahamas Online Magazine.

As a Toastmasters International award-winning speaker, Kendy has spoken throughout South Florida and the Bahamas on topics of faith, empowerment and self-improvement.

She was ordained as a minister at Hope United Church in 2015 where she serves in the women's ministry, Foundation Class instructor, the children's ministry and other ministry areas.

She holds a bachelor of business administration degree in International Business and Management, and is the chief operating officer at a construction company.

She is the daughter of Kenneth and Trudy Ward, the sister of Denise Poitier and Quincy Ward, and the proud aunty of Zylen, Zaire, Zeden, Zion and Zaq.

Books In This Series

Knight in Damaged Armor

Oh Romeo, Romeo

Shiloh James is the quintessential good girl. Despite the devil whispering in her ear, she has decided to wait and trust that God can send the perfect man into her life. He would be a righteous and good man. He definitely would not be the National Basketball Association's premier bad boy, Romeo Knight.From Shiloh's first encounter with Romeo there was something incredibly explosive between the, but not in a good way. Romeo Knight was annoyingly arrogant, incredibly selfish and inexcusably defiant. He was a wild haired, tatted up menace to society. Absolutely nothing like the Boaz she dreamed of. But dreams are one thing... and Romeo Knight was all together, something else.When Romeo's hot temper gets him indefinitely suspended from the NBA, God instructs Shiloh to help him. Although reluctant at first, she yields to the Holy Spirit, and slowly but surely she watches Romeo transform into the man God called him to be. Now she must determine if Romeo Knight is ready to be the man who will posses her heart.

Excerpt of Book 3

(Uncorrected Proof)

Reign Storm

ONE

I was in the bank, praying in tongues under my breath. No, I'm not super spiritual. Matter of fact, I'm the exact opposite. I need Jesus every day, but I especially need Him when people mess with my money. I was trying to hold onto my temper, but it was proving difficult. My business account was minus $10k. Like poof. Vanished. Gone. Yeah, I didn't really see this ending any other way than me going off. That's why I was praying asking God to be a strong tower that I could run into and He could lock me in so I didn't snatch the taupe off the bank manager's head.

I'd woken up with Jesus on my mind. I got out my bed and studied God's word. Then I went into my "war room" for some one on one time with God. I was feeling the Spirit, and ready to witness to the first person I ran across, telling about how Jesus had saved me from me and could do the same thing for them. I jumped in the shower, got dressed, ate some cereal I had borrowed from my brother who lived next door to me, and then hopped in my Jeep to start another fabulous day.

I had an eight o'clock breakfast interview with Estelle who was in town for a weekend concert at Atlantis Resort on Paradise Island. She was the cover story for Rebirth Magazine, the premier magazine of the Bahamas, which yours truly just happens to own. My blog was blowing up and so was my boutique in down town Nassau. I was making that paper. So somebody in that bank had to explain to me where my money had disappeared to.

After leaving breakfast with Estelle, and getting the 411 for my mag, I checked my balance online like I do every day. Yes, I checked my bank balance every day. We were so poor growing up we couldn't afford Ramen noodles. Yes, the 10 for $1.00 Ramon noodles. We didn't have enough dollars for even those. In elementary school I wore the same uniform for three years. The summer before seventh grade I grew six freaking inches! Nothing fit me, but my brother couldn't afford to buy me new clothes. He couldn't even afford to buy me a bra for the breast that had magically grown out of my chest overnight.

You cannot imagine how embarrassing it was to go to school just jiggling all over the place. The boys in my class teased me mercilessly. I never wanted to go back to being that kind of poor ever again in this life and I knew that I sure wouldn't be in the next. Did I love money? No, the love of money is the root of all evil. I love Jesus, and Jesus said love your neighbor as yourself. How are you loving your neighbor if you're stealing from them? Somebody had to find my money because I was trying not to go totally ballistic on these people in this bank.

"Ms. Bryant, please calm down." The bank manager stood almost one foot shorter than my six feet. He kind of reminded me of... What's that guy's name? The one married to that chick from Cheers, the one that played The Penguin on Batman and in that movie with the governor dude. Danny Davito. He looked like a coffee colored version of Danny Davito as the Penguin in Batman. The vertically challenged bank manager dude was really getting on my nerves because he was saying a whole lot of nothing. He should have been telling me where my money was instead trying to get me to "calm down".

"Calm down!" I stopped myself before the string of expletives running through my head left my mouth. I bit my tongue real hard, until it almost bled. I tried to inhale but I could not breathe. I was seeing fire. I said to myself forget it. Every time I tried to do good evil is present. Paul sure didn't lie when he penned those words to the church at Philippi. No, maybe it was the church in Corinth. No, it was the church at Rome. There was no calming down at this point.

"Ten thousand dollars disappeared from my account and you want me to be calm! Where is your safe?" I stood up and stormed out of the manager's office.

"Ms. Bryant!" The annoying manager yelled after me as I headed to the vault.

"What are you doing?"

I thought it was obvious what I was doing. I was going in their vault to retrieve my ten grand.

"You gonna give me the key or I'm gonna have to take it from you?"

"I'm going to call the police!" The bank manager's voice shrilled.

"I'm not afraid of the police." I continued toward the vault. That's when the security guard jumped in front of me and tazed me. My body started jolting and convulsing. Then I was on the ground and super toy cop was hand cuffing me. I couldn't believe this was happening, and I was going to have to explain it to my brother.

Inspector Sky Johnson stood glaring at me. The vein in his neck was pulsing and his forehead wrinkled. His gray eyes looked like storm clouds. He was mad, and that was putting it mildly. If I was ten years old, I knew he would tear my black butt up. I wasn't exactly sure what he was going do with me, but I knew it would be bad. I felt like a bad child, which was kind of appropriate, seeing that I had acted like one.

My brother, Sky, is like super-duper good. I would go as far as to say that he's pretty much perfect. I mean he hasn't always been like that, but ever since that night Pastor led him in the sinner's prayer he hasn't struggled like I struggle with being good.

Our mother walked out on us when I was eight and Sky was eighteen. I was really hurt, and I took it out on my brother. I acted out. Started cutting school, shop lifting, and fighting anyone and everyone. He just didn't know what to do with me.

I'd been gone for a couple days, and returned to our little match box sized efficiency off Mackey Street to find my six foot four inch, thugged out (at the time) brother crying. I couldn't see his tears, but I heard his voice. We never went to church. We never knew about God or about Jesus or salvation period. He was crying out to a God he didn't know anything about, but the truth is that whether or not we care to admit it we know innately that there is a God.

That God that he cried out to heard his prayer, heard his desperation, and heard his heart. The next day Reverend David Knight knocked on our door, and he was the answer to my brother's prayer. The fire and brimstone preacher hailed from our country's second city, Freeport, and was in holding a week of revival services on Clifford Park. He and his team were going door to door in the neighborhoods inviting people to the revival. That's how he came to our door and into our lives. That was Sky's introduction to God. Since then loving God and doing right by God has never been difficult for him. Me, on the other hand, well as you've probably guessed, I am a different story.

"Say something, Sky." I was growing impatient with his silence. I knew it would have been better if I had remained quiet. I couldn't help it, though. I mean say something or do something. Yell at me, at least, but just don't be quiet.

My brother was only ten years older than me, but seemed more like a daddy than a big brother. Like I said he's been taking care of me since I was eight. I owe him a lot. So, I felt badly that I showed out at the bank because he is a cop, and I had more than my fair share of run-ins with the Royal Bahamas Police Force. No, it wasn't the first time that I had become overly "passionate" about a situation and showed out. My temper is my Achilles heel. I need deliverance.

"I can't believe you, Reign." Sky shook his head in disappointment. "You do know your little episode was on the news right?"

I had heard something about me making headlines. Not exactly the way I was used to breaking news.

"Sky, what did you expect me to do? Someone stole ten thousand dollars from me."

My brother started glaring at me again. I glared back at him. I wasn't scared of him. He had me sitting up there like I was a little kid waiting for my punishment. Yeah, I was sorry I'd acted out in the bank, but, seriously, was all of this really necessary?

"I expected you to act like a sane adult and not like someone straight out of a Madea flick."

"Did you just call me Madea?" I interrupted him. Sky rolled his eyes and exhaled loudly.

"No, I said you acted like you were in a Madea movie.

Reign, come on, that was real extra today. Man, do you know how many strings I had to pull so your butt would not get thrown in jail for that little stunt you pulled."

Of course, I knew exactly how many strings he had to pull. I wouldn't have done what I did if I didn't think that my big brother could bail me out. Duh.

"I'm sorry." I was kind of, sort of sorry. I was sorry that my brother was looking like he was about to have a heart attack. Unfortunately, I was not sorry that I had shown out at the bank. And I still didn't have my money back.

"Reign," Sky gritted his teeth.

I scooted the chair I was sitting in a few inches away from him. My brother didn't go around hitting women, but he looked pretty upset so there was no telling what he might do. I just wanted to be out of harm's way.

"You are thirty-five years old."

"And you're forty-five. What is your point?" Even though I was in the wrong, I was catching an attitude. What was he doing bringing my age into this?

"My point is that you're too old for this, Reign. This is something you would have pulled in high school. Matter of fact, I believe you did pull something like this in high school when you thought Sasha girl stole your lunch money. You marched to that girl's house, walked inside, went straight to her bedroom, into her sock drawer and took her little bit of savings."

I shook my head at Sky because it did not happen like that. The money was not in her sock drawer. It was under her mattress.

"I'm still missing your point, Inspector."

"My point, Reign, is grow up. Ok? Grow up. The next time I get a call to come and "rescue" my sister, I'm not gonna come. I'll see you later."

I watched Sky walk out of the interrogation room we had been using for our little meeting. I was stunned. My brother and I had never had this conversation before. No matter what I did or said, or didn't do or didn't say, Sky always had my back. He was always down for me. So, I didn't understand what he meant by the next time someone called he wasn't coming to rescue me. I didn't believe him.

I left police headquarters and decided to make a quick stop at the boutique to check on things before heading home to wrap up the Estelle article. The magazine was going to print the next day. I needed to have my article finished. I found a space to park a couple of blocks away from the boutique. Down town Nassau was the tourist hub on the island. There was never any parking, but the heavy traffic meant that my store was guaranteed to rack up more than a few sales a day.

We specialized in trendy fashion to cater to the natives, but I also had a line of clothing made from the indigenous Androsia print fabric that tourist loved. We also carried some hand crafted jewelry made from seashells fished straight out our crystal clear water. The jewelry was actually designed and hand crafted by local artist, Rajon. The talented artist mostly did oil paintings and sculptures. She was just getting into jewelry, and I decided to support her because her jewelry was just that fabulous. I was so engrossed in my thoughts that I almost walked right into a little white Nissan Sentra that zipped down Bay Street.

When I walked into the store I was surprised to find my main ace, Avery, there. Avery Grant and I met our freshman year at Spellman College. It's ironic that we grew up on the same little island and had to travel to another county to meet. That's probably because we came two worlds that couldn't be more different. As the daughter of a chief justice and president of the College of the Bahamas, Avery came from old money. Everybody in her family is rich. I already told you my story. We ain' had nothing.

Avery was stuck up, self-centered and annoying as heck when we meant. Oh man, she worked my nerves. She looked down her nose at me and anyone like me. I wasn't having that. I had to teach her some things, and somewhere along the way we became friends. It's been seventeen years now and she has finally fallen off that pedestal that she had put herself on. It was a journey, though.

"Reign, I need something to wear to this awards diner Vince and I have to go to with my parents tonight. Nothing fits me."

I snickered as I examined Avery. Avery could wear the heck out of some clothes. She was always fly. The problem (in her head) was that she had just had my goddaughter ,Ava.

"I'm sure that's not true, and you probably just want an excuse to spend money unnecessarily."

"I'm serious, Reign. I literally tried on everything in my closet."

I looked at Avery again. She looked like a perfect size six to me. Being an inch shy of six feet, I had never been a size six. Not even when I was a kid. I was always tall and big for my age. Avery was petite. We were night and day in more ways than one.

"Kia," I turned to the store manager, "where's that white dress?"

"White! I can't wear white. It makes me look bigger."

"Girl, I know what I'm doing. Go try this on." I took the dress from Kia and handed it to Avery.

She rolled her eyes at me, but she did go into the fitting room.

"So, Vince, is still trying to convince me to do this vow renewal thing."

Avery and Vince have had a very turbulent relationship, and that's me really down playing things. Avery was used to dating those glamorous brothers. You know the rapper, singer, actor, athlete dudes. Vince doesn't fall into any of those categories. He's regular. Avery didn't want a regular dude, but her heart didn't get the memo. She hooked up with Vince for what was supposed to be a fling. She was seeing two other dudes at the same time, but Vince thought it was exclusive. Of course, this was pre-Jesus Avery. In fact, this is her come to Jesus story. I digress. Vince found out about the other dudes and bounced.

"I'm with Vince. I think vow renewal is appropriate. Y'all got married in your parents living room, and you didn't invite me."

"Petty Betty, we didn't invite anyone. Besides, who has a seven-year vow renewal? That seems kind of awkward."

"Who cares if it seems awkward. You know that you've always wanted a big, fairytale, princess wedding. This is your opportunity to have it."

"I don't know, Reign."

"Do what your husband says."

"I'm talking about this dress."

Avery stepped out of the dressing room. The dress looked great to me. Just like everything else that Avery put on.

"I look fat."

I know I had said it before, but I had tell her again because obviously she didn't get it.

"You are not fat, Avery Grant Cargill."

Avery scrutinized herself in the mirror for five more minutes before deciding to take the dress.

"Thank goodness! Kia, ring this up please. Thanks."

"Ooh Reign,"

The way she said "ooh Reign", I thought Avery was going to mention something about the "incident". Instead she said, "I've got someone I want you to meet."

I rolled my eyes. Ever since Avery and Vince got married Avery was trying to hook me

and our other BFF, Priscilla, up with some ineligible bachelor. Lucky Priscilla hooked that fine behind Randy Knight. So now I was Avery's only focus. I shook my head at Avery.

"Come on, Reign. He is perfect for you. His name is Adam."

"Adam! I am not going on a date with your brother!"

Avery sucked her teeth.

"You know I would never hook you up with my brother because he's married."

"He's still married. I was sure they would have separated by now."

"Reign!" Avery socked me on the shoulder. I shrugged.

"Back to Adam. He's a really great guy."

"He's so great that's why he's single."

"He's been single by choice for about a year. His daughter's mother called off their engagement moments before the wedding..."

"Daughter's mother? Avery Grant, you know I don't do babies or baby mamas!" I sucked my teeth.

"Girl, what are you talking about? You've never had a boyfriend and you've never even been on a real date."

"Hey!" I yelled at Avery. "Shut up! I don't need all of Nassau knowing my business, and I have been on dates before." I protested.

"You cannot not count going out with me, Vince and Craig as dating!"

"Stop yelling, Avery! I am right here, and I can hear you perfectly!"

"I'm only yelling because you're yelling." Avery lowered her voice and smiled at me sweetly. I rolled my eyes at her.

"I am not going out with what's his name. Kia, ring her up. I'm out of here."

"Don't get mad, Reign. I just want you to find someone as amazing as..."

I didn't hear the rest what Avery was saying because I had left. I loved my girl, but I was sick and tired of her riding me about being single. Before Vince (and even while dating Vince) Avery dated a lot. She thought something was wrong with me because I didn't date. I don't know when or how this whole not dating thing started. It wasn't like I was always saved and made a vow of celibacy or anything like that. I just never meant a guy that I liked that liked me back. Okay... I never meant a guy that I liked like that period. Well, there is this one dude, but we ain't gonna talk about him.

I hit puberty really early and was always at least a foot taller than the boys my age. Like I said I was the butt of their jokes. When I was twelve I looked like I was eighteen so a lot of grown men would try to get with me, and I wasn't into that at all. It was like a catch twenty-two. Boys my age weren't interested in me because I looked too grown, and grown men were interested in me but I wasn't grown.

There were no "do you like me circle yes or no" in elementary school, no "let's go steady" in high school, and nobody rocking, knocking my boots in college. I'm sure there could have been, but I could never bring myself to get with someone just for the sake of getting with someone. There has never been anybody who has caused me to pause in mid-sentence when they walked into a room. I hadn't meant that person who made my breath catch in my throat, caused my heart to skip a beat and made my palms sweat. I hadn't met him yet, or I thought I hadn't met him yet. Yeah, there is this one dude, but like I said we ain't gonna talk about him.

TWO

I tried calling my brother a couple of times on the way home, but he would not answer his phone. That was a second first. Sky always took my phone calls. I was starting to think that he was serious about not unconditionally having my back. What was that about? I couldn't believe him. He should be used to my foolishness by now. It wasn't like I was getting into some mess every day. It was just every week. I let out an exasperated breath and decided to call Rev.

"Reign, what's going on?"

Reverend Paul Rolle was like a father to Sky and I. We met him the night we went to that tent revival, and he has been a part of our lives ever since. He was really old school, but he had a heart of gold. I watched him with his wife and kids, and by watching him I learned how a man should treat a woman. He was the consummate provider. As I watched him with his congregation I saw God's love for us exemplified. I knew that Rev probably saw the news so I wasn't going to play coy with him.

"I messed up today didn't I?"

Rev chuckled. I could see him sitting in his favorite chair in his office, shaking his head.

"You know you did. You don't need me to tell you that. It was funny, though."

I started laughing and then he started laughing. I laughed so hard my eyes teared up.

"You are not supposed to laugh. You're supposed to tell me how sinful I am."

"Child, in Christ there is no condemnation. There is conviction, though, and I know the Holy Spirit is convicting you or else we wouldn't be having this conversation."

"He was talking to me while I was going off, telling me vengeance is His, and I ignored Him. I knew it was so unlike Him the whole time, but the devil made me do it."

"Reign!"

"Okay! I did it. Now I'm sorry because Sky is so mad at me, and because how am I supposed to ever be able to witness to anybody about Jesus after the way I acted."

I sighed. I was always impulsive and irrational. I spoke before I thought about it, and most times it got me into a lot of trouble. Like today.

"Reign, Paul said that we kill the flesh daily. That means that this Christian walk is a daily battle with the things we're not supposed to do. You're not gonna win every battle, but you fight the best you can."

"I didn't put up much of a fight, Rev."

"I know you didn't, but I suspect things will be different in the future. Especially since Sky is threatening you."

I smiled because I felt better. Rev always brought things into prospective for me.

"I think you're right."

I said as I pulled into the driveway of the triplex Sky and I had bought a few years before. Sharing that little itsy bitsy apartment coming up made us very adamant about not sharing a space as adults. At the time, I couldn't have afforded to buy a place on my own anyway. So the triplex was the best alternative. I lived in one apartment, Sky lived in one and we rented the other. The place basically paid for itself.

Rev continued to delve out some spiritual advice to me as I walked up the drive way to my door.   I went to put the key in the lock, and was stunned to find the door slightly ajar.

"The door's open." I said, cutting off Rev's next sentence.

"Reign, don't go inside."

I knew that we had just had a really deep and sobering conversation, but there was no way that I wasn't going to go inside. What I did do was disconnect the call, went back to my car to get my gun, and proceeded into the house, cautiously. As I entered the house into the foyer, I didn't see anything amiss. I moved further into the house and again didn't see anything out of place. Then I heard a slight noise coming from my home office. Then I saw a blur run by me that knocked me slightly off balance as it made its way to the door, and before I could really process the pros and cons of my actions I was out the door, running behind the black blur.

It was the middle of the day. It wasn't even two o'clock yet and this fool had the audacity to break into my house. I was so happy I had put on a pair of riding boots, which was much easier to run in than heels, as I sprinted after the fool. I had always been fast, but dude was really fast. I didn't think I was going to catch him, and I actually thought about just shooting him. The Holy Spirit intervened, though, and this time I listened. Suddenly I got a second wind of some sort and caught up with him. I tackled the dude like I thought I was on a football field. We went rolling down the sidewalk and came to stop with me on top of him. I straddled the punk, pinning him to the ground. He would have fought me, but I think the staring down the barrel of a gun made him think twice about it.

My cell phone was in my car and I really didn't think I was going to get dude to cooperate and walk back to my car. I needed to call my brother. Before I could even give the situation any further thought I heard sirens, and saw police cars speeding down my block. Thank goodness I was on the phone with Rev. I knew then that he had probably called the police. I was never so relieved to see Nassau's finest arrive mostly because they could take care of Mr. Robber, but partly because they weren't coming for me.

"Ma'am, we've got it from here."

A uniformed officer said as his partner helped me up off the robber. I wanted to kick dude where the sun don't shine, but again the Jesus in me intervened. I watched the policemen handcuff the robber dude. I didn't say much because I was catching my breath. I watched my brother's new partner, Inspector Storm Knight, swagger over to me.

He was dressed in his usual black cargos and black v-neck tee. Storm and my brother were about the same height, but Storm had way more muscles than Sky. He looked like he lived in the gym. He probably did live in the gym. Storm's skin was the color of my favorite brew of coffee, and just like I liked my coffee, he didn't come with any cream or sugar for that matter. Storm never smiled. I mean never, ever smiled. His name was very appropriate. He was a big, black storm cloud. So depressing. He was fine, though. Super-duper fine. All the Knight brothers were fine, but I think Storm was the best looking of the five. I'd only known him a short time, but I knew he was going to have something smart to say.

"Wow... this must me some kind of record for you. Two police calls in one day."

I rolled my eyes at him.

"Shut up."

Sky and Storm (I know. That's cheesy weird right) had only been partners for a couple weeks, but they were fast becoming friends. Mostly because they thought just a like. They were both old school, but Storm was even more old school than my brother. He was into that bare foot and pregnant thing that I just couldn't get with. It was cool if that's what he wanted his woman to do, but he didn't have to try to impose it on everyone else. He was opinionated and aggravating.

"What do you think you're doing with this?"

He took my gun from me and replaced the safety. Oh, how could I forget that he thought women didn't need to know how to defend themselves. I remember the look of distaste on his face when I showed up with Sky to meet him at shooting range.

"I was catching me a bad guy." I tried to joke, but Storm didn't have a sense of humor. He put my gun in his waist band.

"What are you doing?" I snapped with attitude.

"That attitude is why you don't have a man, and I'm taking this in for evidence."

I could not believe he said that to me. I wanted to smack him.

"And your chauvinistic attitude is why you will never have a woman."

"I'm single by choice, baby girl."

"Boy, please there is not a woman on this island that would put up with your archaic ideologies."

"I see you've been reading the dictionary during all those nights you spend alone." He smirked. I glared.

"Come on. Let's go see what this butthole tried to take from your house."

Storm began to walk towards the house. I didn't move. I wanted to scream, spit and throw something at him. How dare he talk to me like I was a five-year-old! When he realized I wasn't following him, he spun around. He marched back towards me, grabbed me by the elbow and begun to pull me along. By now you can probably guess what my reaction was like. I used one of my martial arts move to spin out of his grasp, and kneed him. I don't allow anyone to put their hands on me. No one handles me like that. Let's just chalk up my reaction to reflex. Storm doubled over in pain. His subordinates rushed to his aid, and I walked away, heading towards the house just like he'd asked me to.

Acknowledgement

I give praise and thanks to God from whom all blessings flow. Father, thank You for the gifts of imagination and story telling. This book has been a long time coming. So, thank YOU for patiently waiting for its arrival. Thank you to my family and friends for your unwavering support. I hope that you all enjoy Priscilla and Randy's story.

Connect with Kendy

www.facebook.com/authorkendyward

www.instagram.com/queenkendyward

www.twitter.com/kendyward

therebirthoftruth.blogspot.com

Made in the USA
Columbia, SC
01 February 2021

32061556R00141